"Well, tha____ to me like ____ something."

Royce ducked his head sheepishly. "I, um, might have accidentally led him to believe that."

"What? Why would you do that?"

"Because I'm not supposed to leave here unless I have someone who can take care of me."

Merrily blinked at him. "Me? You want *me* to move in with you?" she asked disbelievingly.

"I know it's selfish," he said, taking her hand. She jumped, lightning flashing up her arm. "But I'm desperate. I'll make it worth your while."

She gaped at his handsome face. This gorgeous man wanted her to move in with him, at least temporarily. He didn't have to just disappear out of her life, after all....

Dear Reader,

There's more than one way to enjoy the summer. By picking up this month's Silhouette Special Edition romances, you will find an emotional escape that is sure to touch your heart and leave you believing in happily-ever-after!

I am pleased to introduce a gripping tale of true love and family from celebrated author Stella Bagwell. In *White Dove's Promise*, which launches a six-book spin-off—plus a Christmas story collection—of the popular COLTONS series, a dashing Native American hero has trouble staying in one place, until he finds himself entangled in a soul-searing embrace with a beautiful single mother, who teaches him about roots...and lifelong passion.

No "keeper" shelf is complete without a gem from Joan Elliott Pickart. In *The Royal MacAllister*, a woman seeks her true identity and falls madly in love with a *true* royal! In *The Best Man's Plan*, bestselling and award-winning author Gina Wilkins delights us with a darling love story between a lovely shop owner and a wealthy businessman, who set up a fake romance to trick the tabloids...and wind up falling in love for real!

Lisa Jackson's *The McCaffertys: Slade* features a lady lawyer who comes home and faces a heartbreaker hero, who desperately wants a chance to prove his love to her. In *Mad Enough To Marry*, Christie Ridgway entertains us with an adorable tale of that *maddening* love that happens only when two kindred spirits must share the same space. Be sure to pick up Arlene James's *His Private Nurse*, where a single father falls for the feisty nurse hired to watch over him after a suspicious accident. You won't want to miss it!

Each month, Silhouette Special Edition delivers compelling stories of life, love and family. I wish you a relaxing summer and happy reading.

Sincerely,

Karen Taylor Richman
Senior Editor

Please address questions and book requests to:
Silhouette Reader Service
U.S.: 3010 Walden Ave., P.O. Box 1325, Buffalo, NY 14269
Canadian: P.O. Box 609, Fort Erie, Ont. L2A 5X3

His Private Nurse

ARLENE JAMES

SPECIAL EDITION™

Published by Silhouette Books

America's Publisher of Contemporary Romance

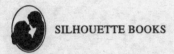 **SILHOUETTE BOOKS**

ISBN 0-373-24482-7

HIS PRIVATE NURSE

Copyright © 2002 by Deborah Rather

Visit Silhouette at www.eHarlequin.com

Printed in U.S.A.

Books by Arlene James

Silhouette Special Edition

A Rumor of Love #664
Husband in the Making #776
With Baby in Mind #869
Child of Her Heart #964
*The Knight, the Waitress
  and the Toddler* #1131
Every Cowgirl's Dream #1195
Marrying an Older Man #1235
Baby Boy Blessed #1285
Her Secret Affair #1421
His Private Nurse #1482

Silhouette Books

Fortune's Children
Single with Children

The Fortunes of Texas
Corporate Daddy

Silhouette Romance

City Girl #141
No Easy Conquest #235
Two of a Kind #253
A Meeting of Hearts #327
An Obvious Virtue #384
Now or Never #404
Reason Enough #421
The Right Moves #446
Strange Bedfellows #471
The Private Garden #495
The Boy Next Door #518
Under a Desert Sky #559
A Delicate Balance #578
The Discerning Heart #614
Dream of a Lifetime #661
Finally Home #687
A Perfect Gentleman #705
Family Man #728
A Man of His Word #770
Tough Guy #806

Gold Digger #830
Palace City Prince #866
*The Perfect Wedding #962
*An Old-Fashioned Love #968
*A Wife Worth Waiting For #974
Mail-Order Brood #1024
*The Rogue Who Came To Stay #1061
*Most Wanted Dad #1144
Desperately Seeking Daddy #1186
*Falling for a Father of Four #1295
A Bride To Honor #1330
Mr. Right Next Door #1352
Glass Slipper Bride #1379
A Royal Masquerade #1432
In Want of a Wife #1466
The Mesmerizing Mr. Carlyle #1493
So Dear To My Heart #1535
The Man with the Money #1592

*This Side of Heaven

ARLENE JAMES

grew up in Oklahoma and has lived all over the South.
In 1976 she married "the most romantic man in the
world." The author enjoys traveling with her husband,
but writing has always been her chief pastime.

Prologue

Royce leaned forward and placed his hands on the railing, staring into the silent darkness. On a warm summer night like this, nocturnal creatures usually kept up a steady chorus, crickets, coyotes and the occasional small owl on the prowl for an unwary field mouse or ground squirrel. Tonight, however, an unnatural silence reigned, and Royce knew why. Someone waited out there.

He gripped the squared edges of the wood railing. Rough and solid beneath his palms, it conveyed a sense of permanence, of ownership. Beyond the deck where he stood and the black, irregular skyline of scrubby forest that flowed down the hill upon which he had built his secluded home, San Antonio spread out in a rumpled quilt of white and amber lights, stitched together by the sinuously askew seams of major streets and highways. He often stood on the large, terraced deck, gazing out over the city he both loved and nightly escaped, a city he had helped to build, often with his own two hands. This night, however, he studied the ground below, the murky black shadows of lush forest cedar interspersed with spindly sprays of mesquite and squat, wicked cactus.

She was there. Somewhere. He could not see her, but she was there. He sensed her, still attuned even after these many, many months to his ex-wife's volatile presence. Every time the kids slept over, she made some sort of scene, created some sort of crisis. He couldn't believe that tonight would be the exception.

Quietly, so as not to disturb his daughter, whose room in the large, rambling house overlooked the deck, he turned and moved to the top of the steep, open stairs that would carry him down to the narrow drive that ran behind the house. The warm summer breeze made his T-shirt stick to his back and molded the thin pajama bottoms to his body. He did not want another confrontation, but this madness had to stop.

He was certain that she was there, stalking, watching, planning her next scene, her next outrageous demand, utterly determined to ruin his life, to punish him for failing to make her happy, for failing to make all her mad dreams come true. She was there, wanting, needing, his destruction. Most of all, she wanted to turn his children against him, to ensure that he did not see them if she could, to remove his influence from their sad, unstable lives and, if she could not manage that, then to ruin every visit, every cherished moment that he spent with them, because, more than she wanted money, control, someone to worship at her feet and make all her fears go away, she wanted to remove every vestige of the love she could not claim from his life.

Until he felt the hands at the small of his back, he did not realize that, even more than she wanted to punish him, she wanted him dead.

Chapter One

Pain swirled through his body, dull here, deep there, throbbing, pulsing, ambiguous. He floated on it, drifting blindly from one ache to another, trying to form thoughts, losing them. Then suddenly, hot pincers clamped his inner thigh and began slowly tearing the muscle from the bone. He heard a hoarse, agonized cry. A fellow sufferer or him? Him, he decided, dimly aware of trying to reach the source of his agony. His right arm felt as if it were nailed down, and when he tried to move it, a new pain flooded him.

Someone whom he couldn't see said, "I've got it. I've got it." It was an angel's voice, melodic and female.

Small, cool hands kneaded away the anguish. The white-hot pinching faded. Ahhhhh. The relief felt magical. He was floating again, his whole being focused on the sensations aroused by those hands slowly working their way up his thigh, electrifying his flesh. A new sensation rose—literally. A roiling sea of contrasts tossed him from one extreme to another: shadows and light, heat and cold, pain and indulgence. The relief of unconsciousness and the greed of arousal beckoned with equal appeal.

Lyrical, that voice whispered in his ear again. "There. How's that? Better? Cramp gone now?"

He tried to answer, but his tongue felt thick and unwieldly in his dry mouth. "Ungh."

The wondrous hands vanished. He tried to bring them back, becoming aware of incapacitating weakness and muscles tight with soreness, of a dizzy head and confusion. Where was he? The unusual heaviness on his right side and in his groin weighed him down. Then he felt something brush against his lips. Ah, his erotic angel had not abandoned him. The heaviness in his groin grew more pronounced. He puckered his mouth around a small round something.

"Sip. Just a sip."

Like honey, that voice. Cool, sweet water flowed into his mouth, and he gulped it greedily. Panting with relief, he squinted his eyes, trying to focus.

"Are you in pain? Use this."

Something hard was pressed into his hand. He lifted his head, tried to look at the thing in his palm and got distracted by a new realization. A bed. He was in bed. But with whom? He tried to put a name, a face, a body to that voice.

"Like this."

Slender fingers wrapped around and manipulated his own. The haze parted, and he looked up into a pretty, delicate face, one he had surely never seen before. Dark hair, a long, thick plait of it coiled beneath her ear. Soft, green eyes. The nose was almost too small, the chin almost too pointed, but the mouth... Oh, the mouth. A perfect, pink, beestung bow. A mouth waiting to be kissed. By him.

Heat pulsed in his groin, and instinctively he lifted his arm, the left one, since the right had turned to stone. The hard thing fell away, but he paid it no mind as he clasped his hand behind her head, his erotic angel with the dulcet voice and gentle touch. Straining upward and pulling down, he brought his mouth to hers. Her lips were soft and supple. They parted against his, and he used all his strength to press harder, to taste her. Sweet. So very sweet. He held on to that as long as he could, his only reality in a nightmare of torture and chaos.

Hums and squeaks swirled around him, fire and pain, need and delight. Where had he met her? What was her name, and why couldn't he remember? Despite his best efforts, gloom eddied in the center of his mind, denying him answers and growing in rings of numbing shadow, darker, darker, until the world went black with a noisy clang.

An electronically generated bell *donged* in measured cadence. Merrily glanced away from the notation desk where she sat catching up on paperwork to check the alarm board. Room 18. At the thought of the patient there, color instantly bloomed in her cheeks. Royce Lawler was badly injured, movie-star handsome and dangerously seductive even when drugged out of his mind. Apparently, he had finally obtained full consciousness, poor guy.

Normally, with a patient in this much pain, Merrily would have jumped up and rushed to his aid, but this time, despite her sympathy for the man's injuries, she hesitated long enough to look around for someone else to answer this particular call. In just the time it took to turn her head, however, she knew the search was pointless. Short-staffed as they were, every nurse was busy to the point of insanity. She was on her feet and moving before she could even tell herself that he wouldn't remember a thing that had gone on earlier.

In her short career as an after-trauma nurse, Merrily had been groped, pinched, patted, hugged, leered at and propositioned, but she'd never been kissed like that. By anyone. Her heartbeat sped at the memory of it, the strength, the possession, the expertise. Had he sensed her awareness of him as a man rather than merely a patient? Somehow her usual cool detachment had deserted her when she'd bared his body and massaged the cramp from the thigh of his injured leg.

Cramps were a real problem with immobilized patients. The docs prescribed potassium and calcium to try to prevent them, as even an unconscious patient would try to move to alleviate the vicious pain. Lawler, however, had experienced more cramps than the average patient. He'd kept the ICU nurses hopping after his surgery until the attending physician had figured out the correct supplement levels for him. This morning's cramp had undoubtedly been a result of the move from ICU to the floor.

Given the trauma and the drugs, Merrily told herself as she pushed through the door into his room, he could not possibly remember kissing her—or how she'd knocked over the trash can next to his bed afterward. Nevertheless, her pulse quickened and spots of color burned high on her cheeks even as she put on her most professional demeanor and prepared to assess and assist her patient. She turned toward the bed in the small, quiet, private room, then rushed forward, praying he hadn't torn loose the stitches, dislodged the broken ends of bones or worse.

Royce gritted his teeth and mentally cursed himself. His arm shook with the effort required to brace his twisted body on his left palm, head dangling toward the floor. He was trapped by the traction device that kept his screaming right leg immobile several uncomfortable inches above the bed. The cast on his right arm and shoulder, though unwieldy, was at least maneuverable to an extent, though at the moment it weighed down on him like an anvil. Somehow the IV line tethering his left arm to the bags hanging over his head and the contraption clipped to the end of his left index finger remained intact, though his right hip felt as if it was being pulled from its socket. The nurse's call button dangled from its cord next to the bed. He'd banged his head against it on his way down but had no way of knowing whether or not he'd managed to trigger the thing.

He'd really gotten himself into a fine mess this time, and he wasn't thinking just about the fall he'd taken trying to reach the telephone, which some fool had placed out of his reach on the bedside table. Oh no, it was much more than that. Black memory spun through his head.

Shoving hands pitched him forward, and he fell, arms milling in cold fear. At the first impact on the sharp edges of the wooden stairs, a white hot snap in his right forearm blinded him and his right foot slipped between the open steps. Twisting, he fell forward in slow motion. Stars winked and whirled overhead. His leg wrenched, bones snapping. His shoulder and head impacted the steps in twin explosions of pain. Above him, the deck stairs loomed steep and dark, a pale figure hovering at the top. Deep, deep regret rushed through him in the instant before he died.

He'd really thought that he had fallen to his death. The same feelings he'd experienced then, pain, fear, regret, and now worry and sheer embarrassment moderated his relief at discovering that he'd been wrong. At the moment, worry surpassed all the others.

"Mr. Lawler!"

Rescue had arrived, but embarrassment beat out relief, at least temporarily, and as feet rushed toward him, rubber soles squeaking on clean floors, he closed his eyes. Arms locked around his dangling torso, small, short arms. He knew a moment of grave doubt as he felt a body crouch next to him. A woman, small and slight. He half recognized the smell, sensed the size and shape of her. Then her legs pushed upward and he found himself being lifted. He wrapped his arm about her back and tried to give her as much help as he could, contracting already strained and bruised muscles.

"What happened?" she grunted.

His stupidity and impatience had happened, but he was puffing too hard to gasp anything more than, "Telephone," as he flopped back on the pillow. She tsked, and lifted the bed rail back into place, but the expected lecture did not materialize as she went about settling him and making sure he hadn't done additional damage.

His rescuer didn't know how much additional damage could be done, however, and how much his fault it was. Why hadn't he seen how close his ex-wife, Pamela, was to the breaking point? Why hadn't he known this could happen? Idiot. He had to do something before anyone else got hurt. The list of those with whom he needed to immediately speak was long: his kids, especially Tammy, his parents, Dale, his secretary, his foreman, doctors. Mentally, he moved Dale Boyd, his best buddy and personal attorney, to the top of the list. He had to get that phone. Head swimming, he opened his eyes and looked up into a surprisingly familiar face.

So it hadn't been a dream. His angel was real. As her

hands moved over him with practiced, efficient purpose, he observed that his angel wore flowered scrubs and an oversize lab coat. He saw, too, that she was young, too young, little more than a teenager, it seemed, albeit a very pretty teenager, too young to have been kissed by the likes of him. Surely that part of it had been a dream; yet the impulse to capture that lush little mouth rose in him even now, and he found that annoying. This was not the time for complications like sexual attraction.

"How are you feeling?"

"Like I fell down a flight of stairs," he retorted, shifting in an effort to ease the insistent throb in his shoulder. His voice sounded rusty and hoarse even to him.

"You have a morphine pump attached to your IV," she said, checking tubes, bags and monitors.

"No morphine," he stated flatly. He knew what the small cylinder lying in his lap was. The line snaking up to the blue box of the IV regulator promised instant relief, but he couldn't afford the clouded mind and lassitude it would bring.

"You can't overdose," she informed him briskly, pouring water into a blue plastic tumbler with a straw standing in it. "The machine won't let you." She lifted the straw to his mouth, and he gratefully sucked the small vessel dry.

"No morphine," he repeated with a satisfied sigh. "Not yet. I need to make a telephone call."

She ignored that. "Do you know where you are?"

He tamped down his impatience. "In a hospital. Not sure which one."

"Big General," she informed him, using the universal term for San Antonio's hub hospital, the largest and most sophisticated in the city. "Room 18. I'm Nurse Gage."

A nurse. "You don't look old enough to be a nurse."

She ignored that, too. "Do you remember how you got here?"

He rolled his head side to side in the negative. "I remember being...falling down the stairs at the back of my house."

"You were brought in by ambulance," she told him, reaching for the stethoscope draped about her neck. He noticed that her hands, though tiny, were long-fingered with short, oval nails. She listened to his chest, took his pulse, then asked matter-of-factly, "Do you need to empty your bladder? You dislodged the catheter in recovery, and it was decided to remove it."

Recovery? He pushed that aside, along with the sudden need to do as she suggested. Everything else could wait. "I *need* to make a call. *Now.*"

"Your parents left their telephone number at the desk. If you want, I'll give them a ring a soon as we're finished here."

He closed his eyes, frustration mounting. He didn't want to feel the resentment that surged through him, but he couldn't help thinking that most parents would be standing anxiously at the bedside of an injured son. Only his supremely self-absorbed parents would have more important things to do. Shoving that old anger away, he marshaled his reason and reached down deep for his usual easygoing demeanor.

"Listen, I don't mean to be difficult, but this is important. If you could just hand me the receiver and dial a number for me, I'd be eternally grateful." He opened his eyes, well aware of the impact those big, baby blues could have. He saw it in her face then, the full memory of that kiss. So it hadn't been a dream, then. Damn. Suddenly the urge to empty his bladder became secondary to another.

She stepped back, bumped into the table and IV pole and flushed bright red. Busily righting everything, she said over her shoulder, "You should rest."

"I can't," he pleaded, "until I make the call. Please."

She glanced at him then picked up the telephone receiver, bobbled it and, eyes averted, tucked it into the crook of his neck. Punching two buttons she asked, "What's the number?"

"Thank you," he breathed, gratitude easing the physical need somewhat. He gave her the number and angled his head so he could hear the tones as she dialed. She moved out of sight, then appeared again at the foot of the bed, where she looked at his toes, which were all that the stiff cocoon of bandages encasing his right leg left visible.

Dale's secretary answered on the second ring, exclaiming at the sound of Royce's voice. He made himself answer her questions of concern before saying urgently that he had to speak to her boss. Nurse Gage moved to examine the fingers that extended beyond the cast on his right arm and shoulder, and a moment later, Dale came on the line.

"Royce? How are you?"

"Still among the living."

"What the hell happened out there, man? I couldn't believe it when Tammy called."

Everything in Royce went on alert. "Tammy called you?"

"Yeah, right after she called 911. She probably saved your life, man."

Emotion swamped Royce. He closed his eyes, tears welling behind them. Poor Tammy, caught between warring parents, not knowing whom to trust, what was betrayal and what was not. Her mother had undoubtedly wanted him to die, yet, Tammy had saved him. The great love that he felt for his nine-year-old momentarily choked him. He cleared his throat and said as smoothly as he could manage, "She's a good girl, always has been."

"Yeah. Must take after you," which meant that they should all feel grateful that she didn't take after her mother, Pamela.

What his ex had put those two kids through was enough to break Royce's heart. He'd been fighting her for full custody since he'd filed for divorce two years ago, and the case was finally coming to court soon, though Pamela had used every trick in the book to block it. If he'd believed for an instant that she really wanted, needed her kids with her, he'd have relented, but to Pamela those kids were nothing more than a weapon to use against him. She'd told them hideous lies in an attempt to make them hate him, even that the only reason he wanted custody was so he wouldn't have to pay child support. He hadn't realized just how far she was willing to go, though. Until now.

"I've gotta see you, Dale. How quick can you get over here?"

"How's an hour sound? I've got a conference call on hold. Give me thirty minutes to wrap it up, and I'll head over your way."

Weary to the bone, Royce figured he'd need that hour to regain his strength. "Thanks. I appreciate it, bud."

"No problem. Can I bring you anything?"

"Just get over here."

"Sure thing. And, Royce?"

"Yeah?"

"You don't know how good it is to hear your voice."

"Ditto." He knew he didn't have to say that he'd never expected to hear or speak to anyone ever again.

As Merrily took the telephone receiver from his hand to replace it in its cradle, she noted that he did not wear a wedding ring. The fact that she couldn't resist looking for one disturbed her. Only the conclusion that he obviously didn't remember that kiss he'd planted on her earlier enabled her to do her job.

"Your extremities look good. Full color, warm to the touch. Have you tried to move your toes?"

The question seemed to surprise him. "No." He looked down at the bare toes poking up at the end of the bed. The faint twinge was not what Merrily had hoped for, but she put a good face on it.

"Don't worry about it. The doctor will undoubtedly want to take a few more X rays, but given your condition they'll probably bring the portable unit here."

"What is my condition exactly?"

She looked straight into his eyes, noting the size of his pupils. "Good. The concussion worried them at first, but the CT scan was normal."

"I've had a CT scan?"

"And an MRI, about a dozen X rays and surgery to set bones in your leg. They also put your shoulder back into its socket and set your arm."

His eyes widened. A surreal blue, they were easily the most beautiful eyes she'd ever seen, as beautiful as his face. Handsome seemed a lame term for such male perfection. Four shades of blond, from brass to platinum, streaked the thick, straight hair that flopped over one brow. The face itself was that of an archangel or a superhero straight out of the pages of a comic book, especially with that tortured look hovering just beneath the toasted gold of his skin. Tiny lines fanned out from the corners of his eyes, another testament to the time this man spent out of doors.

"Anything else?"

"Bruises and contusions. The miracle is that you didn't break a rib and puncture a lung."

"No internal injuries then?"

"Nothing serious, but don't be surprised if you pass a little blood."

He nodded, forehead creasing with a frown. "Guess I can be thankful for that."

"I know it hurts," she said. "I can back off the morphine dose if you like. It might give you some relief without putting you to sleep." That boxy jaw set stubbornly, spurring her to explain. "It's better to stay on top of the pain if you can. If you let it get too bad, your mind won't be any clearer and it'll take more meds to control it."

Grimly he closed his eyes and nodded. She made the adjustment and depressed the pump herself before switching the pulse monitor on the end of his left index finger to his right hand. "That ought to give you a little more dexterity."

"Thanks."

"You don't happen to be left-handed, do you?"

"No such luck." He sent her a wry, lazy look that sped up her heart.

"Too bad." She bent to pick up the plastic urinal, only to knock it under the bed. What was wrong with her? She hadn't been this clumsy since Donald Popof had asked her to the prom. Disgustedly she got down on her knees and fished the large plastic jar from beneath the bed. Rising, she hooked the handle over the bed rail and asked, "Think you can manage by yourself?" His gaze met hers blandly, and she knew by his demeanor that the drugs were beginning to take effect.

"Yeah. Thanks."

"You can lie on your left hip if you keep your body

aligned with the traction bar,'' she advised matter-of-factly, ''but don't let the container get too full or we'll wind up having to change your bed. Okay?''

He looked away. ''Okay.''

She went to the sink and dampened a washcloth with antibacterial fluid, then draped it wordlessly over the bed rail within easy reach.

''I'll be back in a few minutes. Can I get you anything?''

Those blue eyes settled on her again, and a small, appreciative smile flitted across his face. ''Food.''

A good sign. She checked her watch. ''Dinner trays will be up in about an hour. Meanwhile, I've got crackers, ice cream and popsicles, if you're interested.''

''Forget the popsicles,'' he said wryly, meaning that she should bring everything else.

Chuckling, she headed for the door, allowing him the privacy necessary to relieve himself.

Royce eased onto his back, more comfortable than he had been since he'd awakened nearly an hour earlier, and let his mind wander where it would. Not surprisingly, it went straight to Nurse Gage. She had displayed unusual sensitivity, first by refraining from scolding him for putting down the bed rail and trying to get to the phone on his own and then by allowing him to tend to his personal needs in privacy. He felt better just knowing that he wasn't completely helpless, and he couldn't help feeling grateful that she hadn't mentioned that kiss.

He wondered if he ought to apologize for it, then upon reflection decided that it was best to let her think he didn't remember kissing her, though in fact it was one of the first things he had remembered. At the time he'd assumed it was all a dream, and that was how he was going to treat it, like a freaky dream that had brought him a moment of pleasure in the midst of physical anguish. He suspected it would be easier for both of them that way, especially her.

What a strange little creature she was, his Nurse Gage, alternately clumsy and efficient, small but strong, brisk and professional but with a gentle sympathy warming the muted green of her eyes. He wondered what she would look like with that long braid unbound. Would it lie sleek and straight across her shoulders or wave and curl?

She either wasn't married or didn't wear a wedding ring while working. Somehow he figured it was the former. Youth aside, she just didn't have the look of a settled, married woman.

He frowned disgustedly at the train of his thoughts. For one thing he had much more important matters to ponder. For another, he was in no position to pursue a woman, even if his health weren't an issue, which it clearly was.

Deliberately he turned his mind to other things. When could he speak to his daughter?

He wasn't married. The thought circled through her brain all the while she stuffed her pockets with saltines and plucked ice cream bars from the freezer. It was only at his door, however, that Merrily confronted the rise of enthusiasm inside her with a stern rebuke.

"Don't be an idiot, Merrily," she scolded under her breath. "He may not have a ring on his finger, but there's a woman around somewhere." No doubt she would ascend at any moment, miniskirt flapping and kohl-darkened eyes sparkling with tears of concern. Shoot, a man like that probably had them lined up to hold his hand and stroke his fevered brow.

That kiss had been nothing more than a drug-induced fluke. He wouldn't be seriously interested in a woman who looked so much like a kid that, at twenty-six, she still had to buy her clothes in the junior department, which was pretty much why she stuck to uniforms, jeans and simple shirts. Nope, Royce Lawler was not for the likes of her, and to think otherwise would be, in the immortal words of her eldest brother, Jody, cruising for a bruising.

Hiding her own interest behind her nurse's demeanor, she went in to play her chosen role of angel of mercy armed with crackers and rapidly softening ice cream.

Chapter Two

"So apparently she found you right away," Dale said, speaking of Royce's nine-year-old daughter Tammy.

Royce nodded and attempted a smile. "Lucky."

"I'll say. She called 911 and me, then tossed a blanket over you and sat with you until the paramedics arrived."

Royce frowned. "I don't remember any of that."

"Pretty gutsy, if you ask me," Dale commented. "She was terrified you were dead. I told her to stay with her little brother, but she said Cory was asleep and she didn't want you to be alone. She was sobbing, poor kid. I tell you, I flew. Got there right after the ambulance. Guess she called her mom, too, 'cause Pam was there when I arrived. Pretty odd, since she lives farther from your place than I do." He eyed Royce and added, "She said something about being at a restaurant on the south side of town. I asked her twice which one, but she never did say."

Royce kept his expression carefully impassive. "Tammy knows I'm going to be okay, doesn't she?"

"Yeah, the doctors told us so before Pamela sent her and Cory back to her house with that nanny she hired, but Pam stayed here until you were out of surgery and came around in ICU."

I'll bet she did, Royce thought cryptically, recalling the moment he'd opened his eyes in ICU to find three disembodied heads bending over him. He hadn't known to whom they belonged or where he was, but when he'd been asked to cough, he'd done so. He'd grunted answers to questions he couldn't remember now, but he clearly recollected when one unfamiliar voice had said, "You took a bad fall, Mr. Lawler. Do you remember anything about it?"

He'd known even then what he had to say, and if asked today, he would say the same thing. "No."

"Huh?" The tall, lanky attorney with the dark-brown hair and eyes looked at Royce as if wondering whether or not he should call the nurse. He and Royce had been friends since high school, despite having attended different colleges. He was the one person in Royce's life with whom Royce could be completely honest—until now.

Royce cleared his throat. "I mean, um, *no* doubt she was hoping I'd broken my neck."

"She did ask what provisions you'd made in your will for her and the children," Dale said wryly.

Royce sighed, guessing, "And she was some ticked off when you told her that as my ex-wife, emphasis on the ex, she was not entitled to be provided for."

Dale chuckled. "She really went ballistic when I informed her that Mark Cherry and I are to be coexecutors of the trust you've established for the kids. Come to think of it, your parents weren't best pleased, either."

"You mean they were here?" Royce asked dryly.

Dale's face went carefully blank. "Yeah, sure, till we knew you were going to be okay."

"Meaning they didn't stick around to be sure I came out of surgery all right," Royce surmised correctly.

It was nothing more than he'd expected. He'd been at odds with his parents for as long as he could remember. Even as a kid he'd felt that he must've been switched at birth. He just didn't seem to have anything in common with his socially prominent, appearance-driven parents. They'd never forgiven him for preferring to work with his hands rather than a calculator, and when his younger brother had eagerly embraced the family banking business, Royce's fate as "the disappointment" had been sealed.

Dale, bless him, quickly changed the subject. "I want to ask for a postponement of the custody hearing. You're in no shape to take on two kids by yourself now, anyway, and you know perfectly well that our position's been iffy from the start."

Royce nodded in reluctant agreement and rubbed his left hand over his face. His shoulder ached, his head felt heavy, and his leg throbbed above the knee. Shifting in a futile effort to find a more comfortable position on the narrow, lumpy mattress, he said what they both knew. "We're no closer to proving she's a threat to the children than we were when we started."

"She's crazy smart, that woman," Dale said with a sigh. "She's been real careful to make her threats in private to no one but you. The only thing we've ever had in our favor is the fact that she's a proven adulteress."

"Which means nothing when it comes to custody issues," Royce said.

"Listen," Dale said, shifting his chair closer to the bed,

"if we could just get one of the kids to testify that Pamela has repeatedly lost her temper with them…"

Royce was shaking his head. Now he stated his position emphatically. "No. Absolutely not. I won't have my children pressured to testify against their own mother."

Dale sighed. "Well, Cory's too young to be believable, and Tammy wouldn't, anyway."

"You don't understand the pressure she lives under, Dale. No one can unless they've lived with Pamela. Everything that displeases her, no matter how slight, is a major betrayal to her. That means one emotional, irrational scene after another until your whole life becomes nothing more than a fruitless exercise in trying to please her, to stop the tirade. Eventually you realize that it's impossible, but you can't get out and you don't dare give up. I know. I'm an adult, and after two years I'm still trying to fight my way free. Imagine what it must be like for a child. I tell you the truth, Dale, if Mark and I hadn't walked in on her and Campo *in the act,* I'd still be married to that vampire."

Dale knotted his hands into fists. "I still want to clobber that guy every time I think of him. You built his house, for pity's sake, and not only does he try to cheat you out of your earnings, he sleeps with your wife—on the living room sofa, no less!"

"And I keep telling you," Royce said, aware that he was beginning to slur his words, "it was the only way out for me. I can't be anything but grateful to the creep."

"Yeah, but if he hadn't dumped Pamela," Dale pointed out, "she'd have left the kids with you and beat a path with him to the Mediterranean."

Royce closed his eyes, a smile quirking one corner of his mouth. "So Claude Campo is smarter than me. He sure wised up faster than I did. Can't blame the fellow for that.''

''You were a senior in college when you married Pamela,'' Dale argued. ''You thought you'd nabbed a hot redhead to spend the rest of your life with. How were you to know she was a basket case that was slowly unraveling?''

Royce smiled. Trust Dale to defend him. ''Anyway,'' Royce said, getting the conversation back on track, ''about Tammy. I don't want anyone pressuring her, not about her mother and not about my fall. You got that?''

Dale nodded. ''Sure, sure. Her animosity toward you is nothing more than an attempt to placate and please her mother. That's what you've always said, and seems to me that her recent behavior reinforces it. I mean, she saved your life. If she hadn't found you and called an ambulance, shock would have....''

''Finished what her mother started,'' Royce muttered. To his chagrin, Dale pounced on that unwise statement.

''I knew it!'' He came up out of his chair. ''You'd never fall down your own deck stairs. She pushed you. The witch pushed you!'' He punctuated the air with the jab of one forefinger, then dropped his hands to his waist. ''We need a private investigator.''

''No.''

''We'll punch holes in her alibi, sink her for good.''

Royce struggled up onto his left elbow to make himself understood. ''No.''

''But you said—''

''You misunderstood.'' Collapsing back onto his pillow, Royce massaged his temples with thumb and forefinger. ''I only meant that Pam's been punishing me for everything that has ever gone wrong in her life. No doubt she believes that if I died it would serve me right. That's what she's been teaching my kids ever since the divorce."

Deflated, Dale turned the armless, molded plastic chair and straddled it. "And they're too young to know that you divorced their mother because you caught her naked, humping a client in your own home."

Royce cut his gaze sideways. "Succinctly put."

Dale sighed and hunched forward, hanging his sharp chin on the edge of the chair back. "So that leaves us right where we've always been. Square one."

"Not exactly," Royce said, disciplining a yawn. Blinking, he fought off the drug-induced lethargy. "I want you to find a therapist for Tammy. She has to have been traumatized by all this."

Dale fixed him with that no-nonsense, lawyer glare of his. "Royce, did Tammy see her mother push you? Is that what this is all about?"

"No. And even if she had, I wouldn't let anyone badger her about it. She needs to talk to someone she can trust, someone neutral. I mean it, Dale, someone neutral. This isn't part of the case. This isn't discovery. This is my daughter. She needs help."

Dale straightened and nodded. "Right. Sorry. I'll get on it as soon as I leave here. You know, though, that Pamela's going to fight us on it."

Royce nodded wearily. "I'm going to ask my doctor and the kid's pediatrician to recommend it."

"That'll help," Dale said doubtfully.

The door swung open then, and Nurse Gage walked through bearing a green plastic tray. "Dinner."

Despite his fatigue, Royce's stomach rumbled and he smiled. "I think I'm hungry enough even for hospital food."

"I didn't know anyone got that hungry," Dale quipped as the nurse slid the tray onto the bed table.

Apparently unamused, she pointed a finger at Dale and said bluntly, "You have been here long enough. He needs to eat, take his medicine and rest."

Dale's thin brows arched. With an amused glance at Royce he stood and threw his shoulders back, emphasizing his height. Executing a smart salute, he winked at the diminutive Nurse Gage. "Aye, aye, sarge."

She barely spared him a glance as she elbowed him aside, lowered the bedside rail and rolled the table into place, positioning it over Royce's lap. Royce chuckled. "Thanks for coming by, Dale."

Defeated, Dale started toward the door, saying cheerily, "I'll be back this evening."

"See you then."

Nurse Gage bent to depress the button that lifted the head of the bed. When his body was adequately contorted, semi-sitting with leg suspended and right arm propped on a stack of pillows, she shook out a thin paper napkin and tucked it into the too-high neck of his hated hospital gown. "Now, then," she said briskly, "let's get you fed."

She lifted the domed cover off his plate, revealing grayish meat and limp, overdone vegetables. Taking knife and fork in hand, she began cutting up the meat. He wondered, with some amusement, right up to the moment she placed the fork in his left hand, if she was actually going to feed him.

Ping, ping, ping, ping.

Glancing at the alarm board, Merrily shrugged into the roomy lab coat she preferred to wear over her simple scrubs. Room 18, Royce Lawler. Lydia Joiner, the charge nurse, groaned.

"Not again."

"What's wrong?" Merrily asked, checking her voluminous pockets.

"Eighteen's on a rampage," Lydia said, rising from the desk. "Found out he's got to have surgery again on that leg, and he's taking it out on the whole nursing staff."

"I'll go," Merrily said, aware that she didn't have to, since she was early for her shift.

Lydia inclined her head appreciatively. "Thanks, kid."

Kid. Always the kid. Lydia was no more than three years her senior, but due to her appearance, Merrily was "the kid." Sighing with resignation, Merrily moved toward Royce's room. The alarm board ping-ping-pinged again as she pushed through the heavy door.

"Thank God!" Royce Lawler exclaimed, tossing the bell remote into his lap. "It's about time somebody with some sense showed up around here. Where the hell have you been?"

Merrily tamped down a surge of gratification at his greeting. "I just came on shift."

"They've moved the damned phone again. Every time they come, they shove that table aside and leave it that way, then I can't reach the phone!"

Merrily pulled the table closer to the left side of the bed and shifted the telephone to the far right edge, within reach. "How's that?"

He dropped his head back onto his pillow. "Thank you. Thank you."

"The problem," she explained, squeezing behind the table to check his IV output, "is that the IV poles are fixed to the head of your bed. I'll see if I can't get a rolling pole in here and place it in front of the table."

"Why didn't they do that to begin with?" he grumbled.

Merrily bit her lip to quell a smile. "Because you are not ambulatory," she explained patiently.

"And I'm not likely to be anytime soon," he complained. "They're going to put a metal rod in my leg. I won't even be able to go through the metal detector at the airport!"

She laughed. She just couldn't help it. He glared at her, but then the furrow in his brow eased and his mouth curved into a wry smile.

"Okay, okay. So it's not that bad. And don't you dare say that I did it to myself. My mother has already pointed that fact out to me—not that I wasn't already aware of it."

"I understand," she said. "When did they remove the fingertip monitor?"

"They didn't. I did," he declared flatly.

"I see." She checked his pulse with her fingers. He lay still and quiet as she counted the beats and marked time on her wristwatch. As she retrieved his chart to make the proper notation on it, he lifted his head from the pillow to watch.

"You aren't going to scold me?"

She didn't look up from the chart. "Would it help?"

He didn't answer. He didn't have to. But after a moment he asked bluntly, "How old are you?"

The clipboard bearing his chart fell to her side. "Why do you ask?"

"Because you have to be older than you look."

She squared her shoulders beneath the crisp white lab coat, trying to conceal how sensitive the subject was. "I'm twenty-six."

"Holy cow! I'd have guessed eighteen, twenty, younger before I got to know you."

Chagrined, Merrily snapped, "What makes you think you know me?"

He shrugged his left shoulder and fell back on the pillow. "I know you're the only one around here with an ounce of compassion. First they tell me to rest, then they keep me up all night with tests. What kind of sense does that make?"

"Fiscal," Merrily answered succinctly. "The hospital labs are so busy with outpatient procedures during the day that they have little choice but to conduct inpatient tests at night. Hospitalized patients, after all, aren't going anywhere."

"Tell me about it," he mumbled. Then suddenly he announced, "I'm hungry."

Merrily folded her arms. She'd noticed the "no intake" sign on his doorside clip. "What time is your surgery scheduled for?"

He looked at the ceiling. "Three."

"Tell me what you want for dinner, and I'll make sure it's here when you get back." She didn't have to tell him that it was the best she could do.

Sighing richly he seemed to consider, then his eyes narrowed and he said, "Pizza with chicken and shrimp, pesto sauce, black olives, pineapple and mozzarella." He lifted his head to see how she'd taken that.

Smiling because she knew he thought he'd stumped her, she said, "Number six, Riccotini's. There's one around the corner. I'm having the salmon and sun-dried tomatoes myself."

"Number nine," he said, tussling with a grin.

"Anything else I can get you? Orange iced tea, maybe?"

"Mmm. About a gallon ought to do it."

"A number six with a large orange iced tea."

"And turtle cheesecake."

"And turtle cheesecake," she echoed. Chuckling, she headed for the door.

"Wait." He waved her back toward the bed and indicated the bedside table with a nod of his head. "In the drawer."

She opened the drawer to find his wallet. "Oh, don't worry about that." Ignoring that, he groped the drawer blindly with his left hand until he found the wallet. Flipping it open, he laid it in his lap and extracted a twenty-dollar bill.

"Dinner's on me," he said, thrusting the money toward her.

"Oh, no, that's all right. I was planning on going out, anyway."

A grin spread across his face. "So? What's your name? Given name, I mean."

"Merrily."

The grin spread wider. "Well, Merrily, I insist on buying your dinner, since you volunteered to pick up mine. No arguments, now. It's the least I can do."

Suddenly he stuffed the bill into the breast pocket of her lab coat. Electricity flashed through her, so strong that she stumbled backward a step—and into the corner of the bedside table, rocking it enough to send the telephone sliding toward the floor. She grabbed for it at the same time he did, and while they managed to keep the phone from falling, their arms became entwined. Her gaze collided with his and stuck.

For a moment the world and everything in it stopped. The second hand on the clock of time froze as they stared into each other's eyes. Then, slowly, he blinked and carefully extracted his arm from the loop of hers. Sinking back onto the pillow, he cleared his throat. Merrily settled the phone.

"What, uh, what time do you think I might get to enjoy that dinner?" he asked, his voice thick.

She tried to keep her tone level, normal. "Best guess, around eight."

He grimaced and covered his eyes with his hand. "I trust you'll still be on duty then."

"Until ten," she confirmed.

He said, "Good."

Good. She tried very hard not to let that please her in any personal fashion.

"I'll, um, be in later to perform the preop."

He let his hand fall to his side. "Sure. Better you than Nurse Disjointer."

Merrily ducked her head to hide her smile as she fled the room.

Katherine Lawler lifted her patrician chin and sniffed, silver hair swinging against her nape. "All I said is that it's a pity he can't sue himself."

"That's what's wrong with this country!" Marvin, her husband and Royce's father, proclaimed. "Everyone's sue happy. Let the blasted insurance pay for it. That's what it's for. Not that it isn't his own fault. He built the damned stairs."

Royce groaned, wondering desperately where Merrily was with that pizza. He hadn't caught so much as a glimpse of her since he'd returned to his room nearly an hour ago. The piteous sound elicited not a glimmer from his parents.

"You sued your own partners," Katherine pointed out.

"That was different! I had to get an accurate accounting, didn't I?"

"You already had an accurate accounting."

"How was I supposed to know that?"

The door opened, and to Royce's immense relief, his angel swept into the room, carrying two small pizza boxes and a brown paper sack.

"Finally!" he exclaimed on a long sigh, relaxing at last.

Her soft, muted-green gaze skidded right past him. Smiling at his parents, she left the pizza and sack on the bedside table. Briskly, she lifted the head of his bed and moved to the sink to moisten a cloth with antibacterial solution so he could clean his hand, saying, "Your postop exam was fine, so you get to eat now."

"It's about time," he said, though in truth he wasn't nearly as hungry as he thought he would be. He chalked it up to the drugs that were keeping him comfortable. He'd had a much easier time coming out from under the anesthesia this time, fortunately.

"Excuse me," Merrily said sweetly to his parents, wheeling the lap table into place. "These little rooms get awfully crowded. Perhaps you wouldn't mind standing in the corner over there. Just in case. He's a little awkward with one hand."

It was all the excuse his parents needed to beat a hasty retreat. Royce could've kissed her. Again.

"We'll let you enjoy your dinner in peace," his father pronounced, lifting a hand toward his mother.

Katherine kissed the air next to Royce's cheek and instructed in her long-suffering tone, "Try not to hurt yourself again."

Then they both went out the door without so much as a glance for Merrily. Glad as he was to see them go, Royce frowned. The least they could have done was spare a word of thanks for the only person around here who actually made him feel better.

"Who do I speak to about getting you a raise?" he asked, closing his eyes in gratitude. "Your timing is perfect. I was contemplating a heart attack in order to get them out of here, but I'm not that good an actor."

Merrily chortled and dug change from her shirt pocket, dropping it into the drawer of the bedside table. "The look on your face said it all. Who were they, anyway?"

"My parents."

Her eyebrows shot up, slender, winged things with a hint of gold in their gentle brown coloring. "I guess I should have recognized them, their photos are in the paper so often."

"Ah, you've made that connection, have you?"

"Who hasn't? Listen, I'm sorry."

"So am I," he quipped wryly.

"I meant, I wouldn't have chased them away if I'd realized they were your parents."

"I use the term loosely," he said. "They're no fonder of me than I am of them. Don't worry about it. You couldn't chase them away with a pitchfork if they didn't want to go. Now, where's my pizza?"

She checked the first box, closed it again and set it aside. "Here it is." She opened the box and arranged it on the adjustable table in front of him, then opened the sack. Plunking napkins down in front of him with one hand, she reached into the bag with the other and extracted a small cardboard triangle containing the cheesecake he'd been dreaming about since he'd first thought of it hours earlier. She set that aside and carefully lifted out first one and then another foam cup with plastic lids. Next she removed two straws, peeled one and pushed it into the hole in the top of the lid on one of the drinks. Sliding the large cup close to the pizza box, she picked up the other cup and reached for her own pizza. A moment ago he'd have given his house, his dream house, for a few minutes of solitary peace. Now the idea of eating alone, of being alone, seemed singularly unpalatable.

"You're not going?" he said disapprovingly, catching her wrist in his one good hand. He realized as his fingers closed around her delicate, finely boned wrist that he wasn't trying to detain her so much as he was looking for that jolt, that flash of carnal recognition that he'd felt before, when he'd stuffed the twenty-dollar bill into her pocket and discovered the unexpected bounty of her breast beneath the loose coat. It flashed through him, right up his arm to the center of his chest and straight down to his groin. It jolted the cup right out of her hand and sent it spilling across his clean, dry floor.

With a small cry, she leaped back, dismay shaping her pretty little mouth into a plump O. Royce craned his neck to glimpse the pale liquid spreading across the glossy tile, then he smiled at her, moved by a mischievous imp whose presence he hadn't felt in far too long and said, "Be glad to share."

But she just shook her head and ran out of the room. With a sigh Royce closed the lid on his pizza. Somehow it didn't look nearly so inviting without Nurse Merrily Gage there to share it.

Chapter Three

"Lane, would it kill you to actually put your dirty clothes into the hamper?" Merrily asked, exasperated.

Her brother peered at her through the steam generated by the long, hot shower he'd gotten out of minutes before. "What difference does it make?"

Merrily stuffed the clothes into the hamper and straightened, brushing her ponytail off one shoulder. "It would save me the effort of picking them up."

He shrugged and went back to combing his hair. "When you sort the laundry you're gonna pile it on the bathroom floor, anyway."

"That's beside the point."

Ignoring her, he tossed aside his comb and hitched up his jeans, admiring his bare chest in the mirror. "Hey, you ironed that red shirt of mine yet?"

"I haven't had time."

"Merrily, I'm going out tonight."

"Wear another shirt."

"I don't wanna wear another shirt. That's my chick-magnet shirt."

"Then iron it yourself."

"Yeah, right. You know I can't iron."

"Maybe it's time you learned."

He chucked her under the chin and grinned down into her upturned face. "Baby sister, that's what you're for." Abruptly turning pitiful, he whined, "Come on, Merrily, I'll ruin it if I try. You can whip it out in no time. Ple-e-ease."

Merrily sighed. "Oh, all right, but from now on you put your dirty clothes in the hamper, agreed?"

Lane turned away. "Sure, sure. Make it quick, will you? The guys are picking me up in a few minutes." He went out of the bathroom whistling.

Merrily bent and opened the cabinet beneath the sink. After extracting the steam iron as well as the cleanser for which she'd originally come into the room, Merrily straightened and looked around her. She'd spent the whole morning cleaning this one room, and now just look at it. Towels lay in a damp heap on the floor. One corner of the bath mat had been kicked up and left so that water pooled outside the shower. A wet washcloth that had been slung over the top of the shower dripped a trail down the pebbled glass wall. Why did she even bother? On every day off, she slaved to clean up this place, but not one of her brothers could be trusted to so much as straighten up after himself.

At twenty-eight, Lane ought to have been living on his own, possibly even married, but he wasn't responsible enough for that. The older two were worse. Lane at least had a social life, if trolling the club scene with his equally immature friends could be called such. Kyle, at thirty, remained the next thing to a recluse. He considered himself superior to the others because he'd earned a master's degree in English, but he hated his job as a high school teacher and had always been more comfortable with his books than people. Jody, on the other hand, had followed their father into the U.S. Postal Service, delivering mail. It was grueling work, but not grueling enough to have turned Jody into the old man he'd become at thirty-two. Since their parents had spent a large chunk of their retirement fund on a motor home and set off to see the country more than a year ago, Jody had virtually turned into their father, taking over the family home as if he owned it and attempting to order all their lives as their strict, conservative parents had done.

That proclivity created friction amongst the siblings. Jody parked himself in front of the television most evenings and issued edicts that his brothers both protested and ignored. Merrily herself operated on the periphery, functioning as housekeeper and cook while holding down a demanding full-time job of her own. The only thing the three brothers seemed to agree upon was that Merrily deserved whatever headaches and exhaustion her life brought her since she'd opted for a career instead of marriage and the protected existence of a housewife that her mother had chosen. They conveniently overlooked the fact that marriage had not really been an option for her. Even if some guy had been interested in her, he wouldn't have braved the guard dogs her father and brothers had always become whenever anyone approached her. She knew it was their way of showing their love for her, but she also knew that if they had their way, she'd be stuck keeping house for one or all of them the rest of her life.

She'd been trying to work herself up to moving out on her own for some time now, but what was the point, really? Her own social life was nonexistent and would likely remain so. Certainly she had friends, but most of them were married with young families of their own. She was Aunt Merrily to a bevy of small children whom she often baby-sat, but their parents didn't really have much time for her anymore, and because of her appearance it was difficult for her to make new friends her own age. She kept telling herself not to be so shy about it, but she couldn't seem to overcome that first dismissive look she always received when she approached other adults. The only notable exception to the rule was Royce Lawler, and even he had thought at first that she was a candy striper or some other teen volunteer at the hospital.

She wondered how he was doing and suppressed a surge of guilt at having left work the evening before without checking in on him. Really, though, how could she have faced him after she'd spilled her drink all over the floor of his room? She hadn't even gone back to clean it up. Instead she'd called housekeeping to take care of it. If she hadn't gone in there thinking they could share dinner together, she wouldn't have embarrassed herself like that. It was stupid, the way she'd started to fantasize about the man, especially since she would probably never see him again. Barring complications, he'd leave the hospital before she even returned to work. Disappointment welled up in her. She bit her lip, but then Lane yelled to get a move on with that shirt, and she shoved aside personal concerns to do what she seemed to do best, taking care of everyone else.

"What the hell do you mean she's not coming in?" Royce demanded of the male nurse easing his bandaged leg down onto the pillows arranged to accept it. Knowing that he was going to lose the traction bar soon was a great relief, but it seemed secondary to the fact that Nurse Gage wouldn't be tending to it. "She has to come in. She's a nurse, and she has patients who depend on her."

"She also has days off just like everyone else," the man told him, his smile flashing white in his dark, squarish face. "I, Carlos, will take care of you today."

Royce tamped down his impatience and forced a smile. "Great. That's great. Uh, when did you say Merrily, er, Nurse Gage would be back?"

Carlos shrugged, saying off-handedly, "Day after tomorrow."

The day after? But he was due to check out of here tomorrow! Wildly he thought of stalling that for a day, but the idea of spending one more night in this torture chamber made him shudder. He might have done it if he'd been able to see his kids, but Pamela had decreed the hospital too traumatic for them, and under the circumstances he was forced to agree, so his only contact with them had been by telephone, when he could convince that suspicious nanny that he was who he said he was and should be allowed to talk to them. No, he had to get out of here so he could schedule a real visit, and the sooner the better, but that brought up a whole other set of problems.

He really couldn't manage on his own, but he would not go to his parents' house. Dale was well-meaning but no one's idea of a nurse, even if he could've spared the time from his busy practice to play that role. So Dale was calling home care agencies looking for someone to stay with Royce for the next few weeks. Royce grimaced at the thought of some stranger living in his house helping him tend to his most intimate needs, but what else could he do? Unless... He realized suddenly what had been in the back of his mind almost from the moment he'd been

told he would be going home soon. It probably wouldn't
work, but he knew that he'd kick himself later if he didn't
at least try.

"Listen," he said as the nurse turned away. "I have a
favor to ask. It's real important to me."

The man shrugged good-naturedly. "Sure, as long as it
is not against doctor's orders."

"It's not against doctor's orders," Royce promised
him. "I just need you to contact Merrily, I mean Nurse
Gage, for me. Can you do that?"

Obviously surprised, the man stroked his chin. "I don't
know. Personally I hate to be called on my day off."

"Please," Royce said. "If you could just get her a message, tell her I need to see her... Look, I'll pay you. It's
that important."

The man seemed insulted. "You do not have to pay
me. If it is that important to you, I will see what I can
do."

Royce relaxed slightly. "Thanks. H-how soon? I mean,
how soon can you call her?"

Carlos Espinoza glanced at his watch. "I have a break
in about forty minutes. I will try then."

Forty minutes. Royce bit his tongue to keep from urging the fellow to make the call now, immediately, instantly. Forty minutes, and then how long before he heard
from her? Would he hear from her at all?

Merrily sat in the kitchen thumbing through a magazine. When the phone rang, she didn't even look up,
knowing that Jody would prefer to get it himself. A moment later, when he yelled for her, she felt a mild spurt
of surprise. Rising from the table, she walked to the end
of the bar that separated the den from the kitchen. Jody
sat in his recliner, staring at the television screen.

"What is it, Jody?"

He didn't look away from the screen. "That call was for you."

She folded her arms. "Why did you hang up, then?"

"Guy said that a Mr. Lawler wants to see you. I said I'd pass the message. That was it."

Royce! For a moment she stood frozen in place. He wanted to see her. She didn't stop to wonder what he wanted or why it was important enough to contact her at home. She didn't question who had actually made the call or when or how she was supposed to make contact with Royce Lawler. She only knew that he wanted her, and that was more than enough at the moment.

"I'm going out," she announced as she moved back through the kitchen. Jody shouted at her that it was too late to be going out, though in truth it was only a little past eight. Ignoring him, she grabbed her handbag from her room and, mindless of the sandals, shorts and simple tank top that she wore, darted out through the garage door.

Her small, two-door car sat curbside in front of the house. Lane, who was in construction, always got the garage because the tools piled in the back of his pickup were liable to be stolen if he left the truck out, or so he claimed. Merrily couldn't help recalling that when their parents had been at home and their mother had parked her car in the garage, Lane's truck had sat beside their father's in the drive and nothing had ever disappeared from the back of his truck then. Now Jody parked in the drive, leaving one side free for Lane to come and go, and she and Kyle jockeyed for position curbside in front of the house.

For once, Merrily was glad that she didn't have to back out of the garage past Jody's SUV and ease between Kyle's sedan and the neighbor's minivan into the street. It was much easier just to jump behind the wheel and take off. By the time Jody figured out she wasn't paying him any mind, heaved himself up out of the recliner and made it to the front door to yell at her again, she was already pulling away from the curb.

The hospital was less than ten minutes away from the house, which was one reason her parents had agreed three years earlier that she should take the job there. She had never regretted the decision. She loved nursing. She was good at it, and the money was generous enough to allow her to pay off her school loans in record time, make a substantial down payment on the sporty little economy car she was driving and stash a sizable amount in savings every month.

As she parked in the employee's lot and hurried into the hospital, she thought again that she really ought to move out on her own. She could afford it. Why she should consider doing so now, however, was something she did not want to address. Instead, she concentrated on getting where she wanted to. The moment she entered his room, however, she realized that she could have chosen a more opportune moment to visit, since the room was already crowded with medical staff, all of whom clustered around the side and foot of his bed.

The traction rod had been removed, and they were in the process of replacing the heavy bandages on his right leg with a stabilizer, which was really just a heavy elastic bandage with steel rods attached and Velcro closures. It would serve in place of the old-fashioned plaster cast, such as the one on his right arm and shoulder, and allow the doctors to periodically check the surgery incisions required to properly set his leg bones. After counting four practitioners, including the doctor, his assistant and two nurses, Merrily knew that she didn't need to be in that room at that moment.

All thought of beating a hasty retreat evaporated when Royce spotted her and exclaimed, "Merrily! Hey. Come on in."

Carlos Espinoza glanced over one shoulder, grinned and said, "That was fast."

So it was Carlos who had left that message.

Royce waved her over, exclaiming, "Free at last! Man, that traction stuff is for the birds."

"If you don't stay off this leg," the doctor warned from the stool rolled close to the bed, "you'll be right back in it."

"Don't worry," Royce replied meaningfully. "I'm not going to do anything stupid."

The doctor looked up at Merrily, who had moved to stand next to the head of the bed, and said, "See to it that he doesn't."

She thought it odd that he should direct his orders specifically at her, but she just nodded. The orderly at the doctor's elbow slid the spread stabilizer beneath Royce's leg, which the two nurses held suspended slightly above the bed. Bright red with white trim, the contraption would be hard to miss in the weeks it would have to be worn. The nurses gently lowered Royce's leg, and though he winced when it met the padded lining of the stabilizer, he winked at Merrily and said softly, "Thanks for coming."

She just smiled and shifted her weight self-consciously. At the exact same moment, Carlos started to turn away from the bed. The two bumped, and Carlos apologized cheerily, though Merrily felt her face glow red with the knowledge that it was her fault. What was it about Royce Lawler that turned all her fingers to thumbs and her feet to blocks of clay?

As Carlos left the room, Merrily grasped at something

to say to deflect attention from her clumsiness. "I see the IV and morphine pump are gone."

"He'll be getting a shot of painkiller when we're done here," the doctor said, threading a strap through the metal loop opposite and carefully tightening it. "And he'll have to continue taking those injections for a while. The anti-inflammatory and antibiotics can be taken by mouth. I'll leave prescriptions at the nurses' station. The leg should be kept dry and elevated as much as possible. I'll see him again in about a week. You'll have to call my office for an appointment."

Again, it seemed as if the doctor was speaking directly to her, but Merrily dismissed that and said to Royce, "Did you get all that?"

"Got it," he replied, smiling. Those heavenly blue eyes seemed to be trying to telegraph her a message, but she wasn't receiving.

The doctor finished what he was doing and got up off the stool. "Okay, that about does it. Nurse Gage, would you lift the foot of his bed, please?" Merrily bent to activate that function of the bed. The doctor went on as the other two practitioners left the room. "I suggest you rent a wheelchair for use at home and when you have to be out in public, which you really should keep to a minimum for several more weeks. I'll see to it that your dismissal packet has a list of equipment providers in it." He peeled off his latex gloves and added, "I'll see you in the morning about six, and you should be ready to go by ten. Takes a few hours to process the paperwork. Any questions?"

He looked first at Royce, then at her. Merrily just looked at Royce, who shook his head and said, "Nope. None I can think of at the moment. Thanks, Doc, for everything."

The doctor smiled and nodded, then he pointedly addressed Merrily again, saying, "Do me a favor, will you? Keep him away from stairs. I don't want to have to put him back together again."

Merrily blinked and opened her mouth to reply, but she couldn't think what to say to that, so she simply closed it again and nodded.

The doctor dropped his gloves into the appropriate waste receptacle. "I leave you in capable hands then," he said, and with that walked out.

Merrily stared at the door as it slowly swung shut behind him. "Well. That was odd." She turned her attention back to Royce. "He kept talking to me like I'm your personal nurse or something."

Royce ducked his head sheepishly. "I, um, might have, like, accidentally led him to believe that."

"What? Why would you do that?"

"Because I'm not supposed to leave here unless I have someone who can take care of me."

"But you don't," she immediately deduced.

"Uh, not yet."

Was this what he wanted to speak to me about? Disappointment skewered her. "Okay, well, I can recommend a couple of reputable agencies."

He grimaced. "I thought of that already, but I can't stand the idea of some stranger moving into my house with me."

Merrily nodded sympathetically. "Maybe you should stay somewhere else for a while, with your parents, perhaps?"

His eyes grew wide with mock alarm. "I'd rather stay here, and believe me, I'd sooner jump out of that window over there than do that. Nope, I just see one option."

"Which is?"

"You."

She blinked at him. "Me?"

"Look, I know it's an imposition, but I don't trust anyone else."

"You want *me* to move in with you?" she asked disbelievingly.

"I know it's selfish," he said, reaching across the bed with his left hand to take hers. She jumped, lightning flashing up her arm. "But I'm desperate," he went on. "I'll make it well worth your while. Whatever they're paying you here, I'll double it."

Double? "No, that's not right," she said distractedly.

"Please, Merrily. I can't get along by myself, and it's a big house, lots of room, beautiful area. Did I say that you're the only one I trust?"

At the moment she couldn't do anything but gape at his handsome face. This beautiful man wanted her to move in with him, at least temporarily. He didn't have to just disappear out of her life, after all. He trusted her.

"I know it's asking a lot," he said, squeezing her hand, "but Carlos says that because of the nursing shortage you can probably take a leave of absence and come right back here to your job when you're ready."

Her job was the least of it, actually. She could get another job. Nurses could pretty much write their own tickets these days, which was why Royce was going to have a difficult time finding someone with really good skills to take care of him. No, the job was the not the problem. The problems, plural, were her brothers. Jody would hit the roof if she told him she was moving out even temporarily, and the other two would lay on foot-deep guilt trips. They'd never taken care of themselves a day in their lives. Maybe it was about time they did.

Why shouldn't she do this if she wanted to? They were

all adults. It might do them some good to start acting like it, including her.

"Look," Royce went on. "I wouldn't even mind if you have company over. I mean, if you have a boyfriend or something…"

"No boyfriend," Merrily murmured, already working out the logistics of it. She had to call her supervisor right away. No one was going to be happy about the short notice, but it couldn't be helped. Then she had to pack, and it would be best to take everything she might need with her the first time, since any time she returned to the house she'd undoubtedly have to contend with one or all of her brothers. She'd get started tonight while Jody and Kyle slept and Lane was out with his friends.

"Maybe there's someone else then?" she dimly heard Royce ask.

"Hmm? No, not really."

He squeezed her hand again, and this time heat burned in her chest, creeping up her throat to her face. Professional, she reminded herself. This was purely professional. Nevertheless, her heart was beating like a big bass drum.

"Can you do it?" he asked, gazing at her with those blue, blue eyes.

Could she? Oh, yes. She nodded, afraid she might gush if she spoke.

"Will you?"

Merrily took a deep breath, drawing her composure around her.

"Please," he added softly. "Merrily, I need you."

Something inside her melted, and she said the only thing that she'd even thought of saying. "Yes. Yes, I will."

"Are you out of your mind?" Jody demanded.

"It's a job," Merrily repeated for the third time, shoving toiletries into the small suitcase open on her bed. Since her announcement at breakfast all three of her brothers had been in a lather.

"You already have a job at the hospital!" Lane exclaimed.

"I've taken a leave," she said, returning to the dresser for her hairbrush.

"You can't move out of here!" Lane protested.

"It's only temporary."

"Who's gonna take care of us in the meantime?" Kyle wanted to know.

Merrily stuffed her nightgown into the bag on top of everything else and closed the lid. "You'll just have to take care of yourselves."

"You're not going," Jody insisted angrily. "Mom and Dad—"

"—are off seeing America," Merrily finished for him, straightening, "and even if they weren't, I'd still be taking this job."

"I forbid it!"

"Forbid away, but I'm an adult, Jody, and I'll do as I please."

"But you can't," Lane whined.

"Why not? You do."

"That's different."

She gaped at him, though why she was surprised was beyond her. "It's not different, Lane. It's not at all different, and it's time the three of you came to grips with that fact."

Jody wagged a finger in her face. "You are my responsibility."

"Oh, shut up. I'm twenty-six years old. I'm no one's responsibility but my own, and if you want to be respon-

sible for something, get a life and be responsible for that.''
She grabbed the suitcase by the handle and hauled it off
the bed while Jody stood there with his mouth open. For
a moment she waited in the hopes that at least one of
them would show a glimmer of understanding, but only
seconds went by before she realized the folly of that. Taking a deep breath, she moved toward the door. She had
hauled the rest of her things out to the car last night,
leaving only those things she'd needed to dress this morning and the gown she'd slept in.

"Who's gonna do my shirts?" Lane wanted to know.

"Take 'em to a laundry," she suggested blandly.

"Who's gonna cook?" Kyle groused.

"There are ten thousand restaurants in San Antonio,"
Merrily said with a sigh.

"I wanna know who this guy you're moving in with
is," Jody suddenly demanded.

That finally brought her to a halt. She glanced over her
shoulder. "This 'guy' took a fall down a flight of stairs,
dislocated his shoulder and broke his arm. He has compound fractures of the leg, not to mention torn ligaments,
a concussion and various contusions. He is helpless and
alone, and he offered me twice what I'm making at the
hospital."

Only Kyle had the nerve to block her path, whimpering,
"But we already need you."

She leveled a disgusted look at him and said drolly,
"You may be helpless, Kyle, but at least you're not
alone."

"I am not helpless," he said, lifting his chin. "I have
a college education."

Merrily rolled her eyes. "So do I." She began moving
toward the door again. "I suggest you hire a housekeeper,

but first get your lazy, college-educated butt out of my way.''

To her surprise he hopped aside. Without so much as a backward glance, she carried the suitcase through the door and out of the house. To freedom.

Chapter Four

"You'll follow us?" Royce asked through the rear window of the SUV, knowing perfectly well that was the arrangement they'd made.

Merrily nodded and waved as she walked toward the employee parking lot, his paperwork tucked neatly beneath one arm. He rolled up the rear window and put his back to it, his injured leg propped on the seat. As the vehicle moved away, Royce put his head back and closed his eyes, disgusted with himself on several levels.

For one thing, just riding in a wheelchair down to meet Dale, who had retrieved his SUV from the house in order to pick him up in comfort, had his heart pounding as if he'd hopped down from the third floor on his one good leg all by himself. For another, he'd just robbed the hospital of a very fine nurse, and he knew that he'd done it for reasons that went far beyond the obvious medical need. The very idea of having Merrily Gage under his own roof, alone with him for weeks, had conjured the sort of dreams that disturbed a man's sleep. And if that were not enough, at the root of it all was the poor exercise of judgment that had initially landed him in this predicament.

It helped a little to know that he'd already determined to hire Merrily away from the hospital even before she'd shown up in his hospital room wearing neatly cuffed little shorts that made her legs seem as long as she was tall and a top that left no doubt about the maturity of her form. Her breasts were small but high and firm. Their natural shape had been lovingly rendered by that clinging knit top with straps so tiny that she could not have possibly been wearing a bra. She had struck him then as the most natural beauty he'd ever seen. And he wanted her.

Merrily Gage was no girl: she was a woman. Suddenly the possibilities of having her in his employ seemed highly enticing, though pursuing even a semipermanent relationship with Merrily or any other woman was out of the question. He couldn't deny that he wanted her, so he half hoped that by the time he was physically able to act upon his desires, Merrily would be gone. Hell, he should've hired some gargoyle to move in with him and tend to his needs, but he couldn't be unhappy that Merrily had agreed to help him. His self-disgust didn't reach that far apparently. For the first time he wondered if he might be the selfish monster Pamela had always claimed he was.

Merrily stopped her car and gaped. "Wow."

The sandstone house sprawling across the hilltop awed her. The circular drive, arched car shelter and landscaped yard in front were impressive. Tall, arched, leaded-glass windows, the many hips of the copper roof and three soaring chimneys lent an unexpected grandeur to the rolling natural beauty of the setting. Obviously, Royce Lawler was no pauper.

Slowly she started the car forward again and followed the SUV. As she parked behind it under the drive-through, Dale got out and unloaded the wheelchair from the back of the SUV. Merrily went immediately to Royce's side. He had opened the rear door and twisted around in his seat so that his legs were outside of the vehicle, and he was trying to slide down to stand on his left foot. Merrily quickly ducked under his left arm and slid an arm about his waist, trying to ignore the jolt of heated awareness that accompanied the contact. With Dale balancing his immobile right arm and her supporting the rest of his weight as much as possible, Royce eased out of the vehicle, turned and sat down heavily in the wheelchair. Merrily adjusted the footrests, extending the right to support his injured leg, while Dale unlocked the front double doors and pushed them open.

Moving behind the chair, she grasped the handles and turned Royce toward the house. Royce tilted his head back to look up at her, and though white-lipped, he smiled.

"I cannot tell you how good it is to be home again."

"I can imagine," she replied. With such a home, she would never want to leave.

She pushed him into the house, looking around her avidly. The floor of the wide entry hall was inlaid with stone. To the right, one could step up into a large, open dining room furnished with a long plank table and ladder-back chairs with padded seats upholstered in faded denim. Over the table hung an impressive rectangular fixture made of rusty wrought iron, and a large stone fireplace took up one entire wall.

The formal living room opened on the left. Plank floors, this time a step down, were scattered with tanned cowhide rugs and comfortable leather couches. Glass-topped occasional tables of the same wrought iron as the overhead fixtures stood at convenient intervals. Some supported small works of art, bronze sculptures and clay pots. Others held lamps with pierced tin shades. The center wall was composed of a massive double-sided fireplace, through which she caught glimpses of denim sofas in another room.

Farther down the central hall, a pair of steps led up to another hallway on the right. A ramp had been placed here to facilitate the wheelchair. On the left, another ramp had been installed over two steps that led down into a large den with bleached plank walls and floors. A recliner that matched the denim couches had been arranged in front of a large television screen recessed into the wall. At the very end of the entry hall and on the same level was another eating area and presumably the kitchen. The entire back wall of the house seemed to consist of enormous plates of glass and overlooked an expanse of terraced decks, a slope of forested ground and, far beyond, the city of San Antonio.

"Our Nurse Gage is suitably impressed, I see," Dale commented dryly, and Merrily promptly snapped her mouth shut, aware only then that she was gaping like an untutored child. "Royce believes that a builder's home ought to reflect the very best of his work."

"Then I'd say he builds some magnificent homes."

"You will notice that the house itself is designed and constructed so it contains many steps but no flight of stairs," Dale told her.

Merrily furrowed her brow in confusion. "But I thought he fell down a flight of stairs here at home."

Dale pointed toward the deck beyond the glass wall at the back of the house. "It's outside. A very long, steep flight of stairs that leads down to the back driveway. That's where he fell.''

"Hel-lo," Royce said irritably. "In case it's escaped your notice, I'm sitting right here. Stop talking about me like I'm not."

Dale grinned and said to Merrily, "Obviously, the patient needs a nap. Let me help you get the chair up the ramp, then I'll show you where to stash this character."

"I can do it," Merrily insisted, knowing that she would have to manage on her own sooner or later.

"I'm not helpless you know," Royce muttered, seizing one wheel of the chair with his left hand and awkwardly turning the chair toward the ramp. He had no hope of getting that chair up that incline, though, and they all knew it. Merrily, however, waited until he had the chair lined up and aimed forward, then set her legs and pushed with her body until they were on level floor again.

Two doors opened off this level. As they passed them, Royce waved a hand to his left and said, "Through there is the powder room, cloak closet, linen storage and laundry room. That's my office there on the right. Up ahead on the next level and overlooking the back of the house are the children's rooms."

Merrily hoped her shock did not communicate itself through her voice. "I wasn't aware that you have children," she said, after pushing the chair up the second ramp.

"Two," Royce answered. "My son, Cory, is five, and my daughter, Tammy, is nine. They live with their mother." That subject seemed to be closed, as he gestured to the right. "These two rooms are for guests. Take your pick. Each has its own bath."

The third and final ramp led to a type of landing and a double door, which Dale hurried ahead to open. By the time Merrily got the chair into the master bedroom, her arms were trembling. Grateful to have a rest, she looked around. The room was huge and contained a sitting area and fireplace, as well as large leaded-glass windows. A door opened onto a bathroom of equally large proportion with similar windows. Another was closed, and she assumed that it led into a closet. A king-size bed with a heavy wrought iron headboard occupied the wall opposite the fireplace. Matching tables with matching lamps flanked it, with a third positioned in front of the window between two side chairs. A rocking chair stood in front of the fireplace, and colorful rugs had been placed strategically over the plank floors. The smooth walls had been painted and stippled to resemble old leather. A wall cabinet stood open, revealing an entertainment center. Bookcases contained not only many books but a number of framed photographs and several small objects of great interest to Merrily. One looked like a lumpy dog sculpted of plaster and colored with crayon.

She had no time to investigate, however, as her patient was showing signs of extreme stress. "Let's get you undressed and into bed."

He was wearing a pair of jeans split up one side all the way to the thigh and a T-shirt with one sleeve and most of that side cut out, as well as a single bedroom slipper. The fact that he didn't argue with her was indicative of his state.

"Dale," Royce said wearily, "would you get a pair of gym shorts out of the dressing room? It's the third large drawer down. And get my robe out of the closet."

As Dale went off to do as instructed, Royce pointed Merrily toward the bath. "You'll find a pair of scissors in the cabinet opposite the mirror. Should be the top drawer."

She went readily into the other room, fascinated by the luxury she saw there and what it said to her about Royce Lawler. Through a batwing door to her left, she glimpsed a huge, jetted tub of hammered copper and an equally impressive shower built of curving glass block. To her right was an area of cabinetry with double sinks back to back, mirrors above each, a built-in dressing table with chair and lighted mirror, and a wall of cabinets containing a pair of doors above a set of wide, shallow drawers, the top one of which came to about her shoulders. Between the dressing table and drawers, the dressing room door stood open, revealing walls lined with more drawers and two closet doors. A bench sat in the middle of the floor. As she watched, Dale extracted a pair of shorts from an open drawer, which he then closed before walking into the closet.

She had known, of course, that Royce Lawler was well out of her league. His family was among the most prominent in San Antonio, after all. This place proved that he was a man of rare good taste with the money to indulge himself in the very best. Obviously he would never be seriously interested in a completely average woman like her. As she opened the well-organized drawer and extracted the scissors, she told herself that knowing this fact liberated her from any foolish dreams. Now she could concentrate on her work and enjoy this rare moment of freedom from her family obligations in these surprisingly sumptuous surroundings.

When Royce instructed Merrily to literally cut the jeans from his body, he did so because exhaustion and pain simply precluded that he get out of them the same way he'd gotten into them. She worked without comment, cutting through the heavy denim fabric while he sat passively and Dale turned down the bed after returning to the room with a pair of loose, gray knit shorts and his Texas orange bathrobe. He wore nothing beneath those jeans but skin and could only feel grateful when she finished her job and turned away, allowing Dale to help him out of the mutilated T-shirt. She returned a moment later to drape the robe over his shoulders. Then she wisely stayed behind him as he rose, allowing the ruined jeans to fall to the floor at his feet, or rather foot, as he couldn't put the right one on the floor, let alone stand on it.

One of the things he liked best about her, he decided, as the robe slid down to shield his nakedness from her view, was the thoughtful, somehow wise manner in which she allowed him as much dignity as possible in dealing with his current disability. Once he sank down into the chair again, Dale whisked away the ruined jeans and worked the shorts up his legs.

Royce struggled once more to a standing position, only to discover that he had reached the end of his strength. Swaying dangerously, he reached back to catch himself on the arm of the wheelchair and found warm flesh. Merrily stepped up under his arm and steadied him while Dale quickly pulled the shorts up around his waist inside the robe. Any other time, Royce would have burned with embarrassment. Just then, however, his injuries were exacting too great a toll to leave him strength even for humiliation.

He turned blindly toward the bed, Merrily on one side, Dale on the other, and somehow managed to hop the short distance to it. They turned him and eased him down to a sitting position. Then, pivoting on his hips and with Merrily carefully lifting his injured right leg, he lay back with a groaning sigh. His own bed. Heaven. Exhaustion clutched him, but his eyes managed to find Dale.

"Will you get her settled?"

"Sure thing, old buddy."

Royce smiled. He could always depend on Dale, but as his eyes drifted closed, an alarming picture branded itself on his brain, his best friend and confidant sliding an arm familiarly around the shoulders of his own personal angel.

Dale placed the two large, mismatched bags in the center of the large, airy room and straightened. "What do you think?"

Merrily dropped the two smaller bags on the bed and glanced around her, smiling. The four-poster bed was high and wide, its pale wood gleaming. A matching dresser stood across the room between the bath and closet doors. The single bedside table matched a larger table that stood before a deep shuttered window flanked by two small wing chairs. A rustic armoire, she had already discovered, contained a small television and CD system. She stood on thick, soft Berber carpet. The generous bath attached to this room was white-tiled, bright and pristine. Her own room at home was small and shabby by comparison.

"This is some house."

Dale chuckled. "Yeah, well, what would you expect from the city's finest home builder? Honestly, you haven't seen anything yet. Wait until you see the pool under that massive deck out there."

Merrily gaped at him. "A pool *under* the deck?"

Dale grinned. "Royce is nothing if not inventive, and he believes in making best use of the natural resources. Another builder might have come in here and leveled this spot before building. Royce had the house designed around the site. Besides, having the pool covered makes it usable year-round. Come on. Let me show you the rest of the place."

Merrily followed, her amazement growing, as Dale led her around the house as proudly as if he owned it himself. "Does he run his business from here?" Merrily asked, looking around the cluttered office.

Dale shook his head. "Not really. He has an office downtown, and he usually drops in there several times a week just so the staff doesn't forget what he looks like, but he's usually out on the job sites. A lot of stuff winds up in here, though."

"So I see."

They moved on to the breakfast room, which commanded a sublime view, as did the large den and kitchen, which connected to the formal dining room through a sunken hallway. The kitchen, in Merrily's opinion, was the very heart of the house, and she couldn't disguise her eagerness to get in there and putter around. The cabinet bases and countertops were stone, the floor and cabinet fronts highly polished wood, the fixtures brushed steel and copper. A center island, over which hung a large wrought-iron pot rack laden with copper and cast iron pans, provided more than ample work space.

The pool, accessed via the garage or the sunken game room was a marvel. The space was open on two sides, but the framing existed for panels that would close it in during the weeks of winter. The massive deck above it was a marvel of engineering genius, but when Merrily stood at the top of the stairs and looked down at the distance Royce had fallen, a shiver crawled up her spine.

"A guy will be out tomorrow to put a gate at the top of these steps," Dale told her. "Royce always meant to do it, but it was somehow overlooked during the building of the house, and he never got around to correcting that."

"It's a miracle he wasn't killed."

Dale nodded and said, "He might have died if not for Tammy."

"His daughter?"

Dale nodded and looked toward the back of the house. "She apparently saw him fall from her room, and she immediately called 911 and me. Then she got a blanket, covered him and stayed with him until help arrived."

"She did everything right. Must be a bright, brave little girl."

"A troubled little girl," Dale said.

Merrily waited for him to go on and, when he didn't, gently prodded him. "The accident must've been very traumatic for her."

"Just one more trauma of many, I'm afraid." He looked away then, hand sliding into the pocket of his slacks to nervously jingle its contents. Finally, he jerked the hand free and made an agitated gesture with it. "Look, you're going to find out soon enough so I might as well tell you. Royce's divorce was and continues to be extremely acrimonious, and that's had a detrimental effect on both his kids, but especially on Tammy."

Merrily bowed her head, disappointment pulling at her. Somehow she had expected better from Royce Lawler. "That's too bad."

"It's not Royce's fault," Dale quickly assured her. "That ex of his is a walking pestilence in my opinion. She's done everything in her power to turn those kids against him. They've been locked in a bloody custody battle for the past two years."

Merrily's head came up sharply. "He's trying to take the children from their mother?"

"He's trying to *protect* them from her. Pamela's just plain crazy."

"Well, if that's true, then why has it dragged on all these months?"

"Because Pam is as smart and manipulative as she is nuts."

Merrily wanted to believe that. She couldn't picture Royce being cruel enough to deprive a loving mother of her children, but she didn't really know him, and the luxury of this place merely served to point up that fact. Still, she was here to perform a service, not to judge. Shrugging, she turned away from the stairs and started toward the house, saying, "It's none of my business, I'm sure."

Behind her Dale muttered something that sounded like, "It will be."

He followed her into the house and was waiting in the kitchen when she returned from looking in on a soundly sleeping Royce. "It, um, just occurred to me that you're going to have to do the cooking."

She brightened immediately. "Really? I thought there might be a cook."

Dale shook his head and swiveled around on the stool to watch as she strolled into the kitchen. "The housekeeper comes in two afternoons a week, and a guy comes by every Thursday to take care of the lawn, but that's it."

"Well, I guess I'd better take a look at the larder, then," Merrily said happily, "see if there's anything I can cook."

"Make a list," Dale told her, "and I'll pick up whatever you need."

Both the refrigerator and the pantry, as it turned out, were extremely well stocked. Still, she noted the lack of a few items. Finding a pad attached to a clipboard that hung just inside the pantry door, she jotted down her list, which she then presented to Dale. He glanced over it, eyes widening.

"Okay," he said doubtfully, "but I'm warning you now, that Royce isn't going to drink herbal teas."

Merrily chuckled. "Maybe not, but I will. And you might be surprised. In addition to having medicinal purposes, many herbal teas are quite tasty."

"Royce still won't drink 'em," he stated firmly.

"I think he will."

Dale lifted both brows. "Wanna bet?"

She leaned her elbows on the counter, smiling. "I might." He grinned, and suddenly she was struck by how handsome he was. Funny, but she hadn't noticed before. "What did you have in mind?"

"How about dinner?"

She considered that and nodded, flattered enough to be enthusiastic. Going out was out of the question, however. "I win, you furnish takeout," she said. "You win, I cook."

He stuck out his hand. "Deal."

She placed her own hand in his, surprised by its size. He was so thin that he didn't look as large as he obviously was. Though taller than Royce, Dale had somehow seemed less substantial—until now.

"Shall we put a time limit on this wager?" Merrily asked brightly, taking her hand back when it seemed that he would go on holding it indefinitely.

"Good idea. How does a week sound?"

"A week it is."

Dale shook his head, chuckling. "Like taking candy from a baby."

"You think so?"

"I know my boy Royce."

"And I," Merrily said confidently, "know my herbal teas."

Dale cocked his head then, studying her blatantly. Finally he nodded. "Like I said, I know Royce, maybe better than he knows himself, and now that I know you a little, I think I understand better why he's so insistent that only you can help him get better."

"Oh?" She couldn't for the life of her imagine what he meant.

"You, Nurse Gage, are more than a pretty face," he said sincerely. "You have a very calming manner about you."

Please, she smiled. "You can't pay me compliments like that and go on calling me Nurse Gage. Let it be Merrily from now on."

He grinned. "My pleasure, and of course I'm Dale."

"Thanks for all your help today, Dale."

"Yeah, sure." He slid the list into his shirt pocket. "But if there's nothing else, I have to get going."

"We'll be fine," she assured him.

"I'll be back around six with these things. If you think of anything else you need in the meantime, I'm numbers three, four and five on the speed dial. If you don't get me at the office or at home, try the cell, in that order."

"All right. Thank you."

"No problem," he said, flipping her a wave as he strode toward the entry. "Oh, and when you concede defeat, I'd like a good steak."

Merrily just laughed, feeling that she'd landed in a very good place and perhaps had made a friend, too. Looking around her, she sighed with satisfaction, then she got busy making lunch for herself and her patient.

Chapter Five

Royce glanced at the syringe in Merrily's hand and grimaced. He hated the way that stuff made him feel, almost as much as he hated the pain and the weakness. Besides, if Pamela decided to send over the children this morning as he'd begged her to, he wanted to be wide awake and in possession of all his faculties. She wasn't likely to do it, mainly because she knew it would give him some peace of mind to see them, but just in case, he wanted to remain lucid.

"I'm not taking that stuff," he told Merrily flatly.

She just smiled patiently and said, "We've had this discussion repeatedly."

"It'll put me to sleep. I don't want to go to sleep."

Sighing, Merrily sank down onto the side of the bed. "I understand that you don't want to be knocked out, but you need rest. As you get stronger, you'll naturally sleep less. If we medicate regularly, you can spend your days comfortable but awake—for the most part.''

"For the most part," he echoed doubtfully. "You mean, occasionally.''

"Every day will get better," she promised, "but you know you need this, so why do we have to argue about it?''

"Arguing is better than sleeping," he said, beginning to enjoy himself. She smelled good, his Nurse Merrily, lemon and vanilla, like the pudding she'd served him with dinner last night. He wondered what she'd say if he asked her to stretch out on the bed next to him. She began speaking again, and his gaze glued itself to her mouth. Watching her speak seemed to ease his pain a little. He suspected that a true kiss from her would be more drugging than any injection.

"Arguing is not helpful," she was saying, "and that's what I'm here for, to help you. It's also why the doctor prescribed these injections.''

What a mouth she had, eminently kissable, absolutely luscious. He still remembered how it felt, even while out of his head and in pain, to press his mouth to hers. Just thinking about it now lessened the ache in his shoulder and leg. Better the doctor should prescribe her. "Why can't I just use the pills?''

"They aren't strong enough," she answered, those luscious lips forming each word carefully. "Tell you what, take the injections today, without argument, and we'll try the pills tomorrow. Okay?''

At the moment he'd have agreed to anything that would have kept her talking. "No more shots?''

"Only at bedtime.''

"You drive a hard bargain," he grumbled.

"I just want to spare you pain.''

"It's not that bad," he lied.

She lowered her head, keeping her gaze fixed. "I know I look young, but do I also look stupid?"

He smiled, despite the persistent ache. "No."

"Well, then."

Resignedly he rolled onto his back and pulled his good arm from beneath the cover. He did hurt, and he was tired, and Pamela was not going to bring the children over. And he was having inappropriate thoughts about his nurse. Merrily swabbed his upper arm with a small square of alcohol-soaked paper, pinched the muscle into a bulge, uncapped the needle with her teeth and plunged the needle into his flesh. He didn't feel a thing and told her so.

"That's the point," she said, deadpan, recapping the needle.

"Ha-ha. Nurse humor." Smiling, she started to rise. Without thinking, he clamped his hand down over her thigh. "Don't go." She froze, her delectable bottom poised a mere inch above the bed. The heat of her thigh warmed his palm and sent blood surging to another part of his body. He removed his hand, and she subsided. "Talk to me awhile," he pleaded. "I'm tired of talking to myself."

"What do you want to talk about?"

"Don't know. How do you like the place? Comfortable enough?"

"The house is fantastic, as you well know," she told him with an appreciative smile. "I adore your kitchen."

"Thanks. You like to cook, don't you?"

"I love to cook."

"Me, too."

"Really?"

"It's one of the things I'm missing most, frankly."

"I thought you'd have someone to prepare your meals for you."

He shook his head. "Uh-uh. When I was married, we had someone because she insisted, but even then I did all the cooking on the weekends." He smiled, remembering. "I'd spend all morning making silver dollar pancakes for the kids."

"She?" Merrily said. "You mean your wife."

The sweet memory evaporated. "*Ex*-wife," he corrected, shifting into a more comfortable position.

Merrily looked away. After a moment she said, "Well, you have a wonderful kitchen. In fact, the whole house is wonderful."

"Wait until I can show you the pool."

"Oh, Dale already has," she said quickly.

Irritation flashed through him. Dale. "Has he?"

"Yes, he showed me the whole house, except for the kids' rooms."

Royce tried not to grind his back teeth. He had asked Dale to help her get settled, not squire her around the house. "What else did he do?"

"Nothing much," she answered blithely.

He turned his head, sure he'd heard something more in her voice. "I don't think I believe you."

She raised both eyebrows, and then she laughed. "All right. He made a bet with me."

Royce frowned. "A bet? About what?"

She leaned toward him, one arm braced against the mattress, weight held against the palm of her hand. "I'm not going to tell you." With that she pushed off the bed and stood. "You need to sleep now."

His eyes did feel heavy, and a lightness was creeping over him, but he wasn't ready to let go just yet. "Why won't you tell me what the bet was about?"

"Because it wouldn't be fair."

"To whom?"

"Either of us."

Us. "You mean you and Dale."

"Mmm-hmm."

"What was the wager? I mean, the payoff."

"Dinner."

Royce narrowed his eyes. "He asked you to dinner?"

"No."

He relaxed, and lightness swirled through him, invading his limbs. "Tell me." His tongue didn't want to move properly.

"I will," she promised, smoothing the covers with her hand. "In a few more days."

He wanted to argue about that, but she stepped back, moving out of his sight. "Don' go yet," he muttered.

She appeared again at the foot of his bed, her smile the sweetest he'd ever seen. "All right." She walked over to the chair in front of the fireplace and turned it toward the bed. "I'll sit here awhile."

"'Kay." His eyelids drifted closed, too heavy to keep open. An easy sigh floated up out of his mouth. Merrily was here, and he could sleep.

Royce groaned, becoming aware of a stiff muscle in his neck and the all-too-familiar aches. Heavily he rolled to his back. Pain shot through his right shoulder. The blasted cast made it nearly impossible to lie comfortably. He'd have given half of what he owned to be able to bend his knee and flex his elbow. Opening his eyes, he knew at once where he was. Home.

"How did you sleep?"

His gaze shot to the side. Merrily. She had pulled the

rocking chair close to the bed and curled up there like a kitten, a magazine in her lap. He smiled. "Okay, I guess."

"I guess. Since you slept through lunch. Obviously, you needed the rest even more than I thought." She set aside the magazine and got up. "Hungry?"

He thought she looked good enough to eat, but he said only, "Starving."

"I'll take care of that as soon as you take your medication." Moving to the bedside table, she poured a glass of water from the pitcher she had obviously placed there earlier. She lifted the tail of her plaid cotton shirt and pulled a pill bottle from the pocket of her comfy jeans. Uncapping the bottle, she shook an antibiotic tablet onto the corner of the table. Next she helped Royce sit up and handed him the pill.

His head swam. His arm throbbed. He stared down at his palm. The oblong tablet looked as if it had been made for a horse rather than a human, and he remembered with a grimace how the things stuck in his throat.

"Do you need something for pain?" she asked.

He was hurting in more places than she knew at the moment. For one thing, his bladder felt as if it were about to burst. He slapped the pill into his mouth, took the glass of water that she offered him and washed the thing down. It felt like a brick in his throat. He handed back the glass and said bluntly, "I have to go to the bathroom."

"Want the urinal?"

"Hell, no," he snapped. "I want to walk into my own bathroom and use the toilet."

"Will you settle for a ride into your own bathroom?" she asked lightly, going after the wheelchair.

"Do I have a choice?"

"Nope."

"That's what I thought," he grumbled, scooting laboriously to the edge of the bed. She parked the chair next to him, and as she bent forward to throw the covers back out of his way, her shirt gaped open just enough for him to see the mounds of her small, firm breasts and the scrap of lace molding them. Suddenly his need elevated to extreme. He put his left foot on the floor and pushed up. Too quickly.

"Whoa." She caught him around the waist, helping him get his balance and sustain it until his head cleared. For a moment he considered falling back onto the bed and taking her down with him, but the ache in his limbs reminded him how foolish and fruitless that would be. He pivoted and sat, dropping his left arm over his lap as she adjusted the footrests. Rising, she moved behind the chair and pushed him forward.

The chair rolled through the wide door into the cool bath, then turned into the shower room. He leaned forward, reaching out to push open the batwing doors with his good arm. A second set of such doors shielded the toilet. She helped him pull those forward so that they locked in place. "I can handle it from here," he told her gruffly.

This was the worst part of being injured, the lack of privacy and the inability to take care of the smallest, most ordinary intimacies without assistance. Thankfully, Merrily sensed that. Without argument, she set the brake on the wheelchair. He lifted the left footrest with his good foot, then grabbed the batwing door and pulled himself up. Hopping on his left foot, he entered the alcove. Merrily swung the short, louvered doors closed at his back.

Leaning his good shoulder against the wall, he managed to shove down his shorts. Then he positioned himself in front of the toilet, balanced on his one good foot. Unfortunately, he was in no shape to take care of business at the moment and his strength was fast waning. Closing his eyes, he tried to think tranquil thoughts, but the vision that popped up before his mind's eye was Merrily bending over his bed, her shirt gaping open to reveal the creamy mounds of her breasts.

Gritting his teeth, he opened his eyes and muttered, "This is what I get for hiring such a pretty nurse." Something clattered loudly in the shower room. "Merrily?" he asked anxiously.

"Sorry. No harm done. I, uh, knocked over the towel stand."

Realizing that she'd overheard him, he smiled. At least he wasn't the only one uptight at the moment.

Some minutes later, he was ready to collapse but, nonetheless, relieved. As he eased into the chair, Merrily appeared from the other room. She briskly wheeled him to the sink so he could wash his hand. He looked up into the mirror, shocked by his haggard appearance. Suddenly he realized that his teeth felt almost as fuzzy as his jaws looked.

"There's a toothbrush, comb and electric razor in that second drawer," he said, indicating the cabinet. Merrily immediately went to fetch them. He brushed his teeth easily enough, but halfway through shaving the strength in his awkward left arm began to fail seriously. Without a word, Merrily took the razor from his hand and began applying it to his jaw. "You seem to have done this before," he commented over the whir of the razor, noting that she held the shaving heads just right against his skin.

"One time my brother Lane broke his right thumb and sprained his left wrist trying to do a handstand. He was drunk, of course."

"Ah."

"Then there was the time Jody burned both his palms

on a hot car radiator. I not only shaved him, I brushed his teeth for a whole week."

"And Jody would be?"

"My oldest brother."

"Sounds like you've taken pretty good care of those brothers of yours."

"Too good maybe," Merrily conceded with a sigh. "You should have heard the fit they pitched when I told them I was moving out for a while."

Royce lifted both eyebrows and asked, "Didn't you tell them it was a job?"

"Sure. They're just overprotective, that's all. Plus, without me they have to do their own cooking, cleaning and laundry."

Wondering just how overprotective they were, he asked wryly, "Did Dale show you how to activate the home security system?"

"Yes, but I didn't think it necessary to set it unless we leave the house. Right?"

Stroking his now smooth jaw, he muttered, "As long as I don't have to fight off three angry older brothers. I'm not up to it at the moment."

She snorted and began to comb his hair back. "As if. Lane thinks he's bad when he's drunk, but the truth is he's a mouse. Fighting's way too much effort for Kyle— I doubt he even knows how to make a fist. And poor, dull Jody, though he thinks of himself as on a par with our father, is all bluster."

Putting the comb aside, she began cleaning the razor. She was nothing if not efficient, his Nurse Gage. Royce looked himself over in the mirror and decided he looked some better. "How come you're still living at home together?" he asked.

Merrily shrugged and began putting everything away.

"It's a patriarchal thing. My dad likes to say he's from 'the old school.' Mom never worked outside the home, and he always insisted that he wanted his kids close because families are supposed to stay together, but I think it was more a matter of control. Now I suspect even he might agree that he overdid it a bit. When he retired, they bought one of those big motor homes and hit the road. They couldn't seem to wait to get out of here. Of course, he made me and my brothers promise to stay in the house and take care of one another."

"Sounds to me like you do most of the taking care of."

"Yeah," she admitted, "seems that way to me, too, which is part of the reason I'm here."

"Part of the reason?"

She shrugged. "The timing was right."

He felt a spurt of disappointment. The timing was right. Why did that rankle? What had he expected her to say, that she couldn't resist his darling blue eyes, that she was determined to hang around until he was healthy enough for her to jump his bones?

Meeting his gaze in the mirror, she asked, "Ready for something to eat?"

"Absolutely."

"Want to sit at the table by the bedroom window while I get together some food?"

"Okay."

She wheeled him into the bedroom and parked the chair at the small table where he sometimes sat to read the paper of an evening. She handed him the magazine she'd been reading, one of his architectural publications, and said, "I won't be a minute." She looked to the console mounted in the wall beside the bed and asked, "Think you can get to the intercom if you need me?"

"Yeah, I think so."

"I've asked Dale to get you a cowbell and a pair of crutches."

"A cowbell?" The crutches he could understand, but a cowbell?

"You could keep it with you," she said, "and if you need me but couldn't get to the intercom, all you'd have to do is ring. I figured it would have to be a pretty big bell or I wouldn't hear it in this big house."

Wryly, he shook his head. So he was to be belled like a rank bull. She didn't know how appropriate the metaphor was. In this case, however, the bull was hobbled. "So long as I don't have to eat hay," he joked.

"I think we can do a little better than that," she said, swinging away.

Ten minutes later he stared down into a bowl of soup ringed with crackers. "I don't suppose this is the first course?"

"That hungry?"

"I was hoping for a steak about two-inches thick, maybe a baked potato, loaded." He peered into the pale-amber liquid in his cup and added, "And coffee, strong, black coffee."

She put her hands on her hips and said in a very kindergarten-teacherish way, "Tell you what. If you'll eat your soup and drink your tea, I'll pan sear that ham steak you've got in the fridge, and bring that up."

He picked up his spoon, loaded it and said dryly, "Just get it up here by the time I've finished the soup or I'm liable to start on the napkin next."

She turned on her heel, noting aloud, "Patient has a hearty appetite."

"Mmm-hmm." He swallowed the warm soup. It was pretty good, actually, not the canned variety. The cup he eyed with more trepidation. Halfway through the soup, however, he decided to give it a try. Lifting the cup, he sniffed. Didn't smell like any tea he'd ever had, but it wasn't unpleasant, a touch of cinnamon, perhaps. Cautiously he sipped and tasted something very fruity underlaid with honey. Not bad. He sipped a little more and went back to the soup, polishing it off in just a few bites. The crackers went the same way, and when Merrily returned with the ham steak and the teapot, his cup was empty, too.

Smiling, she plopped the steak down in front of him, fork and knife crossed atop the plate. As she refilled his cup, she asked, "Feeling okay?"

"Pretty good actually," he said, picking up the fork. A moment later he realized that his clumsy left hand and a simple fork weren't going to get the ham sliced. Merrily picked up the knife and waited. He stabbed the fork into the ham steak, holding it in place, and she quickly sawed off several bites for him. Impatiently he forked the first into his mouth. "Mmm." After gobbling down the rest, he planted the fork in the steak again. Merrily immediately cut the remaining steak into small pieces. A few minutes later, he laid his fork across his empty plate, drained his cup and sat back with a sigh. "Ahhh."

"How are you feeling now?"

"Excellent. Full and relaxed."

She smiled and began stacking the dishes. "This may not be the best time to ask, then, but what would you like for dinner?"

"Hmm." He thought it over, trying to remember what he had in the pantry. Finally he shrugged. "Surprise me."

"How's Chinese?"

He lifted both brows, impressed. "Great."

She straightened, her hands going to her waist. "Have a favorite dish?"

He decided to test her expertise. "Pressed duck?"

Her smile turned cagey. "I'll let Dale know."

He felt his brow furrow before he could derail the reaction. "Dale?"

"Mmm-hmm. He'll be paying off on a debt." She tapped the rim of his cup, asking, "How did you like it, by the way?"

Confused, he waved his hand. "Fine. What is it, by the way?"

"A piece of cake," she replied smugly.

"I beg your pardon?"

She chuckled. "Actually, it's herbal tea."

"Herbal tea!"

"And the reason you're feeling so mellow right now." He couldn't keep the shock off his face. "Don't worry," she went on cheerfully. "I checked to be sure there would be no interactions with your medications."

That had never occurred to him. "I don't drink herbal tea. I mean, I didn't drink herbal tea before this."

"I know. Dale told me."

Realization dawned. "And you bet him that you could get me to."

She just smiled. "Sure you still want Chinese?"

He wanted to feel used and manipulated, but he couldn't. She'd hadn't tricked or nagged him into drinking the tea. She'd just left the damned cup next to his plate and let him decide for himself whether he liked it or not—and he had, did, like it. He laughed. "Tell him to use Chung Pao's Garden. It's not the best pressed duck in town, but it's the most expensive."

She laughed. "Actually, we didn't really say when the loser would have to pay up, so for tonight you may have to settle for the chicken I've got thawing."

"Only one?" he joked.

"I'll see if I can't find *something* to go with it," she promised. "Meanwhile, if you'd like some more tea…"

"No, thanks. I'm mellow enough."

"Fine. I'll just take care of these, then." She picked up the dishes and turned away.

Suddenly he decided to get back a little bit of his own. "You know," he said affably, "it's almost worth falling down a flight of stairs to have herbal tea served to me by such a beautiful woman."

She bobbled the dishes and several hit the floor, bouncing harmlessly on the carpet. Gasping, she dropped to her knees to gather them up again. Royce bit his lip to keep from laughing, but then she stretched, reaching for a spoon, and the pull of denim across her neat little rear end hit him in the groin. No longer feeling quite so mellow, he averted his gaze, but it crept back again a moment later as she rose to her feet, the tray balanced carefully in her hands.

"Sorry," she muttered, hurrying from the room.

He felt rather like a heel, considering that he was the one who ought to apologize. She was just too easy to bait, his sweet little nurse, and too good at what she did—and too easy to like, too easy to need. If he wasn't careful, he'd never again become as self-sufficient as he'd once been. Determined that would not be the case, he decided it was time to begin ordering his world again. He had done it before under much more egregious circumstances. Falling down a flight of stairs was nothing compared to losing custody of his children.

The first order of business was to bring as much normalcy back to his situation as possible. Looking down at his bare chest, he decided that the most obvious course was to dress himself. With some difficulty he turned the wheelchair from the table and maneuvered it across the room. It took a while to find an old T-shirt and get the scissors from the cabinet in the bath, but by the time Merrily returned, he had the shirt laid out on the bed and was trying to work the scissors with his left hand in order to cut out the right sleeve.

"Can I do that?" she asked, and he tossed down the scissors with disgust. So much for taking charge of his life again.

Quickly, expertly, she cut away the right sleeve and enlarged the armhole. Then she handed the T-shirt to him and sat down on the side of the bed, leaning back slightly, her upper body weight supported on her stiffened arms. Smiling to himself, he fumbled with the shirt until he could slip the newly cut hole over his cast, then he shoved his left arm through the intact sleeve and wrestled the thing over his head. The satisfaction was worth the effort.

Merrily sat up straight, asking, "Ready for a nap?"

He grimaced at the bed and confessed, "I'm tired, okay? But what I'm most tired of is lying in bed."

Instantly she suggested, "How about the recliner in the den?"

He closed his eyes. "Yes, please, Nurse Gage. Bless you, Nurse Gage."

She skipped behind his chair and started it moving. "Oh, don't thank me yet. Wait until I've beaten you at gin rummy."

"Gin rummy?"

"Can you think of anything else you'd rather we do?"

He could, but thankfully he wasn't up to it. "What makes you think you can beat me at gin rummy or anything else?"

"Wanna bet on it?"

He grinned. Stupid he was not. "No, thanks."

"Good answer."

Laughing, he sat back and enjoyed the ride.

Chapter Six

"I think we can manage with this," Merrily said, waving the long, narrow box of plastic wrap, "at least until the shower sock I've ordered arrives, but since you can't get your cast or right leg wet, we'll have to settle for half a shower."

"Half a shower," he echoed uncertainly, the lines bracketing his mouth and shadows darkening his eyes telling her that he was tired, despite having napped again before dinner, which had consisted of roasted chicken, rice pilaf and bean salad, Dale having pleaded inconvenience. She was content to allow him to set a date for paying his debt.

"Unless you'd rather have that sponge bath, after all," she suggested hopefully to Royce.

He made a face that perfectly expressed his feelings on that subject, even if his previous objections had not. "So how do we go about this half shower?"

"Well, I've been thinking about it, and it seems to me that since the ledge around the tub is so wide, you can sit on the inside corner of it with your back against the wall. We'll prop up your right leg on the edge to keep it dry and you can balance yourself by placing your left foot inside the tub. I'll soap you and use the sprayer from the tub to rinse you off."

"I'll soap me," he insisted, "and you can hand me the sprayer. Otherwise you'll have to get in the tub."

"I don't mind. I'll just roll up my pants and shuck my shoes so I can stand in the water. We only need a couple of inches."

"Fine," he snapped, "but I think I can wash my own body."

"Okay," she replied carefully, going down on her knees to begin wrapping his right leg with plastic, "whatever you say."

She knew that he was grouchy because he didn't feel well, and she didn't take it personally. Instead, she concentrated on mummifying his right leg, bulky stabilizer and all, in plastic wrap from his kitchen. At the top of the plastic "sock" she fastened an elasticized hair band with a metal clasp, after carefully testing it to be certain it wouldn't cut off his circulation. It would never survive a real shower, but it was the best she could do under the circumstances. Rising, she wrapped the remaining plastic around the top of his shoulder and under his arm to get the edge of the hard cast there.

"We'll have to be careful with the sprayer," she advised. "These plaster casts are just too sensitive to water."

"Maybe we can keep the plaster dry, but you're gonna get wet," he warned.

"I won't dissolve."

"Of course not. You're too damned stubborn for it," he muttered.

"Maybe," she said lightly. "Let's get these clothes off you. Can you manage the shirt?"

"I can, but if you think I'm going to sit around naked in front of you, think again."

Merrily struggled with both a smile and a blush. "You can drape a towel across your lap."

He sighed. "Yeah, okay."

She went for a stack of towels while he struggled out of the mutilated T-shirt. When she returned, the shirt lay over the arm of the wheelchair. "If you'll stand, I'll wrap this bath towel around your waist and we'll get those shorts off." He struggled to a standing position, and she wrapped the towel around his waist. Reaching beneath the towel, he tugged and shoved the shorts down. Finally the garment dropped to the floor. While he held the bath towel in place, she spread a hand towel on the edge of the tub, instructing him to sit down upon it and use it to facilitate his slide around to the corner.

"Without losing *this* towel?" he said doubtfully, indicating the towel around his waist.

"Just turn it around."

He shifted the towel and sat down. Carefully he scooted around the edge of the tub to the corner, keeping his right leg up and a hold on the towel now draped across his waist. When she saw that he was comfortable and secure in this position, she turned on the water and, while it ran, removed her shoes and rolled up her pant legs. Sitting on the outside edge of the tub, she put her feet into the water and chose a bar of soap from the stainless steel wire dish fixed to the side of the tub.

"This okay?"

"Whatever," he mumbled.

Working quickly, she soaped a washcloth, then diverted the water flow to the built-in sprayer with its long, coiled hose. Leaning forward, she adjusted the water stream to a trickle, then she handed him the washcloth and used the sprayer to carefully wet him down. He began scrubbing everything he could reach, above and beneath the towel, while she tried to look elsewhere, anywhere but at the broad expanse of his smooth, muscular, tanned chest.

"The last time I bathed with a beautiful woman," he commented wryly, "it was a lot more fun."

She dropped the sprayer and water shot up in an arc, drenching her. Grabbing it, she shut if off again, her face burning, while he laughed.

"Told you that you'd get wet."

"My fault," she said quickly, wiping her face.

"You've got to stop that."

She looked up. "What?"

"Getting flustered every time I compliment you."

Her gaze dropped away of its own volition. "Did you compliment me?" she asked nonchalantly, trying her best not to sound as breathless as she felt.

"I did, and ignoring it won't make it go away, you know."

"I know. I...I mean, thank you...for the compliment."

"You're welcome." He handed back the washcloth, adding tiredly, "I think that's the best I can do for now."

She started soaping the cloth again. "I'll take care of your leg."

"Just rinse me off," he ordered, obviously too tired to manage it himself.

"If you say so." She rinsed the cloth, dampened it with fresh water and rose to her feet, stepping closer to him in order to remove the soap from his right side. He'd been careful not to touch the cast on his shoulder, and she was just as careful. Finding it difficult to reach the back of his shoulder, she shifted to one side. Her foot slipped slightly on the bottom of the tub.

"You're going to fall," he warned, lifting his left hand to her waist. She gulped as the damp heat of his hand pervaded the fabric of her shirt.

"So long as I don't fall on you," she muttered.

"Oh, I don't know. I think I might enjoy it," he teased, voice husky.

Gulping, she ignored that and turned to retrieve the sprayer, he kept his hand on her so that it rode across her abdomen and back again as she faced him once more. For the life of her, she could not breathe. It was as if he'd poured scalding heat into her lower body and it now rose up into her chest. She fumbled with the sprayer, adjusting the output, as she leaned forward so she could rinse his back. Straightening again, she began rinsing the soap from his torso. Her gaze strayed down to the now tented towel across his lap, and she dropped the sprayer, yelping as water hit her in the chin.

"Get out of the tub before you break your neck!" he barked, releasing her in order to grab the sprayer.

She didn't have to be told twice, scrambling out of the tub while he angrily rinsed beneath the towel. With trembling fingers, she dried off as best she could and released the drain in the tub. Royce shut off the sprayer and thrust it at her. She hung it up and turned off the water supply.

"Towel," he ordered, holding out his hand, and she passed him a fresh, dry bath towel. He rubbed at his face and hair while she used a hand towel to dab at water spots on the plastic shielding his cast and stabilizer.

"I'll get you another pair of shorts. Don't you move until I get back."

"Fine."

She returned a few moments later to find that he had exchanged the wet towel across his lap for the dry one. They performed the procedure that had moved him into the corner of the tub in reverse. As he rose from the outside edge of the tub, balancing his weight with his good hand on her shoulder, she reached around him to secure the towel at his waist and preserve his modesty. He suggested that she slide the opening of the towel around to the side so he could get a hand on it himself, and she complied, but as he grappled with the towel, awareness sharpened and the room heated. Finally he got a hold, and she straightened, her arm about his waist to steady him.

Suddenly she was looking up into his much too handsome face. His blue eyes held hers for a moment, then dropped to her mouth. For an eternity she held her breath, every other concern suspended as she waited expectantly for his mouth to cover hers. Then he sucked in a deep breath, and sanity rushed back, bringing embarrassment. Realizing that he was trembling, she quickly eased him into the wheelchair.

"You can put these on later," she said, striving for her best nurse's voice as she swept up the shorts and dropped them into his lap. "Let's just get you into the bedroom."

"Fine by me," he gasped as she released the band around the thigh of his injured leg and began unwrapping the plastic.

"I'll straighten up here after I've gotten you into bed," she told him, tossing aside the big ball of crumpled plastic food wrap and moving around to the back of his chair.

"Don't worry about it," he said wearily. "Mercedes comes tomorrow to clean the house."

"She won't be cleaning up after me," Merrily told him, pushing the chair into the bedroom. He didn't argue with her.

"I don't even want to think about what I'm going to smell like when this cast comes off," he grumbled.

"I'll put a clothespin on your nose and stand by with a spray can of deodorant," she teased.

He chuckled tiredly. "Ever ready with the ingenious solution."

"Part of the job."

"No, that's just you," he said lightly.

She parked the chair next to the bed and set the brake. Then she folded back the covers, swept the bed with her hand and straightened the sheets. He handed her the shorts, saying, "Let's just leave these close by where I can reach them later. I think for now I'll just slide over into the bed and trust you not to peek beneath the sheets." The shorts slid right out of her hands and landed on his right foot. He just shook his head. "It was a joke."

"I know," Merrily replied lightly, bending to snatch up the shorts. As she tossed them onto the bedside table, she hoped he wouldn't notice the color burning in her cheeks.

Sitting forward on the edge of the chair, his good hand clasping the towel at his waist, he said almost apologetically, "I'm going to need your help for this."

"That's what I'm here for." Bending, she placed both arms around him. He pushed up, and she helped him turn his back to the bed and sit down. She stooped to lift his injured leg as he lay back then folded the covers up over him. "Okay?"

"No," he said. "I've been a bear today, and you've been the soul of patience."

"That sometimes happens when you don't feel well."

"It's more than that."

"I understand," she said. "You're worried about your children."

"Very much," he confirmed, but then he reached up with his left hand and captured her ponytail, pulling her closer. His blue eyes were clouded with pain and exhaustion, but beneath that burned something more. "The more immediate problem, however, is you, sweet nurse," he told her softly. "You're a huge temptation. You know that don't you?"

Her eyebrows shot up. "T-temptation?"

"A huge temptation," he reiterated. "We're both lucky I'm too incapacitated to do anything about it." Releasing her, he rubbed his thumb lightly across her lips before abruptly dropping his hand. "How about some of that tea of yours?" he asked, shifting his gaze. "I could use a little extra relaxation at the moment."

"I...yes." She leaped to her feet and whirled away, her heart tripping like a jackhammer—and almost went sprawling over the wheelchair. She heard a choking sound, knew that he was trying not to laugh at her clumsiness and fled, barely keeping herself from breaking into a run. When she returned several minutes later, he was sound asleep. She drank the tea herself in her own room and tried not to think what it might be like if her too handsome patient should one day yield to temptation.

Her patient was finally on the mend, which meant that Merrily had to find new ways to entertain him. Card games quickly palled, so they worked several crosswords together and even played a board game fetched from his daughter's room.

Part pink confection and part teenybopper, that room spoke volumes to her about the daughter he so obviously loved. Comic books shared shelf space with coloring books, dolls with stereo equipment and the latest "boy group" CDs. The few articles of clothing that hung in the closet ranged from designer label blue jeans to pajamas bearing the likenesses of cartoon characters. A little girl poised on the edge of adolescence, Tammy Lawler seemed caught in that awkward space between child and preteen, torn between two selves. How much of it was the natural result of growing up and how much had to do with the divorce of her parents? Merrily wondered if Tammy knew how much her father fretted over not being able to see her. Surely if she did, she would come to him. Poor kid, and poor Royce. He obviously agonized over the distance between them, though that was no reason to try to take the children from the mother—unless, of course, all that Dale had said was true.

After the board game, which he won, they watched a movie on cable, one Royce had seen and thought she would enjoy, which she did. They were still sitting in the den when Dale showed up with some books and another package of herbal tea. He stacked the books on the end table near the spot where Merrily sat on the couch. The packet of tea he tossed into Royce's lap with a mock scowl.

"Traitor."

Royce grinned. "Hey, I'm just a poor, helpless soul weakened by suffering."

"Yeah, right. About as helpless as a snake without rattlers." The rangy lawyer turned a woebegone look on Merrily, saying, "Don't let him charm you, kid. He's still got his fangs."

"Turn it the other way around, genius," Royce rebutted dryly. "It's the snake who gets charmed."

"Ah, well, that explains it, then." Dale wagged his finger at Merrily, who found that she enjoyed their banter immensely. "No fair, Nurse Merrily. You have beguiled the snake into drinking your nefarious brew. I'm thinking of crying foul.''

"Cry duck,'' Royce advised dryly, "pressed duck.''

Merrily laughed, but Dale made a face. "Ha-ha. Our bet doesn't concern you, and the payoff doesn't, either.''

"Doesn't concern me?'' Royce scoffed. "You know, if the horse wins the race he at least gets his oats.''

"Fine. I'll send you a box of oatmeal. Merrily can have pressed duck at Chung Pao's Garden with me.''

Royce's face immediately darkened, and Merrily knew what he must be thinking. Who would care for him if she went out? He was helpless alone. Tilting her head at Dale she reminded him, "The bet was carryout against home cooking, I believe.''

"So I'm offering a free upgrade.''

"And what about me?'' Royce grumbled, confirming her assumption. "What're you going to do, lock me in a closet? Or maybe you were thinking of pushing me down the stairs yourself this time and finishing me for good?''

Merrily gasped, her pleasure evaporating. "You were *pushed!*''

Dale and Royce exchanged wary glances. Royce cleared his throat. "I didn't say that.''

"Yes, you did.''

"It was a joke,'' Royce offered weakly.

Merrily stared at him, trying to imagine that anyone could hate him enough to push him down a flight of stairs. "What happened?''

"I-I'm not sure.'' His gaze shifted away. "I don't really remember.''

"Do you know who it was?''

"Like I said, I don't remember very much.''

"Oh, please,'' Dale said with blatant disgust. "We both know it was Pamela.''

"That's your theory," Royce retorted. "Don't you think that if I knew for sure what happened that night I'd do something about it?"

"Not if it meant Tammy having to testify against her own mother," Dale stated softly.

Royce looked away. Merrily's heart squeezed. That poor child. Had she actually seen her mother push her father down those stairs? If so, then Royce was protecting her by keeping quiet about what happened. Dale evidently thought that was the case.

"What about that therapist I asked you to find for her?" Royce asked.

Dale sighed. "Her pediatrician agreed to the recommendation, but Pamela's refusing to cooperate. We'll have to take it to the judge."

"And in the meantime, Tammy suffers," Royce said bitterly. He shoved his hand through his hair. "If I could just talk to her myself, I might be able to help."

"I know," Dale said, "but Pamela's keeping her under wraps. I called and went by there today, but first the housekeeper said they were all out buying school clothes, and later Pamela herself claimed Tammy was taking a nap."

Royce snorted. "As if. Tammy last took a nap when she was about sixteen months old. How am I going to get her over here, Dale?"

"Wait until they miss the next scheduled visitation, then petition the court to enforce its order," Dale said offhandedly.

"But they've already missed visitation."

Dale spread his hands. "You were in the hospital. Pamela can say it was too traumatic for them or you or whomever. Just give it through the weekend."

"And then wait for the court to act," Royce added

bitterly. "I know how the farce plays out. Pam will stall for weeks while the paperwork wends its way through the courts, then at the last moment she'll comply, and her attorney will point out how cooperative she's been, making me out to be unreasonable and demanding."

"Okay, we have one other option, then, but you're not going to like it," Dale said. "I can petition the court on a hardship claim, maybe gain us a little sympathy, say that in your weakened state you need the solace of your children and plead for immediate compliance."

Royce made a face. "Oh, that's classy, a grown man using his children like that."

"You aren't using your children," Dale pointed out calmly. "You would never use your children. You love them. That's allowed by the courts, you know, even preferred."

Royce sighed tiredly. "Whatever works quickest," he conceded.

"I'll see what I can do," Dale said. Turning to Merrily, he smiled and pointed his finger. "You and I, Nurse Merrily, will talk later about pressed duck."

"You," Royce said forcefully, "will leave my nurse alone. Now get out of here, you ambulance chaser, and let me get some rest."

"Is he always this sweet?" Dale asked Merrily gaily.

"Oh, sweeter," Merrily said with a smile.

Dale parked his hands at his hips and slid a look at Royce. "I'll bet."

Royce looked at Merrily and commented dryly, "Slow learner."

"Oh, really?" Dale countered. "I'm the one having dinner with our Merrily."

"Why don't *you* take a little fall," Royce suggested.

"If you break enough bones, maybe you can have several meals with her."

"That's your thing, pal of mine. I've never stolen pages from your book before, so don't look for me to start now."

"Suit yourself."

"Always." Dale turned to Merrily with a wink. "Until later, dear nurse. Call if you need me."

Royce snorted, and Merrily laughed. "I will. Good night."

"I'd say the same to you, but you're stuck here with him," Dale quipped, "so I'll just say, 'later.'" With that he started for the door.

"Not later enough," Royce called, but he was smiling ruefully.

"Is he always such a tease?" Merrily asked after Dale was gone.

"Yes."

"Well, he's a good friend to you."

Royce nodded. "I don't know what I'd do without him—or you."

"Me you can replace at any employment agency," she told him, rising to her feet. "A real friend is irreplaceable."

"Are you not my friend as well as my nurse, then, Merrily?" he asked softly as she moved around behind his recliner to retrieve the wheelchair.

"Of course I am."

"Of course you are," he said, releasing the footrest and sliding to the edge of the recliner, "which is precisely why I can't imagine letting anyone else do for me what you do."

"I don't do anything any other nurse couldn't or

wouldn't," she told him, positioning the wheelchair and setting the brake.

Leaving the packet of herbal tea on the arm of the recliner, Royce pushed up to his left foot and hopped around until he could sit. "Right. I can just see Nurse Disjointer climbing into that bathtub with me."

Merrily giggled at the thought. Lydia Joiner was built like a brick wall, wide and sturdy, and she always wore white stockings and an old-fashioned skirted uniform. Releasing the brake, Merrily pushed the chair toward the door.

"Would you like me to bring the books Dale brought to your room?"

"No, I'm too tired to read tonight—even though I slept most of the day. Again."

"You'll get stronger," she promised as they moved into the hall. "Just be patient."

Merrily didn't know what else to say, but it didn't really matter as they had reached the ramp up to the bedroom hall, and it required all of her strength to get him and the chair up it. They were almost to the second incline when Royce suddenly asked, "Are you going to start dating my best friend?"

She stopped, the chair giving a little lurch. "What?"

He put his head back so he could look up at her and said, "He's a bit of a ladies' man, our Dale. I don't see it myself, but women seem to like him. Even Pamela liked him at first, but he never flirted with her the way he flirts with you."

Heat washed into Merrily's cheeks. "Oh, I don't think he *flirts,* really. It's just teasing." She bent to the task of pushing his chair up that second ramp, and within seconds they were on level floor again.

"You didn't answer my question," Royce pointed out at once. "Are you going to start dating Dale?"

"I...I don't know. I...no," she decided abruptly, just then realizing that she'd be horribly uncomfortable on a date with Dale Boyd. "No, I'm not going to start dating him, and I can't think why you'd even ask."

"I ask because he's obviously interested in you."

"It's not obvious to me."

"Well, I know him better than you do, and it's *very* obvious to me."

She shook her head, figuring that she knew what this was really about. "Look," she told him. "I would never neglect my duties here."

"I didn't suggest you would. I'm only trying to ascertain if you have any romantic interest in a certain attorney."

"And I just told you that I do not."

"Why not? He's single, successful, charming, fun, a good, reliable friend."

Was he trying to sell her on the idea? She let the chair roll to a natural stop at the foot of the last ramp. "I'm sure he's all those things," she began, "unfortunately he's just not..." *You.* Shaken by the utter foolishness of that thought, she gripped the handles of his chair and shoved it up the ramp in one mighty heave.

"Your type," Royce concluded for her.

"Yes."

He nodded, but as he was looking forward, it was impossible to discern exactly what that nod meant. "You'd better tell him, then."

"Tell him! That seems rather presumptuous, don't you think?"

"Nope."

"But he hasn't even asked me out."

"Hasn't he?"

"I think I'd know if he had."

"I don't."

Both irritated and perplexed, she shoved the chair through the door to his room, then walked around it to stare down at him. "Where is this coming from?"

He just looked at her for a moment, then he gripped the wheel of his chair with his left hand and propelled it forward. "Observation," he said, "and envy."

"Envy?" she parroted.

He stopped the chair and said roughly, "Dale is healthy, unencumbered, completely free to do as he pleases."

"And you're not?"

"And I'm not," he confirmed.

"Surely you don't begrudge him a date because of your own temporary circumstances," she scoffed.

"No. I'd begrudge him a date with *you,* though," Royce confessed bluntly.

Merrily's heart turned a cartwheel. With her pulse beating so hard she could barely get a breath, she moved in front of his chair again and licked her lips. "You'll be healthy a-and…"

"Healthy, yes," he interrupted, looking away. "Unencumbered, no. That's not a temporary situation. I'll never be free of Pamela, not completely."

"I…I don't understand. You're divorced."

"Legally." He turned his head then, pinning her with a brutally frank look. "But don't kid yourself that Pamela will ever be completely or even substantially out of my life."

Merrily's hopes plummeted. Did he still love his ex-wife then? Could he still love the woman who had pushed him down the stairs? Was that why he wouldn't admit she had done it?

"Pamela is…well, emotionally and mentally, she's… needy in the extreme. I don't know how to be free of that. I want to be, but…"

"She's the mother of your children," Merrily whispered.

"Yes, but it's more than that. Once Pamela gets her hooks into you, then you stay hooked. For life. Whether you want to or not."

Merrily sighed, knowing all too well what he meant. How many times had she wanted to stop caring about her selfish, immature brothers? Yet even now she wondered and worried how they were doing, even though every time she called home they made her angry all over again. Yes, she comprehended perfectly what Royce was telling her. He was attracted to her, but he loved his ex-wife and always would, however foolish that might be, however much he didn't want to.

"I understand," she said, determined not to let her disappointment show. "Thank you for telling me. Now let's get you to bed, shall we?"

Sighing, he nodded, and she went back to doing her job, her aching heart tucked away carefully.

Chapter Seven

"Your parents are here."

The midday news report had just begun. Royce used the remote to switch off the television before he leaned to the left and twisted around to find exactly what Merrily's announcement had warned him he would, his parents standing bracketed in the wide opening between breakfast room and den. Merrily hovered just to one side, sympathy glowing in her soft green eyes.

The days they had spent alone here, except for a short trip to the doctor's office, occasional visits by Dale and the unobtrusive attentions of his housekeeper and yard man, had been unexpectedly pleasant. Merrily's natural serenity and quiet sensitivity created an island of peace and rest in the maelstrom that was his life. If not for his worry concerning Tammy and Cory, he might have been happy, despite the great inconvenience of his injuries and the simmering sexual attraction that continued to erupt into boiling intensity at the oddest moments.

Just the night before, in that limbo time after the lights have been turned out and sleep actually settles in, a tickle in his throat had made him begin to cough. A mere moment later, Merrily had slipped into his room. With only the light from the hallway to guide her, she'd padded on bare feet to his bedside and offered him a lozenge. Her thick, heavy hair had hung past her shoulders. Except for those bare feet and that loose hair, all else had been as usual. The whole episode hadn't lasted five seconds, and yet he'd lain awake well into the night, rigid with helpless desire.

And now there she stood offering him silent understanding at the long-expected arrival of his parents. He could've kissed her. Then again, most any time of the day or night, he could gladly kiss that sweet Cupid's bow of a mouth.

"Thank you, Merrily."

"Oh. Yes, thank you," his mother offered belatedly, moving forward into the room.

"Can I get you anything?"

"No, thank you, Merrily," he answered for all three of them, "not just now." He'd be hanged if he'd allow his thoughtless parents to make work for her.

"I'll just take a pass at the liquor cabinet," his father said, immediately getting a rise out of his wife.

"You haven't even had your lunch yet," Katherine objected.

Marvin Lawler glanced at his expensive wristwatch and retorted decisively, "Call it the appetizer then." Katherine huffed and deposited her tiny envelope bag on the sofa opposite Royce's recliner as Marvin helped himself to a shot of bourbon from the wet bar in the corner, asking, "In the mood for a nip, Royce?"

"No, thanks. Alcohol doesn't mix well with the medication I'm taking."

"Ah. Of course."

Katherine folded her arms. "About that girl, Royce. Don't you think she's too young to be living here with you?"

Royce smiled grimly. "Why, thank you, Mother. I'm bearing up, and how are you?"

"Don't be facetious," Katherine Lawler snapped. "A man can get into trouble with a girl like that."

"Merrily is twenty-six years old."

"Hmph. And just exactly what does she have to recommend her besides that pretty, girlish face?"

"Oh, I assure you, Merrily is much more than a very pretty face," he said, unaware that he'd raised his voice until he heard the satisfying clatter of a pan in the kitchen.

"What on earth was that?"

"Merrily starting lunch, I'd imagine," he answered smoothly. Then he dropped his voice and added, "She's quite a good cook, actually."

"Maybe we should consider hiring her, then," his father said, refilling his glass. "Our girl can't cook more than rice and beans and the occasional flank steak."

Their "girl," as Royce well knew, was fifty if she was a day and had been hired away from one of the city's finest restaurants.

"Merrily isn't a professional cook, Father. She's a college graduate with a degree in nursing, and I wouldn't know what to do without her. Now I have a favor to ask of you."

"Oh? Something your little Mary can't do, then?" his mother said archly.

"Merrily. Her name is Merrily, and believe me, Mother, if she could do it, I would never ask it of you."

"Humph."

"What'd you have in mind, Royce?" Marvin asked, finally leaving the liquor cabinet with his third "appetizer" in hand.

"Bring the kids to see me. It's been nearly two weeks." Royce knew perfectly well that his parents saw their grandchildren regularly. He wouldn't go so far as to say that they got along with Pamela, whose mercurial nature made her a problematic prospect for inclusion within the social circles in which they functioned, but that same social status assured them of entree into Pamela's warped world.

Marvin and Katherine had the rare grace to look uncomfortable, glancing first at one another and then at odd points about the room. Finally his mother cleared her throat. "We, um, we would, Royce, but…well, frankly, Tammy refuses to see you."

"Dale actually suggested we broach the subject a few days ago," Marvin went on. "Naturally he blames Pamela, but it was Tammy herself who exclaimed she didn't want to come back here to this house."

Royce closed his eyes, grief and concern welling up in him. "Poor baby," he whispered. "If she could only see that I'm going to be all right."

"I suppose it's the shock of finding you at the bottom of those stairs," Marvin concurred.

"Poor child's probably afraid of falling herself," Katherine put in righteously.

"I've had a gate installed at the top of those stairs," Royce informed them, all too aware that they blamed him for his fall. Then again, they routinely blamed him for everything that made them unhappy.

According to Dale that was why he had accepted Pamela's recriminations for so long. On some level it had seemed natural to him, no matter whether her complaints were just or not. His parents had assigned him the role of scapegoat in childhood, and he'd still be playing it if he and his field superintendent Mark Cherry hadn't walked in on Pamela having sex with Claude Campo on the living room sofa. To his shame, Royce knew that it wasn't so much that the wife he could no longer love had cheated on him as it was that his friend and employee had such painfully firsthand knowledge of it. He couldn't maintain the fiction of his marriage after that.

In his parents' eyes, however, he would always be to blame for the failure of his marriage, and perhaps they weren't so far wrong this time. He had chosen Pamela, after all, and to compound his mistake he had stayed with her far too long, hoping that a child would settle her and satisfy her. By the time he'd accepted that a true marriage was unsustainable, Pam was pregnant with Cory, and no amount of resignation or determination could have healed the relationship. Still, he'd convinced himself that he could endure the coldness, the scenes, the constant criticism for the sake of his children. If only Mark hadn't been with him that day, he'd have turned around and walked away without a word. He hadn't cared for a very long time what Pamela did, so long as he had his children to come home to every day. Now he couldn't even get his little girl to speak to him on the telephone.

"Perhaps if you changed your will?" his mother had the nerve to suggest.

Anger roared through him. "To favor Pamela, you mean. Well, that ought to lengthen my life span."

Katherine gasped. "You don't really believe—" She broke off, her gaze traveling past him, and Royce became

aware of Merrily's presence. Marvin shifted uncomfort-
ably just before she spoke. "Excuse me."

Royce craned around in his chair. "What is it, Merrily?"

"I was wondering if Mr. and Mrs. Lawler would like
to stay to lunch. It wouldn't be any trouble to make four
portions instead of two."

"No, thank you," Katherine refused primly, shooting
up from the couch. "We have reservations."

Marvin set aside his drink and climbed to his feet,
mumbling, "I'm sure you understand."

"Oh, I understand," Royce replied pointedly. People
like them might gossip about murderous tendencies but
they didn't have them or acknowledge them within their
own family. On the other hand, his parents probably did
have reservations for lunch. Hell, they probably made reservations for breakfast.

Bobbing from the waist, Katherine kissed the air next
to his cheek. "Do try to behave yourself until those bones
mend," she admonished, heading for the exit.

Following, Marvin clapped a hand on Royce's uninju-
red shoulder and growled, "Good bourbon," he pronounced. High praise, indeed.

"I'll show you out," Merrily offered, but Marvin
waved her off.

"Never mind, young lady. We know the way."

"All right, then."

"Thanks for coming," Royce called wryly behind
them.

"Lunch in ten minutes," Merrily said quietly.

"That's longer than my parents' duty visit," he
cracked. Then he reached for the remote control. He still
had time to catch the market report and the weather fore-
cast, but the television screen might as well have been

blank and the newsman speaking in Latin for all the attention Royce gave the program. His concern for his daughter was growing. Tammy had to know that he was all right. She had to be made to see that all would be well. It probably wouldn't do any good, but he had to try again. His hand went to the telephone receiver. Holding it in the cradle of his fingers and palm, he began to laboriously punch in the numbers with his thumb.

"Pamela, please don't hang up!"

Merrily balanced the tray in her hands and stood behind his recliner, listening unabashedly. It wasn't the first time since she'd been here that Royce had called his ex-wife, but always before Merrily had politely excused herself or silently walked away. This time, however, she couldn't quite bring herself to leave.

"I have to talk to you, for Tammy's sake. I'm trying to put my daughter's needs ahead of my own now."

Merrily bit her lip, disliking the desperation in his tone.

"If Tammy doesn't want to come on her own," he implored, "then come with her, but for God's sake, have a little pity, if not for me then for her."

Merrily bowed her head. As much as she wanted to believe that this was about his daughter, he definitely had the sound of a man who would do or say anything to see a woman.

"Can't we just forget the past and do what's best for our children?" Royce pleaded. "They need a father as well as a mother. For their sake, I beg you. Please come."

Merrily closed her eyes. Well, he had warned her. No matter what she had done, he still loved the woman and was hurting over the breakup of his marriage and family. He might have a certain yen for her as his nurse, but that was no doubt just a product of their enforced proximity coupled with his lost love.

"Pamela, please don't force me to take you to court," he was saying. "That's not how I want to do this, but you know I will if I must. Just have a little compassion, can't you? Pam—" Abruptly he broke off. Then he threw the phone as hard as he could. Fortunately it hit the sofa and bounced harmlessly onto the rug. He beat his fist against the arm of the recliner. "Damn! Damn! Damn!"

Calmly, Merrily walked around him, placed the lunch tray on the small, folding table next to his chair, picked up the telephone receiver, dropped into the pocket of her apron and left the room without saying a word.

A foul mood had him by the throat, and he'd known it for more than two days now but was no closer to breaking free than he had been from the outset. Merrily had tiptoed around him the entire time, barely speaking to him, though he couldn't imagine why. He hadn't been any more difficult than he had to be. He hadn't shouted, not at her, anyway. He hadn't complained. Overmuch. He hadn't demanded that she entertain him, despite the most crushing boredom he'd ever known. Hell, he hadn't even mentioned how irritating it was to have Dale over here every evening pretending to visit him but unable to keep his eyes off *her.*

When the phone rang—again—he waited impatiently for Merrily to come and tell him who wanted to talk to him. She'd taken to carrying the darn thing with her as she moved around the house doing whatever it was that she did all day long, and obviously she was getting a good many personal telephone calls. As he drummed the fingers of his left hand on the arm of the recliner and counted off the seconds, he reflected sourly that this was obviously one of *those* phone calls.

Did she have a boyfriend, after all? Was it Dale? True, she'd said that she wasn't attracted to his good friend, but that could change. Dale had a way of growing on a person, even his mother said so. Katherine disapproved of Dale Boyd, whose background couldn't have been more different from his own, but for some unfathomable reason, though she spluttered and sniffed and posed, it was obvious that she liked and respected the now successful attorney. If Dale could charm snobbish, prickly Katherine Lawler, he could darn well charm sweet, caring Merrily Gage.

Royce heard the bong of the doorbell and thought with a triumphant "Ha!" that she'd have to hang up with her mysterious caller and tend to other needs now, not that she hadn't tended admirably to his needs from the beginning, those that *could* be tended. And if he didn't stop thinking about those that couldn't, he was going to go nuts. Wouldn't that be a kick in the head for his poor kids, two crazy parents? Brooding on that, he waited more impatiently than ever for Merrily to come and tell him who was at the door. The next moment he heard laughter, male laughter and more than one male. Sitting up straighter, he twisted in his chair expectantly.

"Mark!"

Mark Cherry, his field superintendent and good friend, smiled a hello, his hard hat parked against his side beneath one arm. It was Mark's way to say little and take care of business. Royce liked him immensely. Three other men crowded into the open doorway with him. Vincent's dark, weather-beaten face displayed a wide, infectious grin. The oldest of the men, Vincent had emigrated from Central America more than a decade earlier, and Royce sensed

that behind that ready smile of his lay a deep well of
sadness born of some pretty horrible persecution. As a
foreman, his rapport with the mostly Hispanic work crews
was invaluable. Waldren, a big man with a wavy shock
of light-brown hair shot through with silver, a pretty wife
and a son on the middle school football team, enjoyed the
distinction of being the hardest worker in the whole company. Patient to a fault, he'd pretty much adopted young
Cooper, who at twenty was still wet behind the ears, eager
as a newly weaned pup and about as cute. Royce could
think of only two other people he'd have been as happy
to see.

"Hey, boys, come on in."

They did just that, and as they chose seats around the
room—Mark and Vincent on the couch, Waldren in the
arm chair, and Cooper on the edge of the window seat
that overlooked the side yard—Royce couldn't keep the
smile off his face.

"Okay, so why the hell aren't you working?"

"We came to check on you," Vincent said.

"Damn, boss," Cooper piped up, "you look like a
gang of motorcycle bandits done danced on you with their
boots."

"Hell, I think he looks good," Waldren put in quickly,
"all things considered."

"Gee, thanks," Royce said facetiously. "All things
considered."

Mark just shook his head. "So how are you doing?"

"As well as can be expected."

"Would anyone like a glass of iced tea?" Merrily
asked, and all four men looked past Royce and riveted
their gazes on her.

Cooper hopped off the window seat as if that were a

place a man didn't want to be caught sitting. "Now that would be extremely fine," he said.

"I'll bring a pitcher," she said. "Sweet or not?"

"Sweet," they all said in unison.

Royce watched their faces as she moved away, and as those eyes turned back to him, he could see the unspoken questions in them. "For the record," he stated flatly, "she is not as young as she looks."

"She looks plenty old enough to me," Cooper observed with interest.

"Down, boy," Royce said, trying to sound nonchalant. "She's half a dozen years older than you."

"So? Maybe she likes younger men."

"Maybe she likes boys, you mean," Royce retorted.

"She is a pretty little thing," Waldren observed.

"Again, for the record," Royce stated flatly, "I hired Merrily for her nursing skills, not her pretty face."

"The pretty face doesn't hurt, though, does it?" Mark said.

Royce couldn't deny it. "Not a bit," he replied drolly. The sharp clinking and tinkling of glass from the kitchen made him smile. "The woman can hear a compliment all the way across the house."

They all laughed, then his ever-conscientious superintendent changed the subject to business. That occupied them until Merrily returned, some time later, with five tall glasses and a pitcher of iced tea.

Royce felt a certain amount of gall at first about the fact that his business seemed to be humming along nicely without him. As he began asking questions, however, previously positive reports began to yield some problems that only he could resolve. Mark got out a small notebook and a pencil as Royce made decisions and suggestions and issued orders.

The tea disappeared, and Merrily returned to replace the empty pitcher with a full one, plus a plate of sandwiches. The men wiped those out almost by rote, hands reaching and mouths munching even as they discussed specifics of business. When the sandwiches were gone, she brought a big bowl of salted nuts. Royce tilted and swayed to look around her as she moved silently among them. When she dropped a pill into his palm, he swallowed it without thought and continued the conversation.

Finally concern focused on a certain construction problem that Mark and Waldren had been unable to solve. Some differences in the descriptions of the problem prompted Royce to try to remember where he could find the plans for that particular job. Just as Merrily arrived to sweep away the now empty nut bowl, he recalled exactly where those plans were.

"Darlin', I'm sorry to have to ask you, but do you think you could go into my office and find a set of blueprints for us? They're marked 'Jensen 14-C' and ought to be third from the top in the stack on the chair to the right of the desk as you come in the door." It was only as he waited for her reply that he realized everyone was staring at him, including Merrily. He couldn't for the life of him think why, unless his directions had been too vague or were seen as too great an imposition. "I wouldn't ask if it wasn't important. You shouldn't have any real trouble finding them. They're in a stack of plans on a chair at the right end of my desk. You're looking for one marked 'Jensen 14-C.' Okay?"

She dropped her gaze and said, "O-okay," before scurrying out of the room.

He looked around to find Cooper frowning, Waldren smiling sheepishly and Vincent trading a significant glance with Mark. "What?" he demanded sharply.

Mark just pressed his lips together and shook his head. Vincent cleared his throat and looked away, and Waldren studied a tiny hole in his jeans with the concentration of an archeologist. Cooper, however, folded his arms, flopped back onto the window seat and snorted unhappily.

"All you had to say was she's taken."

"Huh?"

"Shut up, Coop," Mark ordered mildly.

"But—"

"Shut up, Coop," Waldren repeated, and Cooper clamped his mouth closed as if he was trapping flies.

Vincent cleared his throat and sat forward on the edge of his seat. "How long you think before you'll be back on the job, boss?"

Royce bullied his mind around that corner and formulated a reply. "Oh, uh, don't know, really. One more week and I can trade this ski slope on my shoulder for a regular cast on my arm and a pair of crutches. I get the last of the stitches out of my leg on Friday, but how long it'll be before the doc says I'm fit for associating with the likes of y'all I don't know."

"Well, don't rush it," Mark advised seriously.

Talk turned to the catalog of his injuries, but no one, thankfully, asked how it had happened. Apparently, whatever Dale had told them right after the fall had been enough to satisfy them on that point. The tea pitcher was empty again by the time Merrily returned with the plans. As she swept the tray away and collected the glasses, he rolled out the thick sheaf of papers on the too-small table and studied them until he found what he was looking for. Mark and Waldren huddled around, explaining why the execution could not match the design, and Cooper wandered over to put in his two cents' worth. Surprisingly, Cooper came up with the solution.

"Lookee here," he said, tapping the drawing with his blunt forefinger. "Why don't we just cut this off at a forty-five-degree angle and brace it from this direction. Plaster it over and no one'll ever be the wiser."

"Except the inspector," Waldren noted dryly.

"I don't think that'll be a problem," Mark said consideringly. "What d'you think, boss?"

Royce looked up at Cooper and drawled, "I think this punk just might turn out to be worth the price of his lunch." He rolled up the plans. "Okay, boys, here's how we handle it. I'll call the architect and get him to rubber stamp a change in the plans. Mark, you handle the inspector, and, Waldren, you speak to the homeowner, soft sell the change, tut-tut about the cost of it, then let them know we'll swallow it."

"What about me?" Cooper wanted to know.

"You," Royce said, "watch your step and come payday you just might find a little extra kick in your pocket."

"Oo-ee, I feel me a hot time coming on in the old town this weekend!"

"Cooper," Vincent said, "in your case, a hot time is a bad sunburn."

They all laughed, even Cooper. Then Royce looked up at them, moving his gaze from one to the other. "Glad y'all came by, boys."

"The men have all been concerned for you," Vincent confided.

"Well, you tell them I appreciate it," Royce said, "and not to worry. I'll be fit as ever soon."

As they started filing out, Waldren said, "Yeah, and we'll be telling 'em you're in good hands, too—mighty sweet little hands, at that."

Cooper fell in behind the big man, muttering, "Now don't that beat all. Take a tumble down a killer flight of stairs and come up in a sweet spot with a little doll like that.''

Royce scowled, and Vincent immediately scampered after the others, hobbling slightly on his arthritic knee. Mark dropped a hand on his shoulder, and Royce tilted back his head in surprise.

''You did call her darlin', you know.''

Royce felt like someone had planted a fist in his belly. ''I did?''

''Mmm-hmm.''

Royce tried to think of an excuse, but none formed. ''Well,'' he said.

Mark just smiled. ''Yeah. That's kinda what I thought.'' Then he winked. ''You take care, now, and don't worry about a thing. We got the business in hand.''

''Yeah, okay, thanks,'' Royce mumbled as the man walked away, but he was thinking just one word that went around and around inside his head, a damning litany that was going to haunt him for some time to come.

Darlin'. Darlin'.

Darlin' Merrily.

Chapter Eight

"You sure you aren't keeping anything back?" Royce asked, speaking into the telephone receiver. "Because I'm completely able to answer your questions or troubleshoot some problem." He broke off for a moment and nodded. "Okay, Mark. Well, you know how to reach me. Sure. No problem." With a sigh he broke the connection and dropped the receiver into the cradle.

Merrily cleared her throat, and his head instantly tilted back.

"Pill time? Too early for dinner."

She winced inwardly at that. Perhaps she'd kept her distance a little too assiduously if he now assumed she would only approach him if it was time for meals or pills. She'd kept her distance even as she'd realized that he was bored to tears. Now that the cast on his shoulder had been removed, he enjoyed a bit more ease of motion, but the broken arm still had to be protected with a bulky cast.

And while the incisions on his leg had healed nicely, he
was not yet ready for a walking cast. So far he was limited
to using the crutches for little more than rising and hopping a few steps. He hated the wheelchair, hated even to
sit in it, but it remained his most viable means of getting
around, but moving around outside of the immediate area
required her assistance. She had unintentionally trapped
him in this room, comfortable as it was.

Folding her hands at her waist, she said lightly, ''I was
going to berate you for the condition of your office, but
instead I think I'll just suggest that you try to do something about it.''

''My office?'' he said uncertainly.

— She waved a hand. ''It's none of my business, of
course, but frankly when I went in there the other day I
was shocked at the mess.''

He lifted an eyebrow. ''Oh?''

''If I were you,'' she went on, ''I'd use this down time
to clean off my desk and get rid of those stacks of paper
that are everywhere.''

''Down time,'' he echoed. ''As opposed to lolling
around at my leisure.''

She folded her arms. ''You're not the leisurely sort.''

''I was beginning to think you hadn't noticed.''

''I was beginning to think you'd decided to sit here and
sulk from now on.''

''Touché.''

She gave him a mock curtsy. ''So how about it? Ready
to do some work.''

''Why not?'' He began struggling up out of the recliner.
Knowing that he preferred to do this himself, she stood
back and watched as he maneuvered himself into the
wheelchair and turned it toward the breakfast room. He
rolled resolutely forward, accepting her help only when

they came to the ramp. Pushing the office door wide, he wheeled the chair into the room and stopped.

A stack of file boxes blocked his way in one direction and a heap of rolled plans in another. Once he could have stepped over the blueprints or turned sideways to slide around the boxes. Now he could only wait for her to step around him and begin shoving the boxes out of the way. While she did that, he propped both elbows on the arms of his wheelchair and looked around.

"I didn't realize it was quite this bad. I'm usually in and out of here in a matter of minutes, sometimes several times a day, and most of the time I can find what I'm looking for."

"Most the time?" she asked with a roll of her eyes. "Most of the time wouldn't cut it in my profession."

"I imagine not."

"What do you want to do first?"

He looked around again, seeming uncertain. "Well, I guess I could start filing some of my correspondence, but I can't reach the top drawers of the cabinets without the crutches."

"I'll be right back," she said, and hurried from the room, having cleared a path to the desk.

Royce looked around him once more, dismayed by what he now saw. Why hadn't he realized how hopelessly cluttered, chaotic and inefficient his private domain had become? How long had it been since he'd done more than whisk in and out of here, clawing his way through the piles to find what he needed at the moment? Well, it was time to get organized.

Using both his left hand and foot, he maneuvered the wheelchair behind the desk, managed to push the high-backed leather desk chair out of the way and got his extended right leg into the desk well. Reaching for the stack of papers nearest to him, he began going through them. To his disgust, much of it was trash. The wastebasket, unfortunately, stood out of reach against the wall, where he had apparently shoved it sometime earlier. He crumpled the advertisement for building supplies in his hand and dropped it to the floor.

By the time Merrily returned to prop the crutches on the corner of the desk, he had accumulated quite a pile. Without a word, she moved the wastebasket to his side and began picking up the wads of paper and placing them in it. Next she moved to the desk and began shifting irregular stacks of papers to spots on the desktop within his reach. She was in the process of gathering up a particularly tall stack when the telephone rang. Steadying the stack of documents with one hand, she reached for her pocket, but he had left the portable telephone in its recharger in the den. He dropped the paper he was holding and reached for the desktop model at his right elbow.

"Hello."

After a brief pause a brusque voice demanded, "Where's Merrily?"

Irritation shot through Royce. "Right here. Who is this?"

"Her brother, that's who. You tell her I want to talk to her."

Royce fought the urge to hang up on the arrogant, demanding brat. Instead he tamped down his anger and shoved the telephone at Merrily, who perched on the edge of his desk and timidly lifted the corded phone to her ear.

"Hello?"

Whatever that brother of hers said, it stiffened her face and made her swivel away from Royce and lower her voice.

"We've been over and over this."

After a moment she said quite calmly, "I am an adult. You can't tell me what to do. None of you can."

A few seconds later she sighed and replied to something that had been said on the other end, "Then wash your underwear, for pity's sake! It's not my fault the housekeeper you hired has quit."

Fully exasperated now, Royce reached around her and plucked the phone out of her hand.

"What do you think you're doing?" he demanded into the mouthpiece.

"Who is this?" the man on the other end squawked.

"Royce Lawler. Who is this, and I want a name?"

"Huh?"

"You heard me."

"Lane Gage."

Merrily hissed at him and reached for the phone as if to take it back from him, but he switched it to the other side, catching it between his shoulder and ear and motioned her away with his good hand.

"How old are you, Lane?" he demanded sternly.

"Huh?"

"I thought all of Merrily's brothers were older than her."

"Yeah. So?"

Merrily slid off the desk, tentatively poised and seemingly as uncertain as her brother sounded, anxiety on her face.

"So I'm repeating my original question," Royce stated reasonably, and then his voice rose. "What the hell do you think you're doing? Merrily isn't your personal maid. She's a professional doing a job—for which, I might add, I am paying her handsomely. You want to whine, you do it on your own time, but don't you dare call your sister here and badger her like this again. Be a man, for Pete's sake.'' With that, he hung up the phone.

Merrily's glare hit him like a laser beam. ''How dare you?''

His jaw dropped. ''How dare *I*? That whiny little jerk was after you to come wash his underwear!''

''He's my brother!''

Suddenly all his pique at her spoiled brother shifted to her. ''I don't care who he is. He ought to have more pride than to call up his baby sister and demand she come home and launder his underwear! And you ought to have more pride than to let him.''

''Maybe so,'' she conceded angrily, ''but it's still my personal business, and you have no right to interfere!''

''Well, excuse the hell out of me. I thought *I* was paying your salary!''

''You haven't *bought* me!'' she retorted, and he wondered why the devil she hadn't displayed that much backbone when talking to her brother.

''I haven't demanded you wash my shorts, either!''

Merrily sighed and sank back down onto the edge of the desk, all the fight seeming to go out of her. ''You don't understand,'' she said miserably. ''It's just that I'm the only girl and the youngest and they all still think of me as a child. Basically they're just trying to protect me.''

''By insisting you come home and do the laundry?'' he asked skeptically. ''Come on, Merrily. Enough with the excuses. No professional housemaid would put up with that kind of whining helplessness. They want you home taking care of them, and they're playing on your relationship to get it. This isn't about you. It's about them and how convenient it is for them to have you around.''

''It's more than that,'' she insisted weakly.

Exasperated, Royce just stared at her for a moment, but

then he realized what he was seeing and his indignation turned to regret and compassion. Of course she wanted to believe that her brothers demanded she come home from love of her, just as he wanted to believe that his kids loved him no matter what venom their mother poured into their ears. He would not be the one to suggest otherwise.

"Darn right," he said, taking her hand in his and pulling her closer. When her pretty face came within easy reach, he skimmed his fingertips down her cheek. "They know as well as I do what a sweet, capable, caring woman you are, and they want to be certain you aren't taken advantage of, but you're perfectly correct that you aren't a child. You deserve respect, and you have every right to order your world as you see fit. Don't let them bully and control you, not even if it's because they love you."

She chuckled softly. "Haven't you learned yet that I don't let anyone bully me? I may not scream and demand and stomp my foot, but I don't give in when I know I'm right, either."

He smiled wryly. Scream and demand and stomp. Merrily didn't even have an inkling as to what extremes a truly demanding, unreasonable woman might go. His mother didn't scream or stomp, but she had beat him to a pulp with her demands, seared him with her coldness, cut him out of her heart as cleanly and dispassionately as any surgeon removing a tumor. Pamela, on the other hand, was just plain crazy. Screaming and demanding and stomping represented the barest tip of the iceberg when it came to that woman's conduct. Merrily couldn't be more different. He saw that with almost painful clarity.

"Darlin', do you have any idea how rare and precious you are?"

"Am I?"

Those soft, mossy-green eyes glowed with a warmth

that reached right into his chest and squeezed his heart. Unfortunately, it also sent blood surging straight down to his groin. Sighing helplessly, he shoved his fingers into the thick hair at the back of her head, wishing he could let out that ubiquitous ponytail and watch the glossy golden-brown locks tumble sleekly about her face and shoulders.

"You must know that you are. You must."

"Thank you," she whispered, and somehow their mouths met, softly at first and then with a deepening ardor over which he seemed to own no control whatsoever. With her simply standing there, bent at the waist, her hands bracketing his head and her mouth pressed to his, the contact ought to have felt slight, minimal, but instead it was as if they melted into each other, blending in some indefinable manner that was new but at the same time wholly natural to him.

Suddenly, in a terrible flash of insight that left him completely bereft, he knew that he'd found a woman unlike any he'd ever known, one who touched something deep inside him. These past couple of weeks living in this house with her, even with this new distance between them, he'd come to know her pretty well. She woke as many intimate needs in him as she tended, but she was as far out of his reach as if he was still married, and she always would be, because Merrily deserved far better than he could give her: a crazy ex-wife, two traumatized kids, a life of constant strife and worry and, yes, even fear, for he shuddered to think what Pamela might do to any woman he came to treasure. Aching with hopelessness, he broke the kiss by bowing his head.

For a moment she stood just as she was, her forehead pressed to his, her hands on his face. Then she straightened a little. "Royce?"

He shook his head, but he didn't look at her. He didn't dare look at her. "I won't do this. It isn't good. It is isn't fair."

"I understand," she said sadly. "You don't care for me."

"I do care for you."

"But not like...*that.*"

He looked up then, to find her standing straight, her spine rigid, arms folded protectively beneath her breasts. How could she doubt her attractiveness?

"Of course like that," he snapped, angry all over again, this time with everyone and everything. "Haven't you looked in the mirror lately? If you did, you'd understand why I care like *that* too much."

"I...I don't understand."

"For pity's sake, Merrily, I want to make love to you! Do you understand that?" He put his hand to his head, regret filling him, so much regret. "You're driving me crazy! I don't want to hurt you, but I can't make you any promises, let alone keep them. All I can do is try to keep my hands off you! Do you understand that, Merrily? If you do, you'll get out of here. Now!"

She whirled and ran. The wastebasket toppled over and spilled its contents. A box of files slid to the floor from atop another. For once Royce did not smile at her clumsiness. How could he when everything he'd ever wanted for himself had just fled him? If she was smart, she'd keep on running.

"I give up," Dale said, holding aloft two large paper bags emblazoned with the logo and slogan of a certain Chinese restaurant.

For nearly a month now, the two of them had teasingly wrangled over the payoff of their silly bet, and finally he had agreed to do things her way. When he'd called that day to let her know that he'd be bringing over dinner, Merrily had been surprised but pleased. She hoped that it would appease her troubled employer. All along, she'd suspected that Dale had insisted she go out with him mostly in order to irritate Royce. It was a devilish little game the two men played, needling one another good-naturedly, and Merrily found that she played it rather well herself, but not now, not lately.

"Well, you held out long enough," she said, trying to sound lighthearted.

"It's not Pao's," he informed her, "but the duck's better. In fact, it's the best pressed duck in town. Trust me on this."

"That's wonderful," she replied, not quite able to muster the enthusiasm warranted. Hoping that he hadn't noticed, she took the bags from him and carried them down the hall to the kitchen. "Smells good."

He followed right on her heels. "What's wrong?"

A false smile rose automatically to her face. She aimed it over her shoulder at him. "Nothing. Why?"

Dale lifted a hand to the back of his neck. "Oh, I don't know. Royce tried to bite my head off over the phone earlier today, and now I'm getting the feeling that I've brought food to a wake."

"Don't be silly," she retorted, right off the top of her head. "Who would bring Chinese food to a wake?"

"Besides the Chinese, you mean?"

"Oh." She placed the bags on the counter. "Of course."

Dale rocked back on his heels. "So it's a lead balloon evening, is it? Every joke going down without a single 'ha'? Every clever quip falling flat? And I spent all afternoon polishing my repartee."

She gave up the determined smile and turned. "I'm sorry."

"Sorry about what?" Royce asked sharply, hobbling into the room on his crutches.

Dale whirled around. "Hey! You're on your feet, er, foot."

His shoulder brushing the wall, Royce moved with painful slowness to the breakfast table where they'd started taking their meals at his insistence. "That," he grunted, "is obvious."

"Still in an upbeat mood, I see," Dale muttered, stepping forward to pull out a chair.

Hopping on one foot, Royce positioned himself in front of the chair and sat. He paired the crutches and leaned them against the table next to him. "What's going on?" he asked after getting his breath back.

"Just paying off a debt," Dale replied lightly. "I brought enough for three, by the way."

Merrily took that as her cue to begin putting out the meal. She brought down tumblers from the cupboard and filled them with iced tea, set them on a tray and carried them to the table while Dale questioned Royce about how he was feeling and got terse responses.

"Sit down, Dale," she invited softly, but he shook his head.

"No, here, let me help."

"I can manage," she insisted, but he was already on his way to the counter for the food. She acquired plates, napkins, knives and forks and returned to the table.

"I *can* use chopsticks," Royce snapped when she laid the fork down in front of him.

"With your left hand?" she queried softly.

For a long moment he simply stared at the fork, then he shook his head and muttered, "Sorry."

"No big deal," she replied, allowing Dale to pull out a chair for her. He passed her a worried look, which she answered with a slight lift of one shoulder.

A tense meal ensued. Dale did his best to keep up a steady stream of light banter, and Merrily did her best to keep up with him, but it was a real effort and not terribly effective. Finally Royce dropped his fork, pinned Dale with a fulminating look and demanded, "What's going on? Why are you really here?"

Dale sighed, laid aside his chopsticks, folded his arms against the edge of the table and said, "I spoke to the nanny today."

Royce sighed and pinched the bridge of his nose. "She wouldn't let you talk to the kids, though, would she?"

Dale looked him squarely in the eye. "I didn't call her, Royce. She called me. Out of concern."

Royce sat back in his chair as if preparing himself for the worst. Instinctively Merrily reached across the table to clasp his hand. "What's happened?"

Dale licked his lips. "Tammy was sent home from a friend's house last night sobbing uncontrollably."

"Ah, God." Royce laid his head back and turned his palm up beneath Merrily's hand, squeezing hard. "What was it about?"

Dale shook his head. "She was supposed to spend the night. Her friend's mom said that they were giggling and playing earlier in the evening but after she put them to bed, she heard Tammy crying. Apparently Tammy wouldn't or couldn't tell the woman what was wrong, so she took Tammy home."

When Royce lifted his head again, tears stood in his eyes. "I've got to see her. I've just got to. She needs me."

Dale clamped his jaw, and Merrily knew that worse was

coming. "I think even the nanny would agree with that now."

"That nanny," Royce went on urgently, "has always been Pamela's creature. You know that. She must be terribly concerned to call you."

"Yes, she is," Dale gritted out, "because Pamela slapped Tammy."

"Slapped her!" Merrily exclaimed. Royce just stared in horror as his friend quickly went on.

"According to the nanny, Pamela shook Tammy, shouted at her to stop crying, then slapped her and sent her to her room."

Royce yanked free of Merrily's hand and brought his fist crashing down on the table, rattling the silverware and making the plates jump. "Damn her! Damn that witch to hell! If I could get my hands on her now, I'd wring her neck! How dare she? How dare she!" His voice broke at the end, and he looked away, whispering, "We have to do something."

"The nanny has agreed to give me a formal statement," Dale said. "She assures me that Tammy's okay for the moment, and she's coming into my office tomorrow morning right after she drops the kids off at school."

"School's started!" Royce exclaimed. Anguish twisted his face. "How could I have forgotten that? I wasn't there for their first day of school this year."

"I didn't want to remind you," Dale said helplessly.

"You couldn't have gone anyway," Merrily reminded him gently.

"But I should have remembered!" Royce insisted.

"Listen to me," Dale said, his voice suddenly quite stern. "I'm taking the nanny's statement to the judge. Those kids will be here by the weekend. I swear. By the weekend."

Royce gulped air and nodded. "Th-thanks."

"It's not enough to get them away from her, Royce," Dale went on in a more subdued tone, "but it's enough to get them here for visitation. It's another log on the fire, buddy, and before long Pamela's going to find her skirts are burning."

Royce nodded again. "Sure. Okay. Great. But I can't relax until I see them. I just can't." He pushed his plate away and reached for the crutches.

"No," Merrily said, rising. "Let me get the chair. I don't want you up for a while. The last thing you need at this point is another fall."

Sighing, he let his hand fall to his lap. "Whatever. I am feeling pretty beat at the moment."

Merrily hurried to get the chair. Then together she and Dale pushed Royce into his room. He struggled out of his shirt, collapsed onto the bed and waved them both away, rolling heavily onto his side with his back to them.

"I just want to sleep," he said. "Finish your dinner and let me be."

"Do you need something for pain?" Merrily asked.

"Will you just leave me alone!"

His anguish reached out to her, but Dale caught her by the arm as she stepped toward the bed and silently shook his head. Merrily considered for a moment and knew that he was right. What Royce needed most now was a moment to lick his wounds. Nodding, she allowed Dale to lead her from the room.

"I'm worried about him," Dale said softly once they had closed the bedroom door behind him. "What did the doctor say at his last checkup?"

"Physically he's doing fine," Merrily assured him, "following the doctor's instructions to the letter, but he's frustrated and worried about his children."

"I don't blame him," Dale muttered gravely.

They walked quietly side by side down the hall until Merrily asked, "What do you think is wrong with his little girl?"

Dale slid a sharp, wary glance in her direction. "I'm not sure."

"Do you think she saw her mother push her father down the stairs?"

Dale looked away. "Frankly, I don't know what else to think."

"Poor little girl," Merrily said. "To actually see her mother push her father down a flight of stairs. What torment she must feel." She glanced over her shoulder at Royce's bedroom door. "As much as her father, I'd say."

"Yes," Dale agreed softly, "as much as her father."

Merrily shook her head and stepped down into the entry hall. "Why would Pamela do something like that?"

Dale sighed and stepped down beside her. "I couldn't begin to decipher the workings of that woman's mind."

They moved toward the breakfast room. "Doesn't she know how much he still loves her?"

Dale stopped dead in his tracks at that. "Loves her? Pamela? Where on earth did you get that ridiculous notion?"

"He as much as told me," Merrily insisted, "not that he had to. It's pretty obvious."

Dale's mouth dropped open. Slowly he began to shake his head. "No. Uh-uh. I can't imagine what Royce might have said to give you that perverse notion, but believe me, you've got it all wrong. Even before he walked in on her with another man she had effectively destroyed his feelings for her with her absurd demands and emotional outbursts."

Merrily stared at him, feeling as if everything had

shifted slightly. "But he said...I don't remember exactly, something about never being free of her."

"Because she won't let go of him!" Dale said insistently. "Merrily, you have no idea what that crazy woman is capable of. It's as if she holds him responsible for every moment of unhappiness she's experienced since she met him, even though she can't seem to be happy no matter what the circumstances."

"But just the other day I heard him on the phone begging her to come over here."

"And bring the kids, no doubt. She's made his life a living hell, especially in relation to his kids. She uses them to punish him. I'm telling you, she's dangerous, and one day we are going to prove it. Then Royce, by God, is going to have his kids safe at home again for good. But I'm not sure he believes that anymore. I'm not sure he can, after what he's been through. He'll do anything for those kids, even beg Pamela to let him see them. Do you blame him?"

Merrily bowed her head. If what Dale had said was true, if Pamela really had pushed Royce down those stairs—and Merrily had come to believe that she had, for no other explanation made sense—then it was understandable that Royce would feel helpless in the face of what must be Pamela's obsession. It wasn't that he didn't want to be rid of his ex-wife, but that he felt he could not be.

Suddenly she saw everything in a different light, the inexplicable pull between them, those intensely sweet moments when he yielded to it only to push her away again. He was trying to protect her, just as he was trying, yearning, to protect his children. Silly man. Silly, wonderful man.

"No," she whispered, smiling inside, "I don't blame him."

Chapter Nine

Royce shifted to the left. Restless and edgy, he stared upward into the dark, trying to imagine the stars scattered across the sky like so much flotsam in an ink-black river. He saw instead his daughter's pale, horrified face and his son's small, confused one. With the vision came a whole host of worries, none of which he could alleviate. Helplessly he shifted to the right again and tried to blank his mind.

He had slept more comfortably since the large, hard cast that had encased his shoulder and right arm had been reduced to a smaller, L-shaped one that covered his right arm from palm to mid-biceps. His pain had receded to mere aches and the occasional sharp stab when he did something he shouldn't. But for the worry that constantly plagued his mind and the unwanted desire that left him languishing between gentle delight and sad regret, he might have found a certain contentment—enough, at least, to sleep. Not, however, this night.

Tonight he could not shut off his mind. If he turned his thoughts from his children, they invariably landed on Merrily and what he could not have with her. In his desperation, he wished mightily for a cup of her infernal herbal tea, anything to bring respite from the fears and regrets and desires that consumed his peace of mind and destroyed any possibility of rest.

Merrily would smile with satisfaction if she knew. No doubt she would even rise from her own bed and hurry to the boil the water if he asked her. Then again, perhaps not. In a hopeless effort to maintain some distance between them, he'd been barely civil to the woman, and it was killing him. The way he wanted her shocked him. Not acting on that desire was the most difficult thing he'd ever done. He felt her with every breath he took, there, just out of reach, that delicious little bow of her mouth begging for his kisses. With a groan he squeezed his eyes shut and resolutely turned his thoughts away from Merrily Gage.

The faces of his children once more rose before his mind's eye. Was Tammy crying again tonight? How confused Cory must be! Dear God, when was he going to see them, talk to them, hold them again? It felt like forever since the last time they'd been together, since that last awful night. The reel of memory started to play again, but rather than relive those memories, he sat up and took stock.

Okay. Waking Merrily was out. He would not disturb her rest. On the other hand, he was a mature, reasonable adult, and he wasn't, after all, a complete invalid. Surely he could get himself down to the kitchen and make a simple cup of tea. The wheelchair seemed risky, given the downward slope of his converted hallway, and he wasn't at all sure he could get himself back up those ramps with only his left arm for leverage. The crutches would require a great deal of effort, but he could rest along the way, enjoy his tea in the kitchen, and hopefully be worn-out enough by the time he got back, to finally sleep. The crutches it was.

After switching on the lamp, he stood on his one good foot and hopped around the bedside table to the crutches propped against it. He steadied himself by leaning his newly mended shoulder against the wall while he got the crutch under his good arm. The second crutch provided nothing more than balance, really, because he still couldn't put his weight on that shoulder, but as he attempted to maneuver the thing under his bad arm, he knocked the lampshade over, breaking the bulb to which it was clamped and plunging the room into darkness once more. Cursing under his breath, he attempted to make a ninety-degree turn away from the broken glass, only to stumble against the poorly positioned right crutch, lose his balance and fall heavily onto his bad side.

Such pain streaked through his shoulder and leg that he cried out. Snapping his mouth shut, he rolled onto his back and tried to catch his breath, but one of the crutches lay beneath him and made a most uncomfortable bed. Angry at himself and in pain, he made a sound somewhere between a growl and a groan. Just before he began the laborious process of getting himself up and back to the bed, the overhead light came on, momentarily blinding him. In a heartbeat Merrily was on her knees beside him, pulling the crutch free of his weight.

"I didn't want to wake you," he murmured apologetically.

Ignoring that, she dropped the crutch on the floor beside him and asked, "Where are you hurt?"

"I'm all right," he snapped, thoroughly chagrined by this patent failure, but she began running her hands over his body, anyway. No recriminations, no scolds, just concern.

"Does this hurt?" she asked, flexing the toes of his right foot with her hand.

"No." He sat up, legs splayed straight out and got his first good look at her. Legs and feet bare, long hair flowing down, she crouched beside him in a pale-yellow, oversize T-shirt of some sort. Her position pulled the fabric of the nightshirt tight across her nicely rounded backside. Royce gulped, looked away and managed to mutter, "Watch for glass. I broke the lightbulb."

She swept her hair back with one hand, lifting it away from her face. "I noticed. It's okay. Looks like most of the pieces are on this side of the table. Just let me unplug the lamp, and I'll help you up so I can vacuum the floor."

"I can get up by myself," he grumbled, grabbing the crutch with his left hand and planting it.

She just raised a brow and went to unplug the bedside lamp. When she returned, he had managed to pull himself up onto his left knee. With his right leg extended awkwardly, he really had no way to get himself up any higher. Crouching beside him once more, she gently removed the crutch from his grasp and laid it aside before wrapping her arm around his waist and lifting his arm around her shoulders. "I'm going to give you a little lift so you can get your foot beneath you. Then we'll push up together and pivot toward the bed. Okay?"

"Yeah, okay," he conceded with a sigh.

She lifted with both her legs, and he got his left foot

flat onto the floor by performing a kind of squatting hop. "Ready?"

He nodded, trying not to think how good she felt against him. "Let's go."

She pushed up to her full height, dragging him up with her. He helped as much as he could. Luckily, nothing hurt any more than usual. After steadying himself, he began moving toward the bed, hopping on one foot with her creeping along beside him. The bed seemed farther away than he'd realized, and suddenly feeling none too strong, he made a vain attempt to speed up. The next thing he knew, he was pitching forward and taking her down with him. Thankfully they landed partially on the bed.

"Damn!"

"My fault," she gasped. "I got in your way."

He didn't argue the point as they both struggled to right themselves, managing only to twist their bodies into a tangled heap with him halfway on top of her, his left knee between her thighs. He froze as she wrestled her own arm from beneath her, rolling her breasts against his chest in the process, and just that quickly he went hard as stone, so hard that he couldn't breathe, couldn't move, couldn't think beyond the need standing rigid against his belly and trapped between them. He knew the exact moment she became aware of that need, for her gaze snapped up and locked to his.

Nose to nose, they stared into each other's eyes, fighting the one thing that must come next. Finally he gave in to it. Tilting his head, he put his mouth to hers, and she melted. Conversely, the unruly ridge of his desire stiffened and swelled against the jut of her hip bone, and he found that he possessed neither the energy nor the resolve to discipline it. His lips blended with hers so seamlessly that the very rightness of it filled him with equal measures of wonder and dismay; neither compelled him to draw back.

Moaning softly, she lifted her arms about his neck, and he took advantage of the parting of her mouth to slip his tongue past her teeth. His left hand slid over her right hip and down her thigh, finding smooth flesh almost immediately. The big T-shirt had rucked up nearly to her hips. His fingers found the hem, slipped beneath it and moved upward again, skimming over the scrap of nylon that was her panties. Heart slamming in his chest, tongue exploring the moist, sweet cavern of her mouth, he stroked the silky skin of her abdomen, then pushed higher.

To his frustration, the same garment which allowed such easy access below now blocked his path upward, having twisted and pulled tight just below her breasts. He thought his heart would break if he could not palm those ripe mounds as he had so often fantasized, but as he began an urgent retreat, she suddenly sat up, breaking the kiss and toppling him over onto his back.

Thwarted, he made a sound of disappointment and closed his eyes, breathing heavily. The next instant something soft and light plopped onto his chest. Puzzled, he caught it up in his left hand and lifted his head to look at it. In the same moment that he realized he was holding her nightshirt, he swiveled his head sideways. The sight that greeted him nearly knocked out his eyeballs. There on her knees beside him, she sat back on her heels, naked except for tiny, pink bikinis. Her long, golden brown hair flowed down like warm, living silk. Her small, perfect breasts lifted with every breath, rose-tipped and just plump enough to fill his hands. The trim nip of her waist and flat belly, the delicate indentation of her navel, the smooth, slender length of her thighs, yards and yards of pale, creamy skin, all called to him in the most primal of ways.

He tried to say something—he wasn't sure what—but the sound gurgled in his throat, lost in the swamp of desire. Slowly, gracefully, she leaned forward, reached across him and laid her body against his. Sensations knifed through him from every direction, jolting his eyes closed, convulsing his hand so that he lost the T-shirt. He wrapped his arms around her, despite the cast on his right, and held on.

How could he have forgotten what it was like to hold a naked woman against his body? Then again, had anyone else ever felt like this? He tried to think of someone, anyone, with whom to compare her, but they were all gone, those other women he had known. She might as well have been the first.

For a long moment they merely lay there together, then she rose above him, straddling his hips. He opened his eyes and found her face hovering there just above his. How endearingly beautiful she was, with luminous eyes and a luscious mouth. And, oh, that hair! Gold and bronze, it draped and flowed around them, a silken curtain that puddled against his skin. He lifted his right hand and tangled his fingertips in it, while sliding his left over her body, feeling the subtle dips and curves, the cool smoothness of her skin.

She parked her hands above his shoulders and rocked forward on her knees, lowering her eager mouth to his. He wrapped his arm around her waist and pulled her down onto him. Emotion assailed him: bone-melting delight, gut-wrenching need, deep-as-the-earth gratitude and more. So much more. When she slipped her tongue into his mouth, he went a little crazy, rising up beneath her, cupping her neat rump in his palm as he thrust his pelvis.

It was not enough. His erection throbbed against her belly, making his head spin. Unbidden, a moan he hardly even realized he'd made rolled up out of his chest, an inarticulate plea for more, and instantly she recoiled, pushing up onto her hands and knees once more, concern clouding her loving eyes.

"Did I hurt you?"

Hurt him? *Hurt him?* Hell, yes. "But in the most wonderful way," he told her huskily. It was the wrong thing to say.

She scrambled off of him. "Where?"

For a moment he thought she was joking, but then he realized that she really didn't have any idea what she was doing. He looked at that lithe, tantalizing body and that sweet, innocent face and knew that he would be her first—and that he could *not* be her first. Rolling onto his side, away from her, he tried to pummel his emotions into rational thought.

"Royce? Are you all right?"

"I'm...yeah, but it's time for you to go back to your room now."

She neither moved nor spoke for several seconds. Then she eased closer to him. "I don't want to go back to my room."

He sat up abruptly. "But I want you to," he declared harshly, not trusting himself to look at her. He felt the bed move and knew that she was scrambling into the gown.

"I...I don't understand."

He heard the tears in her voice and fisted his hand in his lap to keep from reaching out to stop her. "I just forgot for a moment why this is such a bad idea. Now, please, just go."

She fairly flew off the bed. He heard an all-too-familiar

thump accompanied by a sharp crack, but even as he
swung around, pivoting on his hip, she was slamming the
door behind her. He stared at that second broken lamp.
This time the neck of the lightbulb had broken off en-
tirely, leaving the still-whole bulb in the wire bracket of
the lampshade, which lay at a tilt on the edge of the bed.
He smiled, but it contained no joy, no amusement. Heart-
sick, he rolled onto his stomach, pulled himself across the
bed and unplugged the lamp's electrical cord.

For a very long time he stayed just that way, sprawled
on the bed on his stomach, the overhead light showing
him clearly what a selfish bastard he was to have ever let
himself touch her.

Perhaps he would send her away, he thought desperately. Surely that would be best. Her brothers would certainly be glad to have her back home, and he might rest
easier knowing that she was not right there in the next
room. He tried to imagine how he might manage without
her and, to his dismay, simply could not, though one day
he was bound to lose her. As soon as this stabilizer came
off his leg, he would have no reason to keep her. Aw,
God. His children. Merrily. How much more could he
bear to lose?

They sat at the breakfast room table, avoiding each
other's eyes over a meal that neither of them wanted, until
Royce put aside his fork, lifted his hand to his forehead
and said, "I'll understand if you want to leave."

Merrily didn't have to ask why, where or for how long.
Although these were almost the first words he'd spoken
to her this morning, she knew that he was speaking
obliquely of what had happened between them the night
before. All she could think about, on the other hand, was
what *hadn't* happened. The embarrassment she felt over

throwing herself at a man who didn't want her made every moment in his presence an agony, but she still had a job to do.

"I'm not leaving," she said succinctly. "You still need my help."

Several heartbeats passed before he said, "It might be best, anyway."

Recrimination spilled out of her mouth before she even knew it was there. "Surely you aren't afraid I'll try to make love to you again." He winced, and she immediately regretted the snide remark.

"No." The word was spoken so softly that she might have missed it altogether if he hadn't accompanied it with a negative shake.

"But you still want me to go," she whispered.

He bowed his head, pulled in a deep breath and quickly looked up again. For an instant their gazes touched, then Merrily glanced away. "Please understand that I'm afraid of hurting you," he said.

"Why?"

"You'd have to understand Pamela to understand that," he answered dismissively.

"Then you do love her."

"Pamela?" Incredulity passed over his face at her timid nod. "Of course I don't love Pamela! Good grief, I despise Pamela!" His brow furrowed, and he went on almost apologetically. "I know I shouldn't. I know that she can't help herself, and if it was just me, I could bear it, I could find a way to cope. But my children..." He shook his head. "Dear God, the hell she's made of their lives. I can't cope with that, and I can't forgive it."

"Then why?" Merrily pleaded, more confused than ever.

He placed his hand flat on the table next to his coffee

cup, his face twisted with the sheer weight of his sincerity and concern. "Merrily, sweetheart, don't you see? I can't bring anyone else into this tragedy that is my life. You're not the sort of woman a man can make love to and then let go. It wouldn't be fair to allow you to become part of the nightmare. You'd turn into another target for her insane animosities. I can't let that happen, not to anyone, but most especially not to you."

She was out of her chair and around the table before he finished, comprehension bringing elation. "Then you do find me attractive?"

His mouth dropped open, and he lifted both eyebrows. "Attractive," he echoed. "*Attractive?* You can't possibly think... Good grief. Come here." He slid his arm about her waist and pulled her down, turning her so that she slid back over the side of the wheelchair and into his lap. Cupping her chin in his hand, he tilted her head back and kissed her until they were both breathless. She found the prickle of his morning beard quite erotic. Then again, she found everything about Royce Lawler erotic. Finally lifting his head, he muttered, "Now tell me I don't find you attractive."

The evidence had been growing for some time and now seemed quite strong, rigid, even. She resisted the urge to squirm against it and looped an arm around his neck, lying back against the other arm of the chair.

"Maybe you think I'm too young," she whispered mischievously, placing her right hand over his heart.

He chuckled tautly. "Not anymore."

"Oh, good." Turning her face into the crook of his neck, she warmed the skin there with her breath. The "evidence" beneath her bucked slightly. Smiling, she shifted, rubbing against him, and his resulting groan brought instant gratification. She sat up a little straighter, cupped his face in her hands and tilted his head back. When she brought her mouth down over his, he reached up and pulled the knitted band from her ponytail, letting it sift through his splayed fingers as it fell. She poured her heart into that kiss, silently exulting when his hand left her hair and moved to cover her breast. She pressed against that hand, rubbed against it like a purring cat. His fingers flexed, squeezing her, and she gasped with the flash of pleasure that struck downward all the way to her groin.

Suddenly he jerked his hand away from her breast and broke the kiss, rolling his forehead against hers. "Ah, angel, what am I going to do with you?"

Sighing, she slid her arms about his neck and laid her head against his shoulder. "Well, you aren't going to send me away."

"Merrily," he began, but she silenced him by pressing her fingers across his lips.

"You can fire me," she told him softly, "but until you're physically able to make me go, I'm staying right here." She felt his lips curve into a smile and dropped her fingers.

"Right here?" he queried softly, coiling his arm around her waist.

"Any objections?" she whispered.

He pressed his cheek against the top of her head, sighing. "No objections. For now. But, sweetheart, you have to understand this doesn't change anything. Pamela is still the spider in the ointment."

"Isn't that supposed to be the fly in the ointment?" she teased.

"Not in Pamela's case," he replied morosely.

"I don't care."

"You should," he warned.

"But you can't let her dictate your life," she argued gently, stroking her hand against his cheek.

He closed his eyes. "As long as she has custody of my children, I don't see that I have any other choice." He folded her tighter against him, adding softly, "You have to know, darlin', that if not for my kids, I'd walk away, go someplace where that woman could never find us and happily start all over."

Us. Merrily rubbed her cheek against his shoulder, glowing inside.

"For now that's enough," she whispered. For now.

Chapter Ten

"At least sit down until they get here," Merrily urged, trying not to hover as Royce pulled up onto the crutches once again.

"I will, I will." His jaw was clenched, his face set with concentration as he positioned his weight. When he was standing firmly, he glanced at her nervously. "That was pretty quick, wasn't it?"

She nodded. "You'll have plenty of time to get up before they see you."

"Are you sure the wheelchair is out of sight?" he asked, plopping down onto the recliner once more.

Merrily smiled. Ever since Dale had called to say that he was finally bringing the children to see their father, Royce had been on pins and needles. He had immediately declared that Tammy and Cory would not see him in "that damned chair." Merrily knew that it was his way of assuring them that he would make a full recovery, so she had little difficulty exercising patience with him.

"The chair is in your dressing room. No one's going to see it there unless they go looking for it."

"All right. Good." He carefully propped the crutches on the side of the chair, grumbling, "I wish I could answer the door myself." He smoothed back his sleek blond hair. "I look okay, don't I? I mean, healthy?"

Merrily walked over and looked down at him. She had cut his hair and helped him shave that morning so he would look his very best, not that the man could look anything other than stunningly handsome. "You look great."

One corner of his mouth tilted up into a smile. "Thanks."

The doorbell sounded, a hearty two-toned gong that echoed throughout the main portion of the house. Royce instantly tensed. Merrily sent him an encouraging smile and hurried from the room.

She understood Royce's anxiety, but she didn't really share it—until she opened the front door and got her first look at Pamela Lawler. The woman was a tall, fashionably attired redhead with a stunning figure and perfect face. Her expertly styled, shoulder-length coiffure did not permit a single auburn hair to fall out of place. Her pale porcelain complexion glowed with health. Lips as red as ripe berries, a pert nose and high cheekbones, golden-hazel eyes fringed thickly with dark lashes and gracefully sweeping brows combined in a patrician oval to present the very image of classical beauty. The stiletto heels, miniskirt and surplice-wrapped blouse with plunging neckline added a heavy dose of sex appeal. Merrily felt like a homely child next to this paragon, and the paragon evidently shared the sentiment.

Pamela tilted her perfect little nose up as if she'd caught a whiff of something offensive and demanded imperiously, "Who is this?"

Behind her Dale shifted impatiently. "Nurse Gage," he said meaningfully, "I believe you are expecting us."

"Nurse," Pamela snorted doubtfully. "More like the baby-sitter, from the looks of her."

Merrily's face pulsed hot as Dale quickly pushed two children forward, presenting them to her. "Cory, Tammy, this kind lady is your father's nurse. She's been helping him since he came home from the hospital."

Merrily hung on to her composure by ignoring the mother and bending forward at the waist to greet the children at their level. Cory was a little darling, a blond, blue-eyed, five-year-old replica of his dad, and though he smiled timidly, he wrapped an arm around Dale's leg as if for reassurance. Tammy had her father's blue eyes and her mother's straight red hair, which had been cropped at chin length and parted in the middle. She also possessed, perhaps, some measure of Pamela's sulkiness, for she folded her arms and glared at Merrily with undisguised belligerence, the smattering of freckles across her nose at odds with the fierce desperation that Merrily glimpsed behind the obvious anger. While Cory wore the standard little-boy uniform of shorts and striped T-shirt with crew socks and tennis shoes, Tammy's ensemble had been given considerably more thought. The pink, flowered capris fit her long, slender frame perfectly, while the orange and pink, cap-sleeved top seemed small by design, showing just a glimmer of bare skin.

"Hello," Merrily said. "I'm so glad to meet you. Your daddy talks about you two all the time. He's missed you very much." Cory's timid smile widened, but something like apprehension flashed in Tammy's blue eyes.

Pamela huffed and pushed past Merrily into the house, snapping, "Let's get this over with."

Cory's smile disappeared; Tammy's hostility wavered, exposing an even deeper undercurrent of pure fear as she gazed up at Dale. Tears formed in her big blue eyes, and she complained peevishly, "I don't want to."

"Tammy," Dale said firmly, "we've discussed this. The judge says you have to visit your father."

"So you can see for yourself that your dad's okay," Merrily soothed. "He's not completely well yet. But he's much better. Don't take my word for it, though. Come in and see for yourselves."

Bravely Cory loosened his hold on Dale's leg and slid forward to stand directly in front of Merrily. Tammy made a face, but she stepped up next to her brother with all the bravado of a soldier going to battle. After trading a troubled look with Dale, Merrily turned and led the children into the house. Following, Dale closed the door.

When Merrily entered the den, she knew instantly that Royce and Pamela were already arguing, though Pamela quickly turned away and Royce, balanced on his crutches, pasted a smile on his face. She gave him an encouraging nod and stepped aside to let the children come into the room. Little Cory took one look at his father and beamed from ear to ear. Royce laughed and wisely sank down on the corner of the recliner as his son ran toward him. Royce dropped the crutches and caught the boy against his left side, hugging him fiercely enough with his one good arm to lift his small feet off the floor.

"Oh, you've grown!" Royce teased, a catch in his voice. "You're so big."

Merrily knew he was close to tears. The look he flashed Dale contained such gratitude that her own throat clogged up. He set the boy on his knee and kissed him.

"How's school?"

"'Kay," Cory answered happily. "I can draw the apha-bit."

"*Draw* the alphabet? Already? That's wonderful. Oh, I'm so proud of you." Royce turned the boy so that he sat with his back against Royce's chest and hugged him again, but his gaze stole anxiously across the room to Tammy, who hung back, her arms rigid at her sides, hands fisted. Royce smiled encouragingly. "Hello, honey. Pretty as ever, I see."

Tammy's agonized gaze fell on him for one long, wrenching moment then jerked away. Royce leaned forward slightly, speaking to her over Cory's shoulder.

"I'm sorry I missed your first day of school this year. Won't happen again, I promise. So how's it going?" When she didn't answer, he pressed on as if she had. "Do you like your teacher? I know you loved Mrs. Sands last year and she promised that you'd like the new one, as well. Was she right?" Sullenly Tammy nodded. "Good. That's good. I want you to be happy, honey, not just in school, all the time."

Tammy stared straight past him, silent as stone. Royce bowed his head. Merrily looked at Pamela, who brushed lint from the collar of her blouse, seemingly as disengaged from those around her as it was possible to be. Dale cleared his throat, hands folded in front of him almost as if he were standing guard over his friend. Royce straightened and tried again.

"Tammy, I want you to know how proud I am of you and how much I appreciate what you did the night of my accident. You were very brave, and you did everything just right." As he spoke, Tammy began to quiver, her spine as rigid as a board. He went on in a smooth, even voice. "You may even have saved my life. I'm a very lucky dad to have you for my daughter, and I love you very—''

Suddenly Tammy jerked around and screamed, ''No! Don't! I don't want you to!''

''You can't mean that,'' Royce said, both pleading and sternness in his voice, but Tammy was looking desperately at her mother, who merely turned and fixed the child with a bland, unconcerned gaze. Royce reached out a hand beseechingly, a troubled Cory balanced on his knee. ''Baby, don't be upset. Listen to me. I do love you. I love you so much, Tammy.''

''Oh, ple-e-ease,'' Pamela drawled, and Tammy immediately began screaming at her father again.

''I hate you! I wish you were dead!'' Sobbing, she whirled and ran.

''Tammy, wait!'' he cried, but she shoved between Merrily and Dan and kept going, zagging into the bedroom wing, her sobs and angry footfalls echoing behind her.

Royce slumped forward as Cory hopped off his knee, a lost look on his little face.

''Are you happy now?'' Pamela demanded shrilly of Royce. ''You've made everyone else unhappy, so you must be very pleased.''

Royce looked up at Pamela. ''What have you told her? Can't you see what you're doing to her?''

''Me?'' Pamela scoffed, throwing out one arm. ''I'm not the one she hates! Is it my fault she realizes what a lousy excuse for a father she has?''

Dale, bless him, quickly stepped forward and swept Cory away, indicating that Merrily should follow. So much for the happy reunion, she thought, and reluctantly left the room with a last concerned glance for Royce, who was imploring Pamela, "Could we just talk honestly about our daughter?"

"It's not about our daughter!" Pamela screamed. "It's about you! You're poison, Royce. Poison!"

In the breakfast room Dale leaned close to Merrily and said softly, "Take him to his room, and see what you can do for Tammy, will you?"

"Sure." Merrily took Cory by the hand and began leading him toward his bedroom as his parents continued to argue.

"Just calm down, Pamela," Royce was saying.

"Calm down? When you've ruined all our lives? I haven't even begun."

Merrily forced a smile and said to the boy, "I'll bet you have some neat toys in your room." Cory nodded, then looked back over his shoulder wistfully.

Hoping to divert the poor boy, Merrily kept up a steady stream of chatter as they navigated the house. Cory marched resolutely ahead, occasionally glancing up at her, his young face masking his emotions as his mother shrieked in the background. As they drew near, Merrily became alarmed at the sounds she heard coming from behind Tammy's door. Quickly she ushered Cory into his room, set him on his bed with a box of tiny cars and a teddy bear for company, and excused herself, saying that she had to check on his sister.

The destructive sounds coming from behind Tammy's door had lessened somewhat, but Merrily wasted no time in tapping and letting herself into the room. A book flew by and hit the wall right next to her head. Calmly she turned to the troubled little girl who had thrown it. For an instant Tammy seemed shocked to see her. Then she scowled defiantly. Merrily glanced around the room. A toppled desk chair lay on its side. Stuffed animals, clothing, bric-a-brac, CDs and other items had been throw every which way. The filmy curtains puddled on the window seat; the rod above was askew. A poster hung in shreds against one wall. It seemed that this most personal item was the only thing Tammy had really destroyed. Merrily offered the child a sympathetic smile, and Tammy abruptly erupted in sobs of such despair that Merrily felt tears start in her own eyes.

"Don't cry, Tammy," she crooned as she started forward, but when she reached out, the girl slipped away and stiffened, wiping madly at her eyes.

"Leave me alone! What d'you know, anyway?"

"I know your daddy loves you."

"No-o-o!" Tammy wailed, her fists lifted to her mouth. "He doesn't! He can't!"

Merrily stepped forward and firmly wrapped an arm about the girl's shoulders. "Why would you say such a thing? I've been here for weeks now, Tammy, and I've seen how much he loves you and your brother. He's missed you more than you can know. Every day he talks about how brave and smart you are."

Tammy lifted painfully hopeful eyes to Merrily's face, but then her bottom lip began to tremble and she stiffened her spine, muttering ominously, "At least Mommy would be happy if he died."

Merrily recoiled. "Don't say that. I-I'm sure it's not true. I know they argue, but surely no one wants anyone else to die."

Tammy ripped away and flung herself against the edge of the window alcove, sobbing uncontrollably. Determined to somehow help the child, Merrily moved to Tammy's side, only to realize that Tammy stared down on the very place where her father had almost died, where she must have surely witnessed his headlong plunge. The hair lifted on the back of Merrily's neck, but the next instant she shook it off.

"Now, you listen to me, Tammy," she began firmly, "whatever you saw, whatever you think you saw, it's going to be all right. I know that your father's...*fall* has been horribly traumatic for everyone, but your father is putting it behind him, and you must do the same."

Tammy looked at her, tears rolling down her oddly impassive face. "You don't know anything," she said contemptuously.

Quite without meaning to, Merrily seized her by the shoulders. "What do you mean? Tammy, if you know something about your dad's fall that you aren't saying, then you should tell someone. Are you saying that his fall was not an accident?"

Tammy blinked and turned her head in order to stare once more out that window. Silent now, she hardly seemed to breathe. Suddenly aching for the girl, Merrily pulled her close, vowing, "It's going to be all right. It's going to be all right."

A small sound alerted her, and she turned her head to find Cory standing with his cheek pressed against the doorjamb, a book clutched against his chest. Sad eyes too large for his little face asked fearful questions that Merrily couldn't begin to answer. Not wanting to let go of Tammy, who stood stiffly and silently against her, she lifted a hand to the boy. Cory ran across the room, zigzagging around the debris of his sister's desperate tantrum, and threw himself against Merrily's side hard enough to rock her. He hid his face against her hip, and she pressed him to her with a hand splayed across his back. He looked up at her and in a tiny, quavering voice asked, "Is my daddy gonna die?"

"No!" Merrily exclaimed, dropping down to her knees

in front of him. "No, he's not," she reiterated more calmly. "Your daddy fell down some stairs and broke a bone in his leg and another one in his arm, but the doctor has fixed them, and soon they'll be all healed. He'll be good as new, able to take care of you again and play with you and go places." She sank into a sitting position, cupped his precious face in her hands and smiled, promising, "He's going to be just fine. You're all going to be just fine."

"No," Tammy refuted dully, her voice little more than a whisper. "No, we won't."

Dismayed, Merrily stared up at the girl, uncertain what to do or say next, but then Cory crawled into her lap and opened the book. Merrily blinked at this oddly normal thing, but he was a little boy, after all, and little boys, indeed, most children, liked to be read to. Reaching up, she snagged Tammy's hand and pulled her, unresisting, down beside them.

"It may not seem like it now," she said in as normal a tone as she could manage, "but I promise you that everything's going to work out." With that she opened the book and began to read aloud, ignoring the chaos around them.

They had finished the book and moved into Cory's room to choose another when Dale appeared in the doorway. He gave Merrily a direct look clearly stating that he'd seen the disarray in Tammy's room and was as troubled by it as she, but then he smiled benignly and addressed the children in a calm, measured voice.

"I'd like you to come with me, kids. Say thank you to Nurse Gage."

Tammy, who had plopped down on the foot of Cory's bed only a moment earlier, reluctantly flung herself back up onto her feet and trudged to the door. Cory just smiled and turned away from the squat bookcase in front of which Merrily knelt. "Thank you," he said shyly.

"You're welcome, Cory," she replied, rising to her feet. "Maybe we can have another story sometime soon."

Tammy looked over her shoulder, her face solemn, but Merrily thought she recognized a question in the way the girl dropped her chin. With a smile and a nod, Merrily hoped to convey that she would put the wrecked room to rights at the first opportunity. Apparently satisfied, Tammy allowed Dale to usher her and Cory from the room. Merrily hesitated a moment, then followed, her thoughts turning once more to Royce.

When she reached the den, Pamela was nowhere in sight, and Royce was embracing his son while perched as before on the arm of the recliner. "I'm so glad you came," she heard him say. "In a few weeks, we'll go golfing. How would that be?"

Held against his father's chest, Cory nodded. "Yeah, we'll go golf the clown," he said, "a-and I'll knock it right in his mouf." For emphasis, he pointed into his own mouth.

Royce chuckled. "I'll just bet you putt that golf ball right into the clown's mouth."

"Yeah, and ring the bell," Cory added, warming to the subject, "'cause I'm a good golfer."

"You sure are."

"I get the wellow ball," Cory declared, staking his claim early.

Royce grinned ear to ear. "You get the yellow," he agreed, "and I get the blue, and Tammy gets the pink. How's that?"

"Yeah," Cory said with a satisfied nod.

Royce smiled down into the boy's face and said with deep feeling, "I love you, son."

Cory wrapped his arms around his father's neck and replied in kind. "I love you, Daddy."

For a long moment Royce simply hugged Cory close. Then he set the child on his feet and turned his attention to Tammy, who had stared at the floor throughout his interaction with Cory. Royce inhaled through his nose and said gently, "Tammy, will you talk to me now?"

The girl blinked but said nothing, her chin set at a mulish angle. "I like your pants," he went on, indicating the pink flowered leggings that she wore with orange sandals and top.

Tammy looked at Merrily then as if to say that it was hopeless, but she spoke not a word to her father. Merrily wanted desperately to reach out to them both, but she was acutely aware that she had no right to interfere. Seemingly of a like mind, Dale folded his arms and bowed his head. Royce lifted a hand entreatingly.

"Won't you at least give me a hug, honey? I've missed you so much."

Tammy turned her head away. Royce sighed.

"I can't force you to talk to me," he said with resignation, "but I know you hear me, Tammy, so listen carefully. Whatever you may think, I do love you."

The girl wheeled suddenly and stalked toward the door. "I love you, Tammy," Royce called after her, "and I always will. Nothing can change that. Do you understand? I'll always love you, no matter what."

The girl halted, and when she glanced up, Merrily saw that tears stood in her eyes. She didn't turn around, and for whatever reason clearly didn't mean her father to hear the words she whispered brokenly, but Merrily heard. "I love you, too, Daddy." Then Tammy ran from the room.

Royce bit his lips and put his head back. It was all

Merrily could do not to go to him then, but she swallowed her own tears and stayed put a moment longer.

Dale cleared his throat, stepped forward and laid a hand on Cory's back, saying, "Time to go, pard. Your mother's waiting in the car."

"'Bye, Daddy."

Royce gulped and bent down to kiss the boy. "'Bye, son. Come back soon, okay? And be nice to your sister. She's having a hard time just now."

"'Kay."

Royce patted the boy's head and sent him off with a smile. As Cory walked by her, Merrily waved at the boy and received a jaunty wave in return. Dale looked at her and then glanced back at Royce, who had looked away as if unable to bear watching his son's departure.

"We'll see ourselves out," Dale said softly.

Merrily nodded and stayed where she was until their footsteps receded into the distance. Only then did she walk over to Royce and put a hand on his shoulder. The gaze he turned on her was pure agony. When he reached out, she stepped into the crook of his arm.

"She hates me," he said, his voice breaking. "That's Pamela's doing, making my daughter hate me."

"She doesn't hate you," Merrily told him calmly, stroking his hair. "For some reason she isn't able to say it to your face, but she said it so that I could hear her, and I've no doubt that she meant me to tell you as soon as she was gone."

"Tell me what?"

"'I love you, too, Daddy.' Those were her exact words. She looked at me and she whispered those words just before she ran out of the room."

Royce stared up at her for a long moment, then a tremulous smile tilted his mouth. "It's a start," he said hopefully.

Merrily smiled to comfort him, but she finally understood what he was up against. It was a nightmare. His little girl, though tortured by the need to do so, felt unable to tell her father that she loved him because her mother wouldn't like it. How desperately that child must need her mother's approval, and how unlikely she was ever to receive it! Still, she had found a way to communicate her feelings to Royce. Perhaps Tammy was more like him than Pamela, after all. Perhaps that was their best hope. But it wouldn't be easy for a child so torn, and Royce had to know it.

Merrily slipped her arms about his shoulders. Tears welled up in his bright blue eyes, and he turned his face against her chest and simply wept, his shoulders shaking. It was precisely then that she knew without any doubt how much she loved him. She'd have given anything, her very last breath and all those between then and now, to spare him this pain, this worry for his children. After a moment he pulled himself together, sniffed back the rest of his tears and wiped his eyes with the heel of his hand.

"How can I help them," he asked raggedly, "when I can't even help myself? My poor Tammy is so torn. Cory can't possibly understand what's going on. And Pamela couldn't care less how difficult it is for them so long as it hurts me."

Merrily had a hard time fathoming such twisted animosity, but she accepted the existence of it. Just the fact that Pamela had allowed her daughter to know that she would be pleased by the death of her father told Merrily how distorted Pamela's emotions were, but it also said something more, something truly frightening.

"She pushed you, didn't she?"

Royce's head whipped around, a look of dismay on his face. "Why would you ask me that now?"

"Something Tammy said."

"*What* did Tammy say?" he demanded, his voice taking on a hard edge.

Merrily answered bluntly. "She said that her mother would be happy if you died." He didn't even blink at that, so Merrily pressed a little harder. "Tammy saw it, didn't she? She saw her mother push you down the stairs."

"Tammy wouldn't have told you that," he insisted.

"But it's true, isn't it?"

"I'm not going to discuss this." Royce bent to pick up the nearest crutch.

"What I don't understand," Merrily went on doggedly, "is why you don't use this to get them away from her. That's what you want, isn't it, to get your children away from your ex-wife?"

"You're right on both counts," Royce said cryptically, using the one crutch to drag the other closer. "I want my children safely away from Pamela, and you don't understand."

"So explain it to me," she pleaded urgently. "Surely if you told the authorities what happened—"

"Leave it alone, Merrily!" he snapped. "I have my reasons, and they're none of your business."

Merrily caught her breath. That was putting it pretty baldly. Her concern was unwanted. Biting her lip, she pressed her hands together before managing softly, "I see."

Royce's face contorted with regret. "I'm sorry."

"I understand."

"No, you don't," he said impatiently.

She abruptly shifted gears. "You're right. I don't understand, but that doesn't matter."

"Merrily, it's just that I can't... There's so much at stake."

She couldn't stand there and listen anymore. The shock of her own vulnerability left her momentarily powerless against it. "If you'll excuse me," she said stiffly, backing away, "I have something to do."

He bowed his head. She turned, walking away without a backward glance. Quickly she made her way to Tammy's room, intending to clean up before Royce could see the havoc his daughter's emotional outburst had wrought. Instead, she put her back to the door and gulped deep breaths, trying to talk sense to herself.

Well, what had she expected? That he was coming to care for her? Hadn't he tried to warn her that a man with so many problems could not spare the emotional energy to fall in love? She would be foolish in the extreme to think otherwise. Still, she couldn't help what she felt. She loved Royce Lawler and wanted to help him. If she could have, she'd fold him and his children into a warm embrace and magically make it all better. She'd shake Pamela until the marbles all lined up correctly inside her head, until the woman could see what harm she was doing to those she should most want to protect.

At that moment Merrily would have given anything to fix what was broken in that family. In the end, however, all she could do was pick up the evidence of Tammy's distress. She began to methodically reverse the physical damage that Tammy had done to her room, painfully aware that it was the only service she was allowed to perform for this man she had come to love.

Chapter Eleven

She refilled his coffee cup without being asked, then retreated behind the kitchen counter. Sometimes it was as if she read his mind, knowing what he wanted or needed almost the moment he became aware of it himself and often even before. He wished that she knew what he was thinking and feeling now; it would be so much easier than having to speak of it. Yet, he owed her the words—and more.

He had seen the ruined poster she had stuffed into the kitchen trash can the evening before and the freshly pressed curtains that now hung in his daughter's room. He knew what Tammy had done and that Merrily had tried to spare him that knowledge. She was the most loving, giving person he had ever met, his Nurse Gage, and he had hurt her with words of careless desperation. The least he could give her now was as much of the truth as possible.

She had been more or less silent since the previous afternoon, speaking only when it was required of her in that gentle, even tone that had so comforted him early in his convalescence. He recognized the pained empathy in it now, as if she actually took on the hurts of her patients. It shamed him in ways. How long had it been since he'd felt empathy for someone else's troubles? When was the last time he'd been able to look beyond his own concerns and distress?

Picking up his fork, he made another attempt at the scrambled eggs. He was getting pretty good with his left hand. By the time the doctor removed the cast on his right, he was going to be nearly ambidextrous. After forcing down a few more bites, he placed the fork on the edge of the plate and sat back, coffee cup in hand. As expected, Merrily arrived moments later to take away the plate. Quickly he set down his cup and placed his hand over her wrist, stalling her.

"Can we talk, please?"

She slid free of him, tucking her hands behind her back defensively. For a moment he thought she would refuse, but then she nodded and pulled out a chair. After carefully positioning herself on the seat, she folded her hands in her lap, tucked her feet up under the chair and said, "Go ahead."

"I'm sorry about yesterday."

"No need to apologize. It was out of your control."

"I mean about what I said to you, or rather, the way I said it."

She looked away from him. "Ah. Don't trouble yourself about it. I understand." She could not, of course, understand, and he could only do so much to help her, but what he could do, he would.

"Pamela's narcissism makes it difficult, if not impos-

sible, for those around her to carry on with anything re-
sembling a normal life. She needs to be adored. That was
my job, to adore her, no matter what she did or what she
said. If she spent every cent we had on something frivo-
lous and impulsive, I was to go on adoring her, even if
the bills went unpaid. And when the collectors began calling, I was never, ever to blame her and to somehow make
them go away without spending more time at work. She
needs what she needs, after all, and her needs are all that
should matter.''

"Not very realistic,'' Merrily agreed, "but you really
don't have to explain all this to me. I saw for myself
yesterday how she is.''

"Oh, she was on good behavior yesterday. Trust me.
What Tammy did, tearing up her room like that, it's the
kind of thing her mother has always done.''

Merrily dropped her gaze. "I hoped you wouldn't know
what Tammy had done. I don't think it was meant to hurt
you. My sense is that it was a product of her frustration.''

He leaned forward and slipped his left hand into the
cradle of Merrily's clasped ones. "You were trying to
protect me,'' he said. "I appreciate that, but honestly, angel, I expected something like that, given all that
Tammy's going through right now. That's what her
mother's taught her, after all, if only by example. It's
nothing for Pamela to destroy things, precious things. She
once burned the kids' baby books because I refused to
buy her a sable coat.''

Merrily looked up at that, obviously aghast. "Not the
ones that record all those important little milestones.''

He squeezed her hands. "Baby photos and all.''

"How could she?''

He smiled wanly. "I'd managed to borrow the money
to start my business. I saw that as something I was doing

for us. She saw only that she wasn't getting any of the money for her needs, so she demanded the coat. When I refused to buy it, she destroyed something that she knew I prized highly, and in her mind it was completely justified.''

''That's so sick.''

He nodded. ''Yes, that's exactly what it is. I tried everything with her, Merrily. Nothing seemed to make any difference. We'd see marriage counselors, and Pam would weep and confess that she hated me at times because I couldn't love her like she needed to be loved. Sometimes the counselor would try to help me prove my love, but that never worked because Pamela's need is irrational. Others saw how disturbed she is and tried to address that, but Pam would claim they were unfair and mean and refuse to continue the counseling. Her coping mechanisms were always unhealthy. She took pills, went off on grand vacations and shopping jags, created one dramatic scene after another, destroyed whole rooms. But the worst was when she started hitting me.''

''Oh, Royce.''

''I didn't dare hit her back. Dale warned me early on that the courts are naturally biased in favor of women when it comes to domestic violence and that she could use any physical move I made against her, even if it was defensive, to have me arrested. You can't know what it's like for a man to show up at work with a split lip or a black eye courtesy of his wife. I used to lie about having accidents, even getting into brawls.''

Alarm sparked in Merrily's soft green eyes. She grasped his hand in both of hers. ''Royce, you must realize how dangerous she is.''

''Yes, I know, but try proving it in court.''

Merrily bit her lip, and he could almost see the wheels

of her mind turning. "Surely Tammy could tell them how her mother behaves."

Royce took his hand away and squared his shoulders. "I will not ask my children to testify against their mother, especially not Tammy. You have no idea how hard that child has worked to please her mother, how desperate she is for some little show of love and acceptance from Pamela."

"But her mother isn't worthy of that kind of effort."

"I know that, but I hope you don't expect me to tell that to my daughter."

"Someone has to."

He arched an eyebrow. "Oh, really? Are you going to be the one to tell Tammy that her mother is a lunatic who doesn't deserve her love? Maybe you can find the words to convince her that she can't fix her mom, that she shouldn't love her own mother. God knows I've tried. But I've also been in Tammy's place, striving every waking moment to please parents who can't be pleased."

Merrily closed her eyes and shook her head. "You're right. It wouldn't be fair to Tammy."

Royce sighed. "At least my folks didn't intentionally set out to hurt me. They're just misguided enough to think that never being pleased is how you make high achievers of your children. Pamela, on the other hand, is vicious. I'm convinced she would destroy our daughter and son just to hurt me if it wouldn't also deprive her of her two greatest weapons against me."

Merrily exhaled strongly. "You must be terrified that they're with her."

"Every moment. I'd never have filed for divorce if I hadn't believed the courts would give me full custody, but Pam can seem perfectly normal—downright charming, in fact, when she wants—and I unfortunately drew a

judge extremely biased in favor of women. It didn't matter
that Pamela was the one caught in adultery, a fact the kids
don't know, by the way, because they're too young to
understand what that means to a marriage.''

"Of course," Merrily murmured, "and if you told
them, you could easily be made to appear the villain."

His shoulders slumped with the weight of his helplessness. "Pamela's managed to do that, anyway. The worst
of what transpired between us went on behind closed
doors. I tried to protect the kids from as much of it as I
could. So it came down to my word against hers in court."

"And she was more convincing."

He nodded morosely and admitted, "When it counted
most, I was the one to lose my cool while she calmly lied,
batted her pretty eyelashes, and walked away with my
kids."

Merrily covered his hand with her own. "I'm so
sorry."

"Thanks, but you couldn't be as sorry as I am. That's
why my whole life to this point has been about getting
my children away from her."

"But, Royce, if she pushed you," Merrily began urgently.

He cut her off. "She didn't."

Merrily's eyes widened, and in them he saw her strug-
gle to reconcile this assertion with everything else she
knew. "You're protecting her for Tammy's sake."

"No. She didn't push me."

"Then what happened? You just fell?"

He looked her straight in the eyes. "It doesn't matter
how it happened. What matters is that Tammy saved my
life, and she feels guilty for that because she knows that
her mother would prefer to see me dead. Pamela truly
believes that I deserve to die because I couldn't make her

happy. In her mind it was my fault that she was forced to look to another man for what she needed. Therefore, I had no right to divorce her, not pay her bills, not let her take out her frustrations on me. She's painted me as the villain of the piece, and though Cory's still too young to really get it, Tammy does, and you can see what it's doing to her.''

Merrily's face twisted in sympathy. "That poor child."

"The worst part is that I don't know how to help her," he admitted. "I don't want to play her mother's game, blaming Pamela for everything, detailing faults and betrayals those kids are too young to hear about. Worst of all, I can't seem to love my daughter enough to make up for her mother's lack of love.''

"What are you going to do?"

He shrugged. "Wait for Pamela to destroy herself, expose her twisted hatred to someone in authority. It's the only way I can see, and it *has* started. Her nanny *did* testify for us, which is how we got the kids here this time.''

"But it wasn't enough to get you custody."

He shook his head. "I'm realistic, Merrily. I have to be. It could take years. Or it might never happen, because Pamela's smart enough not to make the same mistake twice. She knows just how far she can go and how best to take advantage of a situation. That's how she managed to keep the kids away from me for so long. She's been telling everyone that it's just too traumatic for the kids to see me like this, and my insisting that they visit makes me look like the insensitive one.''

"It's so unfair," Merrily whispered.

"Yes, it is," he agreed sadly, "but now you must realize why I can't bring anyone else into this crazy equation. Anyone I care about is another way she can get at me.'' He lifted his right hand. ''That's why you have to go as soon as this cast comes off and I can better fend for myself.''

Merrily lifted her chin pugnaciously. ''Isn't that my decision to make?''

''No. And if it was I still wouldn't let you make it, because I do care, Merrily, and that's dangerous for both of us.''

She regarded him solemnly for a long time. Then she simply got up and carried his plate back to the kitchen. He watched her scrape the leftovers into the disposal, rinse the plate and bend to place it in the dishwasher rack, then fill the teapot and set it on the burner. She went to the pantry and returned with the now familiar packet of herbal tea.

''I think I need a cup of something relaxing,'' she said, tearing open the packet. ''Want some?''

Royce smiled to himself, and if he hadn't been in love with her before, he tumbled headlong into it in that moment. What other woman could make him actually want her damned herbal teas?

''Yes. Thank you,'' he said, meaning it with all his heart.

Glancing at the perfectly good cup of coffee going cold at his elbow, he vowed silently that she would never know how deeply and wildly he did care, for if she ever divined his true feelings she would never go because Merrily Gage was the kind of loving, protective, loyal woman who would always stand by her man. He suspected that not being that man could well be the greatest tragedy of his personal life.

Merrily lifted her head from the pillow at the *bong* of the doorbell. Who on earth would be stopping by at this hour? She'd settled down to watch the ten-o'clock news in her room after Royce had decided to make an early night of it. Worry and nervousness had drained him, and she suspected that he had slept no better the previous night than she had. Raw emotions that neither felt able to discuss had shimmered and flashed between them all day, electrifying every touch and loading every word with hidden meaning. Hoping that he slept soundly enough not to be disturbed by the bell, she slipped from the bed and grabbed her robe off the chair on her way to the door.

The bell bonged repeatedly as she hurried through the house, tossing the robe on as she went. When she jerked open the front door, her jaw dropped. Jody, Kyle and Lane stared back at her.

"What on earth?"

Ever the big brother, Jody stepped over the threshold first. "Get your things," he ordered. "We're getting you out of here."

"What?" The absurdity of his statement hit Merrily only after Jody strode past her, exposing the scorch mark in the perfect shape of a clothes iron on the back of his sport shirt. She clamped her lips tight, but that only turned the giggles to unattractive snorts. Jody wheeled around.

"It's nothing to laugh about."

"Yeah," Lane said, swaggering through the door, "I ditched the guys to come along and rescue you, and you stand there sniggering. What's up with that?"

"R-rescue?" Merrily spluttered.

"Just grab her and let's go," Kyle whined, still standing outside the door. Merrily's mirth disappeared. Jody rolled his eyes, and Lane reached out to seize Kyle by the shirtfront and haul him inside.

"Get in here, you weasel. We gotta stick together in this."

"Just get her before the brute shows up," Kyle grumbled.

"The *brute?*" Merrily echoed, her sense of absurdity giving way to suspicious anger.

At the same time Jody snapped, "What are you afraid of? He's still crippled up, you ninny."

"That's the whole point," Lane said, shaking his hands for emphasis. "We get her out of here while Lawler's still out of fighting form."

Merrily's eyes went wide with disbelief. Her ire growing, she shook her head. "I don't know for sure what's going on, but I do know that you three are idiots if you're referring to Royce Lawler as a brute."

"You don't know what he's done," Kyle told her in a fainthearted, conspiratorial tone.

"Yeah," Lane said, "lucky for you that hot, red-haired chick clued us in."

Hot chick? Clued them in? Red-haired. "Oh, no. It couldn't be...*Pamela?*"

Lane shook his hand as if he'd scorched his fingers. "Ow! Hot to trot and with the legs to get it done. And, man, was she giving me the eye."

Kyle snorted. "You wish."

"Hey, bookworm, for your info, the dolls dig me."

"Ha! Just because you unbutton your shirt and strut around with a beer in your hand, you think you're God's gift to women, but where are they, huh? I haven't ever seen these swarms of women you're always bragging about."

"Will you two shut up!" Jody barked.

Used to taking his orders, both Kyle and Lane immediately clamped their jaws, though Lane made a show of tamping down his resentment by squaring his shoulders, lifting his chin and shaking out his arms. He reminded

Merrily of a scrawny, preening rooster. Jody ignored the display, focusing on Merrily instead.

"I knew I shouldn't have let you come here," he said. "The guy you're working for is a wife beater and child abuser with a short temper and the money to get himself out of a jam."

"That's absurd."

"I'm telling you, sis, it's the truth."

Merrily folded her arms. "And you know this because Pamela told you?"

Jody looked her straight in the eye and said sincerely, "His ex-wife came to us out of concern."

Merrily threw up her arms in pure outrage. "I do not believe this! You three blockheads have been taken in by a very clever liar. That woman is a lunatic."

"She said you'd say that," Kyle pointed out.

"Because it's true!"

"Merrily, he's dangerous," Jody insisted.

"He is not!"

"He's just using you," Lane said.

"And you just want me home to cook and clean and iron your shirts!"

"It's what you're supposed to do!" Lane exclaimed.

"It is not! I am a nurse. What I'm supposed to do is take care of the sick and the helpless."

"We're helpless," Kyle volunteered weakly.

"Clueless is more like it."

"It's our duty to protect you," Jody pronounced, glaring sternly at the other two, "and that's the only reason we're here."

"Give me a break." Merrily parked her hands on her hips. She'd had enough of this nonsense. "Pamela just gave you the excuse you needed to come here and demand I go home with you. Anyone with half a brain would first ask himself what she might have to gain by going to you with this tale, but you don't care whether or not her accusations are true. You just want me back home taking care of the three of you. Well, it's not going to happen. I'm an adult. I can do as I please. I can live where I please. And I'm telling you now that when I leave here I *won't* be coming home with you three!''

Jody's face contorted with impatience. ''Don't be stupid. 'Course you're coming home. Where else would you go?''

''I'll get an apartment of my own.''

''How crazy is that?'' Lane snorted.

Kyle traded incredulous looks with his brother and pointed out, ''You can live at home for *free.*''

''Not from where I'm standing,'' Merrily said.

''You aren't getting any apartment,'' Jody announced in his best bossy-big-brother tone. ''You're coming home where you belong, and that's that.''

''I am not, and you can't make me.''

''Oh, yes, I can.'' To her shock, Jody reached out and clamped his hand around her upper arm. ''You're still my baby sister, and you're coming with us.''

''Take your hands off her!''

The sharp intractability of Royce's voice momentarily froze everyone. Merrily recovered first. Jerking out of Jody's grip, she zipped around him and to Royce's side as he hopped down into the entry hall on his crutches. Blazingly angry, he looked fierce enough to spit nails despite his infirmities.

''What the hell is going on here?''

Merrily answered him. ''These three cretins are my brothers.'' She pointed at each in turn. ''That's Jody, Kyle and Lane, and they think they're taking me home with them.''

"Too bad," Royce retorted scornfully. "If they weren't your brothers I could shoot them."

"Sh-shoot!" Kyle squeaked, scurrying for the door. Lane jerked but stood his ground.

Only Jody displayed bravado by insisting disdainfully, "You can't just shoot us."

"Why not?" Royce asked mildly. "You're in my house uninvited trying to abduct my employee. I'd say that gives me ample justification."

"She's our sister!"

"That doesn't give you the right to take her out of here against her will."

"We're trying to protect her!"

"From what? You're the ones trying to force her to do something she doesn't want to."

"For her own good!" Jody argued.

"You don't get to decide what's in her best interest and what isn't," Royce avowed coldly. "She can make those decisions for herself. Furthermore, if you really cared about her, you'd try supporting her endeavors instead of taking advantage of her. You'd be proud of the person she is and realize that her judgment is trustworthy. You wouldn't treat her like a child who doesn't have enough sense to come in out of the rain, and you wouldn't bully her. That should have stopped long ago, and I warn you, if it continues, you will answer to me." He lifted his right crutch and poked Jody in the chest hard enough to send the other man staggering backward. "I won't be laid up like this forever."

"See there!" Lane erupted, addressing Merrily. "The guy's violent!"

"You'll find out how violent if you try bullying your sister again," Royce warned. "Shame on you, three grown men ganging up on one helpless woman."

Jody's face turned red, but he wasn't ready to give up yet. "Sis, can't you see that Lane's right about one thing, that this guy is just using you?"

"At least I pay her to take care of me," Royce said. "That's more than you've ever done."

"Merrily likes taking care of us," Lane retorted defensively, but then he looked at his sister and asked plaintively, "don't you?"

Merrily sighed, deciding to duck the question by going to the heart of the matter. "I don't think it's good for me to live at home and take care of you all anymore, Lane. It's not good for you, and it's not good for me. It's time you learned to take care of yourselves, and it's past time I started living my own life."

Lane actually seemed to be absorbing and considering this information. From the doorway Kyle said, "I think we ought to call Mom and Dad."

Merrily snorted with disgust. "You do that, Kyle, but when you speak to them, remember that I'm twenty-six and not sixteen."

"Aw, come on, Merrily," Jody wheedled. "It's just that you'll always be our little monkey, you know?"

"Little Monkey!" Royce fairly shouted. "What kind of a nickname is that? Does this beautiful woman in any way resemble a primate to you? If that's how you really see her, then there's something wrong with the lot of you. Little monkey! I'd guess it's designed to convince her that she's undesirable to men so she might as well stay home and coddle you three lost causes. That's an insult, and I, for one, won't put up with it. Now get the hell out of my house!"

He actually advanced, waving his crutch at them. Lane turned and ran. Kyle was already a memory, and without the two of them to back his play, Jody didn't have a leg left to stand on. Clearly, it pained him to abandon the field, but he did so, calling out his parting salvo over his shoulder.

"I hope you don't regret this, little sister!"

"Not as much as you will!" Merrily called after him, hurrying to close the door. Halfway to laughter again, she added in a lower tone, "When you realize what dopes you've been."

"They'd have to actually think to do that," Royce grumbled behind her.

She shot the locks and turned, chuckles bubbling up. Royce had called her a beautiful woman. He'd implied she was desirable, had demanded respect for her, defended her, protected her. As embarrassed as she was by her brothers' idiotic behavior, she couldn't suppress a stab of intense satisfaction. Then she caught sight of the look of pain on Royce's face and every other thought fled.

"Royce!"

He wobbled, then slumped against the wall.

"You walked on that leg!" she accused, rushing to his side.

He let the right crutch fall and wrapped his arm around her shoulders gratefully. The cast added a surprising amount of weight; either that or he was in too much pain to adequately support himself. His next words removed any doubt as to which was the case.

"I think I'd better get off these crutches."

"You've hurt yourself," she scolded, turning him back toward the bedroom.

"I just got a little carried away. It didn't even hurt at the time, and it was worth it to see those three knotheads run."

She clasped both arms around his waist and supported him as he hopped up into the hallway. "It's not all selfishness on their part," she told him. "Oh, I know they don't really believe all that nonsense Pamela was spouting, but Jody at least does think it's his purpose in life to shelter me."

Royce jerked to a dead halt. "Pamela's behind this?"

Merrily nodded grimly. "She paid my brothers a visit earlier this evening, told them you abused her and the children and that they should get me away from you—or something like that."

Royce wilted. "That bitch." He straightened suddenly and began hobbling toward his room, practically dragging her with him. "Probably she just wants me alone and without aid. Then again I might have given away something."

"What do you mean 'given away'?" Merrily asked.

He hesitated, then forged ahead. "The woman's got radar. She can sense any weakness in me. She has to know how much I depend on you."

Merrily suspected it was more than that, and it warmed her straight to her toes, infused her with new strength and determination. "Well, she underestimates me if she thinks sending my brothers here will get rid of me."

"I hate to think what she'll do next."

"What can she do?"

"You don't even want to know."

They reached the end of the hallway and his bedroom. He turned sideways since they couldn't both get through the door at the same time. A few moments later they halted in front of the bed, and she eased him out of the robe he'd donned over those ubiquitous gym shorts. He sank down onto the side of the bed, then lay back with a groan, finding his pillow with his head. His bare chest heaved with a deep sigh.

"Would you like something for pain?"

"No pills."

"Then I'm going to make you some more tea."

He smiled. "I'd like that." Then, just as she was about to turn away, he reached out and snagged her hand. "Merrily, maybe you should go back to your brothers. I'll get someone else in."

"No."

"Honey, listen to me. You know what she's capable of. If anything happened to you, Merrily—" he swallowed "—I couldn't bear that."

She sat down on the edge of the bed. "Now, you listen to me, Royce Lawler, even if I wasn't crazy about you, I'm through letting anyone dictate to me. I'm not leaving. And you can't make me."

His eyes remained troubled, but one corner of his mouth quirked up. "That's what you said to your brother."

"And it's still true."

He lifted his hand to her hair. "Are you really crazy about me?"

"You know I am."

His gaze dropped to her mouth, and an instant later his hand slid around the nape of her neck, pulling her to him. She leaned down and, tilting her head, settled her mouth over his. Moaning, he cupped the back of her head, increasing the pressure. Then she opened her mouth for him, and he folded his arm around her neck as he thrust his tongue inside, pulling her down across his chest. Her breasts swelled, sensitized. Heat pooled in the pit of her belly. She laid her hand on his chest and felt the rapid, pronounced *thump-thump-thump* of his heart. Her own sped up to match it.

Merrily couldn't help thinking how right this was. All these years she'd waited for this man without even realizing it, and nothing and no one was going to drive her away, most especially not Pamela Lawler. She just had to convince Royce of that fact—and she knew exactly how to do it.

Groaning, he turned his head away, breaking the kiss. His chest heaved for several moments, and she realized that the first order of business was to ease any lingering pain for him. She didn't think he'd done himself a serious injury. The bone might not yet be strong enough to support his weight for long, but it had mended to a great extent during the past weeks. The long-unused muscles and ligaments would be the biggest problem just now.

"I'll get that tea," she said, pushing up to a sitting position again.

"Good idea," he replied with a wry smile. "I find I'm even more in need of relaxation now."

She didn't have to look at the bulge in his shorts to know what he was talking about, but she did anyway, compelled by something stronger than common sense. Then, blushing, she rose and hurried from the room, wondering if she had the nerve to do what she was contemplating.

With Royce no longer close enough to command her senses, butterflies began to gather in her stomach and chest, their tiny wings beating madly. He couldn't really feel about her as she'd thought he did. He didn't really want her. She wasn't the sort to drive men wild with passion.

Her shoulder brushed a tin candle sconce on the wall. Disgustedly she watched it tumble to the floor with a noisy clatter. How many times had she already walked safely past the darn thing? As she bent to pick it up, she heard Royce's warm chuckle from the other room, and she smiled in spite of herself. Only he could do this to her. Only Royce.

Confident again, she replaced the sconce. The butterflies flitted away, taking any doubts with them. Tonight, she decided, she was going to begin fashioning her own life as she wanted. Let Pamela Lawler and her goofy brothers do their worst. Only one person had the power to drive Merrily Gage away, and only then with outright rejection. Concern for her well-being was not going to be enough. If Royce didn't want her, he was going to have to say so, bluntly, and until he did, she simply would not believe it.

Standing tall, she walked all the way to the kitchen without another single mishap.

Chapter Twelve

Royce shifted sideways and placed the empty mug on the coaster. Then, fidgeting around and tugging with his one good hand, he managed to divest himself of his gym shorts, which he kicked to the floor. The sheets felt marvelous against his bare skin—he'd never been comfortable sleeping in clothes—but he knew that part of his sense of well-being had to do with Merrily's tea and with Merrily herself. Settling back on the pillows, he took a moment to savor this relative tranquility.

Merrily had delivered his tea with a soft smile some twenty minutes earlier, then disappeared. She hadn't bade him good-night, but he assumed that she had gone back to bed, which was probably just as well, all things considered. The way she had kissed him earlier had sorely tried his willpower. It had been all he could do not to pull her onto the bed and roll her beneath him. Even with his arm in a cast and his leg immobilized, she somehow made him feel well and whole again, fully capable of doing all the things he dreamed about with her. Something of that feeling lingered still.

Thankfully, he'd regained control of his unruly body while she'd been off making his tea, and with a full mug of the stuff now ingested, he felt relaxed and at ease. Some pain remained, of course, but it was minor, and yes, his problems continued unabated, but for the moment they simply hovered on the edges of this rare contentment. He would worry about them later. For now all he wanted to do was relax. But with relaxation came thoughts of Merrily.

For some moments he mused on all that she had done for him, all that she had come to mean to him. Merrily was blessed normalcy. With her, he was his best self. Finding her was almost worth falling down a flight of stairs. God knew that she had enriched his life in countless ways. Surely that was providential. When he was at his most helpless, he'd found someone he could trust, even if she did on occasion smash his good sense to dust with nothing more than an innocent parting of those delectable lips.

She made him forget, sometimes for whole hours, what his life had become. With Merrily he could almost be content, even laid up like this. She always seemed to be busy—Mercedes, his part-time housekeeper, had complained that it was hardly worth her effort to come out these days, as Merrily seldom left more for her to do than the floors and his laundry—but she was *there,* and somehow that made him glad.

He was keeping pretty well occupied himself these days, doing as much business as he could by telephone, relying on Mark to ferry papers and plans back and forth and take care of on-site inspections. His home office had never been in better shape. Organized to a T, he could now immediately lay his hand on any invoice, work order, contract, inspection certificate or floor plan in the place. The girls back at headquarters, who had once dubbed this place The Black Hole, marveled that they could now request a specific item and actually receive it in a timely fashion. He had Merrily to thank for that, too. He shuddered to think what life would be like without her, and yet he had no choice but to let her go.

He should have sent her away as soon as he'd realized how deeply he could care for her. Now he wasn't sure he had the strength, and yet he couldn't allow her to stay once his excuse for keeping her near was gone. Pamela would go after her then in a big way. But he wouldn't think of Pamela again tonight. Tomorrow he'd have another talk with Merrily, make sure she understood what was at stake and how untenable her position here was. Tonight he was going to rest content with the knowledge that she slept just down the hall. With that thought he reached across and snapped off the bedside lamp.

He was snuggling down into his pillow when the door to his bedroom swung open once more, and Merrily swept inside. He lifted his head, catching sight of something filmy that flipped out behind her as she moved out of the light, but then she closed the door again, plunging them into near total darkness. He shoved up onto his elbow, bewildered.

"Merrily? What is it?"

She said nothing, but he heard her soft footsteps moving across the floor. Then she bumped into the corner of the bed. "Ow!"

Completely confused, he reached over and turned on the bedside lamp. Merrily stood at the foot of his bed rubbing her bare shin with one hand. She immediately straightened, and a bolt of pure lust shot through Royce. The baggy, knit nightshirt that she had worn earlier and seemed to prefer had been traded for a somewhat prim but nevertheless telling knee-length gown of soft pink nylon with a white lace inset at the throat. Though not of a particularly seductive design, the garment proved sheer enough to reveal the shadows at the juncture of her thighs and beneath her breasts. The weightless fabric clung to her body with maddening exactitude, delineating her gentle curves. Moreover, she had brushed out her ponytail, allowing her long, thick hair to flow down her back unencumbered. The combination of that feminine gown and that hair made his mouth go dry.

She glanced down at herself self-consciously, and the play of her fingers against the silky fabric demonstrated her nervousness. Her voice gone husky and low, she mumbled apologetically, "It's the best I can do at the moment."

The best she could do. He straightened the arm that supported him, pushing up to its full length, his weight levered against the heel of his hand, and simply stared. Nothing of the child he had once thought her remained. What quickened his blood and sent it rushing through his veins was the wholly desirable woman now standing before him, ripe for loving, for possessing and being possessed. By him. Confirming that assessment, she shyly lifted the hem of her nightgown above her knees and crawled onto the bed.

As if he needed it in words, he asked in a rasping voice little more than a whisper, "Darlin', what are you doing?"

For a moment she said nothing, her gaze trained on the bedcovers, but then she lifted her chin, looked him straight in the eye and announced, "I'm going to make love to you."

His heart lurched inside his chest hard enough to break a rib, but even as that portion of his body hidden below the covers rose to attention, he managed to make a protest of sorts. "Merrily, you don't know what you're doing."

"Just because I haven't done it before doesn't mean I don't know what I'm doing," she argued, and, sitting back on her heels, she lifted the gown and pulled it off over her head. He nearly swallowed his tongue.

Hers was a neat, compact body of toned muscle, smooth skin and delicious curves. Small, firm breasts just made for his hands stood at proud attention atop her tapering rib cage, nipples peaked as if ready for his mouth. The slight dip of her waist and the gentle flare of her hips called to him, leading his gaze downward to the triangle of rich brown hair at the apex of her thighs. The naturalness of her beauty, the pureness of it, amazed him. She was as unlike Pamela, with her purchased, calculated looks, as it was possible for two human creatures of the same sex to be. And no other man had ever touched her in any meaningful way. He knew that with humbling certainty.

"Sweetheart, I don't deserve this."

"I do," she said. Pitching forward onto her hands and knees, she began to crawl languidly toward him until, reaching across him, she bracketed him with her arms, her hands planted against the mattress. Bringing her face close to his, she whispered, "I want this, Royce. Please don't try to send me away."

As if he could. No more than he could stop his hand from lifting to settle in the dip of her waist and slide upward along her satiny skin until it reached the fullness of her breast. "Ah, angel, I've wanted this for so long, but I'm in no shape to do justice by you. I simply can't do a proper job of it.''

"You don't have to do a thing," she promised him, leaning into his hand and nuzzling her nose against his. "Just lie there and leave it to me." She lowered her body to his, not yet giving him her full weight, such as it was. Her hand skimmed across his chest.

"It's not fair, darlin'," he told her raggedly. "You deserve so much more than I can give you."

"I don't see it that way, Royce. All I see is the first man I've ever wanted to make love with."

"Merrily," he whispered, his suspicions confirmed, "you don't know what I'd give to be worthy of that gift."

"Hush," she told him, sliding her body against his.

A groan of sheer pleasure rippled up out of his throat. Then he caught his breath as she pushed the covers to the tops of his legs. Her hand skimmed over him, trembling slightly, and it was as if the tremor passed to him, every nerve quivering first with anticipation and then delight. When her hand ventured past his navel, his whole spine curled, bringing him up off the bed. The sound he made when her hand closed around him would have been embarrassing if he'd been able to feel anything other than sublime pleasure. Though at first untutored, she became expert in about ten seconds and reduced him to a mass of mindless sensation in less than thirty.

Somewhat belatedly, he became aware that she was kissing him, and suddenly his concentration split between what her hand was doing and the sweet cavern of her mouth. That delicious little tongue tormented him, slipping and sliding, much as her hand did, eluding his attempts to capture it. He rammed his hand into her hair, cupping the back of her head and holding her steady as he sucked it between his teeth, then dominated it with his own tongue.

When she shifted fully atop him, straddling his hips, he instinctively moved his hand to her breast again, kneading and plucking until she purred and stretched like a cat, breaking the kiss. He brought her closer again with his right arm across the small of her back and ducked his head to close his mouth around her left nipple. In short order, he had her panting and writhing. He shifted to the other breast, and when he slid his hand lower, his fingers finding the wet, slick core of her, she threw back her head, thrusting her hips with increasing urgency. With the fingertips of his right hand, he flicked the moist nipple of the first breast while rhythmically probing her core with his left, but just when he was sure that he could bring her to climax in this fashion, she reared back, sitting on his thighs. Gasping, her beautiful breasts heaving with every breath, she actually frowned down at him.

"I told you to be still and let me do it."

Laughter erupted in a short, sharp bark. "Yes, nurse."

A smile tugged at the corners of her delectable mouth. "That's better." With the slitted eyes of a siren and the devil's own smile, she reached down a hand and grasped him. Once more he came up off the bed, thrusting upward into her fist. His head was still reeling from that lovely turn of events when she rose up on her knees, positioned herself and pushed down.

Tight, wet heat slowly encased him. Encountering some resistance, she bounced slightly, and his eyes crossed. That delightful maneuver didn't bring her all the way to her final destination, however, so she wriggled her hips and locked his lungs in the process. Another bounce took her all the way home and effectively blinded him, stars exploding inside his head. By the time his vision cleared, he realized that she was sitting atop him, neatly impaled and as still as a statue.

He managed to get enough oxygen into his lungs to gasp, "Did that hurt you?"

Her eyebrows lifted in an incredulous look. "Hurt me?" A self-satisfied smile curled her mouth. "Just the opposite."

He closed his eyes in relief. Then, quite deliberately, she flexed her interior muscles. Inhaling sharply, he clamped his left hand around the nape of her neck and pressed down while thrusting his hips upward at the same moment.

"Ah," she said, and that small sound of enjoyment induced him to repeat the motion. "Oh." After the third such exercise, she pitched forward and began rocking back and forth on her knees.

"Yes," he hissed, encouraging her. "Oh, yes."

She moved again, more quickly, then slower, like a first-time dancer learning the steps. An indistinct desire to aid her had him twisting and thrusting at odds with her. Then he lifted his left knee so that her neatly rounded bottom bounced against his thigh as she moved, and they at last found that natural rhythm as old as time. Within minutes they were both panting like marathoners on the last mile of a day-long run, and ecstasy began to roll through him in languid waves.

Weeks of pain and worry peeled away like the layers of an onion, leaving the vulnerable core of him exposed and free. For the first time in a long, long while, he did not have to watch every word, calculate every move, constantly weigh the consequences. With Merrily he was free to be himself, to be in the moment, to own his own emotions and express them. With Merrily, he was the man he wanted to be, should have been, perhaps even could be yet if the rest of the world would just go away and let them love each other.

He wasn't foolish enough to believe that would actually happen; nevertheless, everything suddenly crystallized. He was free, right now, to love as he wanted, as he could, and because of that freedom, this moment was no longer about him. This was for Merrily. She deserved to be loved and loved well, and for however long he could manage it, that was exactly what he was going to do. He had little enough with which to work, handicapped as he was, but what he had he would give her unreservedly.

Filled with purpose, he carefully reined in his galloping body, tamped down the swelling fulfillment. With only her pleasure in mind, he slid his good hand down her body, stroking and pressing even as he experimented with the angle, length and pace of his upward thrust until he found a combination that made her gasp and rear up, throwing back her head. Locking his gaze on her face, he set about showing her just how much of a woman she was and giving her every reason to celebrate that fact.

Her first climax was as much a revelation to him as it must have been to her. She embraced the growing cataclysm with an obvious sense of wonder and such eagerness that it very nearly put paid to all his best intentions. When at last the maelstrom took her, she was sitting upright astride him, her back bowed, head bent back so far that the top of her head brushed his kneecap, her up-tilted breasts cupped in her own hands, long hair flowing down her back and over his legs. He held himself up off the bed, as deep inside her as he could go, and kept her dangling there on the lip of the universe with the rhythmic motion of his fingers until tears rolled from her eyes and her shudders became so violent that they were almost painful for him. Finally she could take no more and pushed his hand away. Bringing her knees up, she began to rock herself like a lost child seeking comfort, arms crossed over her chest.

Royce struggled into a sitting position, still deep inside her, and wrapped his arms around her slender back, crooning and rocking with her. "It's all right, angel. I've got you. I've got you."

Gradually, she relaxed. Her arms slid down to her sides, and she laid her head on his shoulder. Her tears dwindled and dried. Several moments later she lowered her knees, coiling her legs around his hips. Slowly her movements became more purposeful, directed. Finally she slid her arms about his neck, shook back her long, glorious hair and looked up at him. A new, sensuous knowledge glowed in her eyes, so erotic and keen that it took his breath away. That part of him inside of her leaped in recognition.

Suddenly she pushed him down onto his pillow again, curling her legs backward. On hands and knees, she caged his body with hers, long hair swirling about them as she rocked and rolled against him. She assaulted his mouth, swirling her tongue against his so expertly that she succeeded in diverting a large part of his attention. The end came so quickly and suddenly that he almost didn't pull out in time. Indeed, if he hadn't flopped them both onto their sides and yanked back, he wouldn't have made it. Head reeling, he barely registered the indignant toss of her head or the heat of her glare. Then she smacked him in the belly with the flat of her fist.

"What do you think you're doing?"

He laughed, too happy in that moment to care if the whole world went to hell in a handcart. He could barely gasp out the explanation. "I didn't want—" The words died abruptly in his throat.

He did want, dammit. The image of a hugely pregnant Merrily struggling to catch a glimpse of her own feet filled him with such longing that he could have wept. He'd have gladly, joyously given her a baby if anything about it had been fair or even possible. He gulped down the emotion and pulled her against him.

"It wouldn't be wise to make a baby now," he managed.

"Oh." She dropped her gaze. "Right. I should have thought of that."

"I should've asked before we, uh…"

"Made love," she finished for him.

He tipped her head back with his hand curled beneath her chin. "Yes, before we made love."

She smiled in that slow, erotic way of every woman who knows her own power over a man. "You're pitifully easy to seduce."

He laughed, his vacillating emotions swinging once more to joy. "So I am."

She snuggled against him with a satisfied sigh, one arm looped loosely about his waist. "Well," she said, that single word encompassing the entire wealth of her sensual discoveries this night.

"Well," he whispered, settling her more comfortably against him.

She lifted her head, peering up at him. "Can I stay here tonight?"

He tapped the end of her nose with the tip of one finger. "Just try and leave this bed."

She smiled and pushed up to reach across him and switch off the light. Rolling onto his back, he couldn't resist palming one of those luscious breasts until she twisted away to pull the covers up over them. She sank down beside him once more, pillowing her head in the hollow of his shoulder. He wrapped his arm around her and folded her close. Lying there in the dark with Merrily stretched out naked beside him, Royce could only wonder at the miracle that she had brought into his life. Just when his world had been at its darkest, Merrily had brought him light and love. For a time. He would not think beyond it.

She relaxed against him, sighed, and he assumed that she slept—until she suddenly spoke.

"I have to go into town tomorrow."

She had left the house on her own only once in the weeks since they'd arrived here from the hospital, so he was naturally puzzled. "How come?"

Her head lifted from his shoulder, and he felt the piercing directness of her gaze. "You don't want me to send Dale after condoms, do you?"

The implication that they would share more of this incredible loving delighted him, and the idea of rubbing his best buddy's nose in it drove his head back with laughter, but in the end good sense prevailed.

"No, angel," he agreed, still chuckling, "let's not do that to poor old Dale."

"Good choice," she said, laying her head on his shoulder once more.

He tightened his arm about her, knowing that she was the best choice he'd ever made. That moment when he'd decided that he had to have Merrily Gage for his personal nurse had been his sanest, and the moment she'd agreed, his luckiest.

She yawned loudly, covering her mouth with her hand. "Sorry," she mumbled. "Guess I'm more tired than I thought." Her words trailed off at the end, and within moments she slept.

Royce stared into the darkness, floating on a cloud of satiation. Before he had been content. Now he was happy.

It seemed so odd, foreign, almost unnatural, and logically he knew that it couldn't last. One day soon he would have to let her go, but when that hellish moment came, at least he'd have these wonderful memories with which to temper it, and if he was very, very lucky, he might even have a few more. It was enough. Almost.

"Nnnnaaooo!"

Merrily jerked awake, heart pounding with nameless terror. "Royce?" He thrashed, chest heaving, limbs twisting. "Royce!"

"Ah-ah!"

Suddenly he went still, and Merrily knew instantly what had happened.

"You've had a bad dream."

Panting into the darkness, he clutched her wrist with his strong left hand. "Kn-knife," he gasped. "Oh, God."

Pushing up onto her elbow beside him, she asked, "You dreamed about a knife?"

"Yes. A-are you all right?"

"I'm fine. You woke me, crying out in your sleep."

"Oh, God," he said again. "I dreamed that she was here, in this room, watching us, and when I looked up, she raised the knife, but I was so overwhelmed, so dazed, that I couldn't stop her."

"Pamela."

"Yes."

"And she stabbed you this time."

"No!" He lifted his hand to her hair and, burrowing deep, cupped her nape. "It was you. She stabbed you in the back. You were on top of me. We were making love, and I looked up and she was there. Oh, God, Merrily, what have I done?"

Reaching across him, she found the lamp, fumbled for

and finally located the switch. Light pushed back the shadows. "You haven't done anything I didn't want you to do, Royce," she told him practically, "and Pamela is not here. It was just a dream."

He swept her hair back over her shoulder with the fingertips of his right hand. "It was so real. I've never been so frightened."

"It was a dream," she told him again.

"Or a premonition."

Frowning, Merrily stacked her hands atop the center of his chest and laid her chin atop them, looking up at him. "Do you really think she'd do something like that, take that kind of chance?"

He screwed up his face. "I don't know. I just don't know."

"You're the one she wants to hurt, not me."

"Hurting you *would* hurt me, and that's exactly how she operates. Don't you see that? I cannot allow you to become a target for her."

Merrily spread her hands and laid her cheek over his heart. Everything in her rebelled at allowing Pamela to control their lives. Surely their love was stronger than her hatred. Then again, Royce had never said that he loved her, only that he cared. Perhaps she confused one kind of caring for another, but perhaps one kind of caring could *become* another, given time.

"I'm not leaving you until you're well," she stated flatly.

He lifted his hand to his hair, plowing his fingers through it as far as the pillow. "I don't want you to," he admitted softly.

She ignored the big *but* hanging at the end of that statement and snuggled down at his side, her head moving to the hollow of his shoulder. "Well, that's settled then."

"Angel, you don't know what you're getting into."

She rose up and looked at him. "I think I do. I know the risks and I know the rewards, and as far as I'm concerned it's no contest."

He smiled at that and, reaching up, pulled her head down until their foreheads touched. "And what rewards would those be, Nurse Gage?"

Closing her eyes, she answered his smile with one of her own and slid her hand down his chest to the flat of his belly. His muscles contracted beneath her palm, and he chuckled.

"Ah, *those* rewards."

"Mmm-hmm."

"Any chance I could 'reward' you right now?"

She opened her eyes and slid her hand lower, asking innocently, "For what?"

He sucked in his breath. "For touching me like that. Um. For being the sexiest thing ever to stumble into my life. Literally."

She laughed, a husky sound. "I think my 'stumbling' days are over, or my fumbling ones, anyway."

"Oh. You're probably...ah...a-absolutely... Merciful heaven, d-don't stop!"

"Not until I get my reward," she whispered, shifting her head to bring her mouth to his. He curled his arm about her neck, groaning deep in his chest even as he plied her mouth with his.

She smiled to herself, feeling victorious, heroic, even. Nurse Merrily Gage, private nurse extraordinaire, healer of broken bones and other injuries, banisher of bad dreams. Lover.

But for how long? How long?

Chapter Thirteen

The sudden howling of the alarm made Merrily jump and drop the head of lettuce that she was rinsing in the sink. Water splashed over the edge of the counter top. Dancing back out of range, she slapped a damp hand over her heart, scowling with irritation. Since the night she and Royce had become lovers, the alarm had been armed twenty-four hours a day at Royce's insistence. Merrily had humored him, not that she was afraid of Pamela. To her mind, Pamela was like every other bully. When faced with a determined equal, she would show her true color, which was undoubtedly yellow. As long as the woman effectively held his children hostage, however, Royce was not her equal.

Grabbing a dish towel, Merrily ran for the control panel on the wall of the interior hallway that led to the dining room. If the alarm wasn't turned off within the first minute, the police were automatically notified. She punched in the turnoff code, and blessed silence descended until Royce shouted from the den, "What's going on?"

"I don't know yet," she shouted back. Then she punched the button on the intercom and spoke into the microphone, knowing her voice would be heard from every outside speaker. "Is anyone there?"

"Dale."

"It's Dale!" She shouted at Royce before hitting the microphone button again. "Where are you?"

"What do you mean, where am I?" Dale shot back. "I'm at the front door."

"Well, why didn't you ring the doorbell? Oh, never mind. Hold on a minute." As she hurried toward the door, she tossed aside the towel and said to Royce, who had made it as far as the den door on his crutches, "Relax. Dale's at the front door."

He rolled his eyes and hobbled toward the breakfast table, where she would soon be serving lunch, mumbling, "Why the devil didn't he just ring the doorbell?"

She strode down the hall and opened the door to find Dale leaning against the frame shaking his head. "What is going on?"

"You set off the alarm."

"Sorry about that. Must have accidentally touched the doorknob when I was reaching for the bell," he muttered.

Merrily turned and led the way back into the house. "The silly thing shouldn't be on during the daytime, anyway, if you ask me."

Dale closed the door and followed her. "I take it your employer has decided otherwise."

Nodding, she sighed. "He's afraid for me."

"For *you?*"

She lowered her voice. "He had a bad dream where Pamela supposedly attacked me. She went to my brothers the other evening and painted Royce as this wife-beating child abuser with a hair-trigger temper. They naturally hot-footed it straight over here and demanded I come home with them. Royce threw them out, but now he thinks I've become a target for Pamela's vendetta.''

''Royce *threw* them out?''

She tossed him a grin and made a jabbing motion with one hand. ''More like drove them out at the end of his crutch.''

''How many brothers do you have?'' Dale asked skeptically.

She smirked wryly. ''Three. Choice specimens, believe me.''

''Must be, to let a wounded man on crutches run them off.''

''Who?'' Royce demanded, as they had drawn near the breakfast room.

''You,'' Dale answered. ''You're the only gimp around these parts.''

''True,'' Royce retorted. ''Your handicaps have to do with personality and mental capacity. Sit down, since you obviously came for lunch.''

Dale turned to Merrily. ''If it's no trouble,'' he began hopefully.

''None at all.''

''Don't mind if I do, then.'' Rubbing his hands together, he skirted the table and pulled out a chair.

Royce turned his face up to Merrily, saying, ''Angel, reset the alarm before you finish lunch, will you?''

Merrily sent a told-you-so look at Dale, absently dropped a kiss on Royce's puckered mouth and was heading toward the kitchen when Dale drawled, ''No need to ask how you're getting along, considering obvious developments.''

Merrily froze, realizing they'd just given themselves away. Those quick kisses felt so natural and had become so commonplace that she hadn't thought twice about doing it in front of Dale.

Royce cleared his throat and stated calmly, "You wouldn't know an 'obvious development' if it bit you."

"Maybe, but I sure do recognize one when it kisses you."

"Eat your heart out, Counselor."

"I'd rather remove yours with a spoon."

"You're welcome to try."

"Gonna hit me with your crutch?"

Merrily whirled around. "Oh, please!" She folded her arms. "That will be enough out of you two. Now either play nicely or I'll be forced to send you to your rooms."

"Works for me," Royce goaded, glaring at Dale but speaking to Merrily, "provided you come with me as usual, darlin'."

"You devil," Dale rumbled.

"Royce!" Merrily scolded.

"What?" He turned a perfectly innocent expression on her, not fooling her in the least. "You didn't want him to know?"

"It's not that! It's just that Dale isn't interested in our, uh…"

"Sleeping arrangements?" he supplied pointedly.

"Personal business," she snapped, cheeks flushing with heat.

He lifted an eyebrow, glaring at Dale. "He seems mighty interested to me."

"As interested as you are in letting me know you've staked a claim," Dale said tightly.

"Just cut it out!" Merrily snapped. "You're behaving like a pair of roosters scratching in the barnyard. You're

best friends, for pity's sake, and who I do or do not choose to sleep with is not open for discussion.''

Dale's face suddenly looked chiseled from stone. Royce, on the other hand, grinned cheekily. ''Yes, ma'am.''

He winked, and she knew then that he'd done it on purpose, turned his face up for that kiss, rubbed Dale's nose in their relationship, as if Dale was really interested in anything more than flirtation. Whirling away, she escaped to the control panel, where she armed the system once again, angrily punching in the code. Somewhere along about the third number it occurred to her that Royce had indeed, as Dale had put it, staked a claim, whether he'd meant to or not. He was jealous, and he wanted Dale to know that she was taken. Smiling, she punched in the remaining two digits.

''You're smarter than I thought you were,'' Dale said reluctantly to Royce.

After a moment Royce sighed. ''More selfish, you mean.''

''Well, that goes without saying,'' Dale agreed wryly, and the mood instantly lightened to one of sassy banter. ''But be forewarned, good buddy, I may decide to acquire a private nurse of my own.''

''Want some help figuring out which bones to break?''

''You would know.''

''And I'd be glad to show you.''

Merrily rolled her eyes and headed back to the kitchen. While they verbally sparred, she finished rinsing the lettuce, made some garlic toast, set a third place at the table, and got the chicken salad out of the refrigerator. By the time lunch was on the table, talk had turned to someone who worked in Dale's office, someone Royce evidently knew and in whom Dale had little confidence. They laughed about this character's latest legal foibles. Then Dale put down his fork and pushed away his plate.

"Sugar, that was a great lunch," he said to Merrily. "Your taste in men might be suspect, but your food's always top-notch."

She templed her hands over her plate and asked dryly, "Does that mean you'll be doing the dishes in appreciation?"

Dale gaped at Royce as if to ask, "Do you believe this girl?" Then he folded his arms and retorted, "Fat chance. I'm the one going home alone, remember? Let the fair-haired patient here do the dirty work."

Royce quickly held up his cast. "Not this week."

Merrily rose and began gathering dishes, commenting drolly, "Real princes, you two. I think I'll trade you both for a troll with a pointed hat and a sponge."

"Ouch," Dale said.

"Double ouch," Royce amended.

"Ah, poor baby," Merrily teased Royce. "Did that hurt?"

He slid an arm around her waist, suggesting silkily, "I guess you'll just have to kiss it and make it better."

She smiled and bent down, touching the tip of her nose to his. "Maybe after I finish the dishes," she said in her most sultry tone.

Royce lifted his cast and cut his eyes at Dale, asking dryly, "Wouldn't happen to have an extra-extra-large rubber glove on you, would you?"

"You wish," Dale retorted.

Merrily laughed and carried the dishes into the kitchen. She had placed the dishes on the counter and started back to the table when Royce said, "Okay, law boy. You didn't drop by just for the free lunch. What's up?"

Dale glanced at her as she moved to stand at Royce's

side, all teasing at an end. Royce reached up and idly looped his arm about her waist, waiting for Dale to speak.

"The judge signed an order this morning instructing Pamela to take Tammy to an independent doctor for counseling."

Merrily felt Royce sag against her. "That's good, isn't it?" she asked quickly.

"That's excellent," Royce said, squeezing her. "How did you finally manage it?" he asked Dale.

"The nanny. She began changing her tune when she saw Pamela slap Tammy, but she really started singing when Pamela threatened *her*."

Royce sat up straighter. "Threatened her how?"

Dale shrugged. "Said she'd see to it the woman never worked again, that she was going to tell everyone the woman was a lousy nanny. About what you'd expect from Pamela."

"But nothing physical," Merrily clarified.

"Not overtly, no," Dale said, "but after talking to the judge again, the nanny wisely followed my suggestion and took a job out of state."

"But you don't really think Pamela would physically attack the nanny," Merrily said.

Dale just looked pointedly at Royce then back to Merrily, as if to say, "Isn't it obvious?"

Royce abruptly asked, "When can Tammy see the doctor?"

Dale reached inside his suit coat and removed a folded sheet of paper. "As soon as you pick one from this list that the court gave me and we can get an appointment." He unfolded the sheet and slid it across the table to Royce, adding, "I've added stars by the names of those I was able to get recommendations on and crossed off a couple I've been told don't handle children very well."

Royce studied the list. Merrily did, too, and recognized several names on it. One in particular stood out, though, and she put her finger on it. "This woman is an excellent doctor and one of only two actual psychiatrists on the list."

"You know her?" Royce asked, looking up.

Merrily nodded. "She's a medical doctor specializing in pediatric psychiatry. I've tended several of her patients. One of them was the only survivor of an automobile accident that killed both of his parents. When I met him, he was an eleven-year-old who had tried to commit suicide by throwing himself in front of a moving car. He threw feces at me the first time I tried to check his bandages. Dr. Denelo completely turned that kid around. He's been adopted, and I understand he's an honor student. Dr. Denelo carries a photo of him, along with those of many other patients, and she updates me on him every time I see her. She's very highly thought of."

"I'm sold," Royce said, pushing the paper back to Dale.

"I'll make the appointment," Dale affirmed.

"Tell Dr. Denelo I said hello, will you?" Merrily added. "It might speed things up a bit."

"Can't hurt," Dale agreed.

Royce squeezed her again and looked up. "Thanks, angel. I appreciate your input."

"I'm just glad I could be of some help in this."

Dale refolded the paper and stashed it back where he'd gotten it, shaking his head at Royce, "Looks like your luck has turned in a big way, pal of mine."

"It's about flipping time, if you ask me."

"Here, here. Well, I have to get back to the office." Dale rose to his feet and stepped away from the chair. "Thanks for lunch."

"Our pleasure," Royce said as Dale pushed the chair under the table.

"Absolutely," Merrily agreed, adding, "I'll have to see you out and lock the door behind you."

"Well, have it, then," Dale teased, walking around the table and offering her his arm.

"Hey, now, no funny stuff," Royce warned.

"As if," Dale retorted.

"As if you thought you could get away with it," Royce returned.

"Maybe I could," Dale suggested, waggling an eyebrow at Merrily.

"Hmm," Merrily mused, looking him up and down with squinted eyes. "Maybe a dye job and a little plastic surgery. No, make that a lot of plastic surgery."

"Hey!"

Royce roared with laughter. Dale pretended hurt feelings, sticking out his bottom lip. Merrily just grinned, grabbed his arm and set off, dragging him along with her.

"You sure know how to burst a boy's bubble," Dale grumbled good-naturedly.

"You'll get over it," she said dryly.

"I might," he told her, dropping his voice, "since it's so obvious how you feel about him."

"I'm wild about him," Merrily admitted softly, "absolutely wild."

"Like I said, the man's luck has obviously turned."

"I hope so," Merrily replied with heartfelt sincerity.

"So do I," Dale admitted.

They came to a halt in front of the door, and Merrily let go of his arm, saying, "I'm glad to know that. I could never forgive myself if I came between the two of you."

"No harm of that," Dale told her with a crooked smile, "since you so obviously prefer him."

"You're number two on my list," she offered in consolation.

"Yeah, well, I have a feeling that number two is way behind number one."

Merrily tilted her head apologetically and said softly, "I love him."

Dale reached out and briefly squeezed her hand. "I know."

Merrily bit her lip. "Do you think he does?"

Dale lifted an eyebrow. "You haven't told him?"

She shook her head. "Not flat-out."

"Why not?"

She shrugged and looked away. "The time just hasn't seemed right. He has so much on his mind."

Dale inhaled deeply through his nose. "I take it he hasn't expressed his feelings, either?"

"Not exactly."

"Well, as you pointed out, he has had a lot on his plate."

Nodding, she punched the appropriate code into the keypad mounted on the wall behind the door, then flipped the lock and pulled the door open. "He'll tell me," she stated firmly, "when the time is right."

"My thought exactly," Dale agreed, starting through the door, but then he paused. "By the way, you shouldn't take the risks lightly. Believe me, when Pamela gets wind of this new court order, she's going to go over the edge, so keep that alarm armed. Hear me?"

Merrily nodded. "Don't worry. I'll take care of him."

"And yourself."

Merrily made a face. "She's not going to come after me, no matter what Royce says. She doesn't even know we're together now."

"I wouldn't be too sure of that. The pair of you send

out pretty strong vibes. Besides, if you stay together, she's bound to catch on eventually.''

Merrily lifted her chin. ''I don't intend to go anywhere. Oh, Royce thinks it's too dangerous for us to be together after he's well, but I don't believe that, and even if I did, I still wouldn't leave him.''

Dale smiled and winked. ''My money's on you this time, kid.''

Merrily laughed. ''Never let it be said that you're a slow learner.''

''Amen.''

''It's going to work out,'' she said fervently, ''because he loves me, too. I know it.''

''He'd be a fool not to,'' Dale told her. Then he chucked her under the chin and walked away.

Merrily closed the door, locked it, and rearmed the alarm. No matter what happened she was staying put right where she was. The only thing that could move her now was Royce convincing her that he didn't love her, and she couldn't believe that would ever happen. Royce couldn't touch her as he did, make every night an intimate adventure beyond her wildest dreams, if he didn't really, deeply love her. Could he?

''So how's it going with the new doctor, sweetie?'' Royce asked his daughter. Cory, as usual, sprawled in his lap. The boy must've grown an inch and gained ten pounds since the last time he'd seen him. Seated on the couch opposite the recliner, Tammy shrugged, folded her arms and looked away.

He had been greatly relieved and very pleased when he'd learned from Dale that Dr. Denelo had strongly recommended to Pamela and the judge that the children resume regular visitation. Pamela had insisted that the visits be kept short, and Royce didn't want to appear demanding by insisting otherwise. All things considered, it was probably best that Tammy didn't stay overnight just now, anyway. She had so much to work through, his beautiful little girl, but at least they seemed to be on the right track now.

"I understand the first time was just sort of a get-acquainted session," Dale said helpfully, leaning forward and bracing his elbows on his knees, hands folded together. Tammy sat silent.

"Has Dr. Denelo shown you her doll collection, yet?" Merrily asked from behind Royce's recliner. Tammy shot her a surprised look and nodded warily.

"She gots a train in her waitin' room," Cory piped up, vying to be the center of attention. "It goes under the chairs and around the pot trees, I mean, tree pots, an', an' everywhere!"

"They aren't *real* trees," Tammy retorted in a superior tone.

"Uh-huh, they are," Cory insisted. "I climbed one!" He looked at his father and admitted warily, "It fell over."

"I hope you picked it up again," Royce said, trying not to chuckle.

Cory nodded. "The lady in the window that works there helped me."

Royce couldn't catch his grin. Obviously the boy was referring to the receptionist, who undoubtedly sat behind the usual glass shield. "That was very nice of her."

"I'll bet Mama slapped you," Tammy said spitefully.

"Uh-uh," Cory denied. "The lady told her not to."

Royce glanced at Dale, his ire immediately rising. Merrily said quickly, "Did you get to play with the train?"

Cory nodded. "Yeah, it was fun, but Mommy said I

couldn't have one 'cause—'' He suddenly broke off, his hand going to his chin.

"'Cause Daddy doesn't give us enough money,'' Tammy finished for him.

It felt like a kick in the gut to Royce. "Uh-uh!'' Cory yelled in his defense. "'Cause I was bad and made the tree fall over!''

"It doesn't matter why,'' Royce said firmly. "Maybe I can convince Santa to bring you a miniature train for Christmas, son. I'm sure you'll be a good boy until then.''

"And, Tammy, your father pays more child support than the court mandates,'' Dale said quietly.

Royce shot him a grateful look and changed the subject, speaking to Tammy. "It so happens that Nurse Gage knows Dr. Denelo and thinks very highly of her.''

"Yes, I do,'' Merrily confirmed. "Dr. Denelo used to come to the hospital where I worked, and she used to bring a different doll with her every time to show to the children who were patients there.''

"Why were they patients?'' Tammy asked suspiciously.

"Oh, for different reasons,'' Merrily answered. "Sometimes they were having their tonsils out, or maybe they had a bad case of flu. Once in a while we had a little girl who'd been in an accident of some sort.''

"Were any of them crazy?'' Cory asked, bending his head far back to look up at Merrily. Tammy's face drained of color, and Royce felt his nerves coil tight.

"No,'' Merrily said calmly, "a few were troubled about something. One or two were very, very sick and frightened because of it.''

"'Cause Mommy says she's a doctor for crazy kids,'' Cory went on. "Daddy, do you think Tammy's crazy?''

Royce nearly jumped out of his chair, so angry he could spit. "Absolutely not!"

"'Cause Mommy says—"

"Your mother's mistaken," Merrily interjected smoothly. "Both Dr. Denelo and your father know that there is no such thing as a 'crazy kid,' only those who are confused or afraid or hurting inside."

"I don't care," Tammy snapped, her hands fisting. "I don't want to see dumb old Dr. Denelo or her stupid dolls again!"

"You said she was nice!" Cory accused, leaning forward on his father's lap.

"I did not!" Tammy sprang up onto her feet, adding, "I want to go home now. Mama said we can go home when we want to, and I want to go home now!"

"No!" Cory shouted. "I don't want to go! I want to stay with Daddy! I want to stay all night!"

"That's enough," Royce said, gripping Cory's knee. He could have cried for them, for all of them. Instead, he swallowed down his disappointment and tried to look on the bright side. Tammy liked Dr. Denelo more than she wanted to let on, and Cory wanted to spend the night. Plus, he'd had another visit with his kids. It was a step forward. He hugged Cory, saying softly, "I love to see you, son. One day soon you'll spend the night with me again, I promise, but maybe it's better if Uncle Dale takes you back to your mother's now."

"Sure," Dale said, getting to his feet. "It's about that time, anyway." He offered a hand to each of the children. Tammy ignored him, folding her arms, but Cory reluctantly slid off his father's lap and put his hand in Dale's. "Tammy, are you going to tell your father goodbye?"

Tammy shrugged, then flipped a hand in what might have been called a wave. "'Bye."

"Goodbye, honey. I love you. I love you, too, Cory."

"Love you," Cory echoed as Dale led him from the room, Tammy marching along beside them.

Just as she got to Royce's chair, Tammy stopped. For a moment she seemed frozen, her face stoically blank. Only when she fidgeted, bouncing one knee slightly, did she give herself away. Royce reached out with his left arm, and she melted. He swept her against him, hugging her tightly for as long as she would allow. Then she pulled away and bolted from the room. He put his head back, more grateful for that one moment of raw need breaking through her belligerent exterior than he would have been for all the gold in the world.

Merrily's hand slid down the back of his chair and onto his shoulder. "She's getting there," she whispered.

"God, I hope so," he admitted, reaching up to clasp her hand in his. Merrily came around the chair, and he pulled her down onto his lap.

"She's coming around, Royce. You'll see."

He nodded, praying she was right. Tammy had seemed a little softer, but Cory had been competitive and mouthy rather than his usual reserved self.

"Maybe you ought to talk to Dr. Denelo," Merrily suggested, "fill her in on what's going on."

Royce shook his head. "I can't, not until she asks to speak to me. Pamela can't, either. It's part of the court order, an attempt to ensure that the doctor remains truly unbiased."

Merrily nodded. "I guess that makes sense."

"I guess." He sighed and added, "I feel like I'm running out of time, angel."

"What do you mean?"

"This cast comes off next week," he reminded her, lifting his right arm.

"But your leg's a long way from healed. The doctor just took the pins out."

"And next week I get a walking cast," he whispered, barely able to speak of it. "How do I justify keeping you on then?"

"Why should you have to justify it?" she countered. "If we want to be together we can be, Royce."

He shook his head. "It's not that simple, honey, and you know it. I'd be putting you directly in harm's way."

"It doesn't matter," she argued gently. "I can take care of myself."

"I know," he answered, unwilling to argue with her. Brushing her hair off her shoulder, he bared her neck there where she so loved to be kissed. He had made it his mission to find and uncover all her erotic secrets these past couple of weeks. It had been the most rewarding undertaking in which he'd ever engaged. She had healed him in so many ways, his sweet nurse, given him the greatest pleasure he'd ever known. God, how could he go on without her? But what other choice did he have?

"Let's turn in early tonight," he whispered. She smiled and got up off his lap. Good golly, what a seductive smile the woman had grown in these past weeks. How he would miss it!

"Is now too early?" she asked in a sultry tone.

"Now is perfect," he told her, struggling up out of the chair.

Maybe he'd get lucky and break a few more bones.

Chapter Fourteen

"Well, look who's here," Merrily said, smiling at Dale. "Sorry I couldn't get to the door."

The tall, lanky attorney got up from the deck chair next to Royce's chaise. "On one hand, I suppose it's an improvement to have gimp-boy himself let me in. On the other hand, he's not nearly as good-looking as you." He opened his arms, and Merrily briefly hugged him, laughing. "Hmm, is it possible the worm has turned?" he asked, obviously needling Royce.

"This worm has just scrubbed the shower," Merrily retorted, pushing away a lock of hair that had fallen from the heavy twist atop her head. A black, plastic bag sitting at the top of the stairs caught her eye, and she frowned.

She'd been on her way down to the alley earlier to drop the closed garbage bag in the collection can there when Royce had called her back into the house to answer a phone call. By the time she'd convinced the nurse recruiter, who'd gotten her number from her brother, that she was not interested in leaving her current employment, she'd forgotten about the trash. She made a note to take it down before she started supper. It wouldn't do to leave the thing sitting out after dark. Some raccoon, armadillo or coyote would have it scattered all over the place by morning.

Dale, meanwhile, had brought his hands to his hips and was scowling down at Royce. "You slave driver, you. What happened to Mercedes, anyway?"

Royce sucked the last of his iced tea from the tumbler in his hand, set it on the low table at his right and bent his head back, his eyes hidden by dark sunshades that wrapped around his face. "Mercedes has been downsized or, rather, *Merrilyized.* She cut back her own hours, says she doesn't have enough to do with Merrily here."

"So I pick up after myself!" Merrily exclaimed, throwing up her hands. "Why does everyone have so much difficulty with that concept? It's not like *I* cut the woman's hours, and you pay her too much, anyway."

"Scrubbing the shower equates to picking up after yourself?" Dale queried skeptically.

Merrily rolled her eyes. "It does when I'm the one who got the shower dirty to begin with."

Dale dropped a look on Royce. "Women are so strange."

"Some are stranger than others," Royce said. He looked at her and added, "Some are so delicious you don't care whether you ever understand them or not."

Merrily bent down and kissed the top of Royce's head, noticing that the tips of his ears were slightly sunburned. He caught her by the wrist and pulled her down onto the chaise next to him.

Dale sighed and parked himself in the chair. "I must be doing something wrong."

"Oh, there's a girl out there for you somewhere," Merrily predicted. "You just haven't found her yet."

"Either that or someone else found her first," Dale muttered.

"Pessimist," Merrily accused.

"It'll happen when you least expect it," Royce counseled. "In the meantime, it would help if you'd quit trying to steal my girl." He folded his arm around Merrily's neck and dragged her head closer for a quick, but not too quick, kiss.

"Got you worried, have I?" Dale teased.

"I've been worried about you for a long, long time," Royce drawled, turning his face up to the sun again.

Merrily laid her head on his shoulder and closed her eyes. The evening sun blanketed them with muted-yellow light and warm peace. It was the perfect time of the year for sitting on the deck and soaking up some rays. Warm but not hot, the air felt soft and substantial on her skin. Soon it would grow crisp as the days cooled and drew deeper into autumn. Would she cuddle here in the chaise on the deck with Royce then?

"Well, for once in a long, long time, I'm not worried about you," Dale was saying to Royce.

Royce and Merrily both lifted their heads and looked at him. He sat there grinning like an idiot, staring at the two of them. Royce tipped up his shades and wryly teased, "Why, Dale, I didn't know you cared."

Dale ignored that and said, "As much as I hate to say it, you two are perfect together. You know that, don't you?"

Merrily traded a look with Royce, who then dropped

his glasses back in place and said, "You're certifiable, but you do have your moments of brilliance."

"Of course, your mother doesn't see it that way," Dale said pointedly.

Merrily groaned in concert with Royce. "My parents deigned to visit again day before yesterday," Royce said, "and after Mother made her usual snippy, snide remarks about Merrily, I sort of got fed up."

"What he means is that he flaunted our relationship," Merrily added, quoting, "'Darlin', angel, sweetheart, baby doll.' I almost clobbered him over that one. By the time they left, Katherine was livid and Marvin goggle-eyed. I'm sure his mother thinks I'm a gold digger now."

Royce looked at Dale and surmised, "Mother called you."

Dale chuckled happily. "Fit to be tied."

Royce cursed under his breath. Merrily whacked him lightly for it. "It's your own fault."

"Well, she made me mad, calling you 'that unfortunate child' and 'girl.' I wanted to strangle her."

"Instead you waved me under her nose like a red flag," Merrily pointed out. "Honestly, if her snide remarks don't bother me, why do they bother you?"

"They just do," he grumbled. "She's so damned shallow that if she was a river we'd pave her over." Dale clapped his hands and hooted with glee. "What'd you say to her, anyway?" Royce wanted to know.

"Told her I was cheesed off that you'd beat me out or words to that effect."

"Oh, great!" Merrily huffed. "I'm sure *that* elevated me in her opinion."

"Sugar, for that to happen you'd have to learn to kiss butt in the same league as Pamela," Dale told her dryly.

"Surely she doesn't approve of Pamela," Merrily scoffed.

"Why, according to my mother it's bad form to get upset about little things like infidelity, threats and abuse," Royce said, the lightness of his tone belied by the underlying edge. "Divorce is so tacky, and of course once these things are in the public record one can never quite live them down again. Better to suffer in silence and put up a good front. After all, Pamela *looks* the part."

"And I do not," Merrily muttered, truly insulted now. "I don't think I like your mother very much."

"Angel, that makes two of us."

"Three," Dale said, holding up the requisite number of fingers.

"But I'm crazy about you," Royce told her silkily.

"Two," Dale announced, putting down one finger.

Merrily laughed and said, "I think you've both had too much sun." That reminded her of her earlier observation, and she switched her gaze to Royce, adding, "By the way, darling, the tops of your ears are turning red."

Royce reached up with his left hand to feel the top of one ear. "No wonder they've started burning. I thought it was just Dale's envy boiling over."

"Possible," Dale teased dryly.

Merrily shook her head and got to her feet, saying to Dale, "Take him inside, will you? I want to take the trash down before I start dinner."

"Oh, I'll take down the trash for you," Dale offered, quickly popping up out of his chair, but Merrily waved him off and started for the top of the stairs.

"No, no, you're wearing a business suit," she told Dale. "I'll take care of it. I won't be a minute, and when I'm done I'll put together some dinner."

"Yes!" Dale rubbed his hands together eagerly.

"Is there no one else who will feed you?" Royce gibed as he grabbed hold of Dale's arm and pulled himself up.

"Sure," Dale said, "but you have the best-looking cook."

Chuckling, Merrily went on her way. She lifted the black garbage bag by the top with one hand and opened the gate at the head of the stairs with the other before starting down to the back driveway below. Only moderately heavy, the bag contained mostly nonrecyclable paper products, the odd tin can, coffee grounds and few food scraps not suitable for the garbage disposal, but Merrily took her time, nevertheless. Whenever she did this, which was every few days, she thought about Royce falling down these same stairs, and a shiver ran up her spine.

She reached the bottom of the stairs and turned toward the large refuse container tucked out of sight beneath the stairwell. Lifting the hinged rubber top with one hand, she dropped the black plastic bag on top of the two others already deposited there. Trash pickup was scheduled for the next morning. As she straightened and let the lid fall again, movement on the edge of her peripheral vision made her turn her head in that direction. Gasping, she stepped back just as Pamela reached out and clamped a hand around her wrist.

"I want to talk to you."

Merrily yanked her arm away, mind racing. "You'd better not let Royce see you here."

Dressed from her chin to her running shoes in form-hugging, gray knit athletic apparel, Pamela still managed to look chic and stylish. In jeans, canvas shoes and a T-shirt tucked in at the waist, Merrily felt positively grungy by comparison. Pamela widened her stance.

"I said, I want to talk to you."

"You have the telephone number."

"What I have to say needs to be said face-to-face."

Merrily folded her arms. "So say it already. I have to start dinner."

Pamela mimicked her gesture, emphasizing the hefty proportion of her bust, and walked in a circle around Merrily. "You'll never hold his interest."

Pamela's tone left no doubt that she knew of the affair, and once again a chill kissed Merrily's spine, but she maintained her composure. "Okay. Anything else?"

"What's he told you?" Pamela abruptly demanded.

"About?"

"Don't be coy with me, Nurse Gage. I know where you live."

"Is that a threat?"

"You don't want to underestimate me, little nurse. I've spoken to your brothers, you know."

"And that obviously did you a lot of good."

"I also spoke to your supervisor at the hospital."

Anger at the other woman's high-handedness warred with humor at the absurdity of her assumptions, but Merrily refused to show either to Pamela. "Is there a point to this conversation, or is this just about sizing up the competition?"

The smooth beauty of Pamela's face abruptly contorted into a mask of malice. "You dare put yourself on the same plane with me?" She raked her gaze up and down Merrily in disdain. "You are nothing and no one, without enough sex appeal to so much as rate a second look from the average male."

"Is that so?" Merrily retorted smugly. "Funny, Royce doesn't seem to agree with you."

Anger flared white-hot in Pamela's gold-dominated hazel eyes, but the next instant they had gone as cold as the metal itself. "Don't delude yourself. Sex means nothing.

It's an itch that's easily scratched. You're convenient for Royce, too convenient, but that's all it is.''

"If that were so," Merrily reasoned, desperately trying to hide her despair, "you wouldn't be here."

"On the contrary," Pamela rebutted smoothly. "That's precisely why I am here. I want you out of this house."

"Which proves that you just can't stand the competition," Merrily said.

"I want you gone because you're a convenience to him," Pamela insisted, "a convenience he doesn't deserve."

"And who appointed you his judge and jury?" Merrily wanted to know.

"He did," Pamela answered, "when he married me."

"He divorced you, too."

Pamela took a menacing step forward. "Do you think that gets him off the hook? He deserves to pay for what he's done to me!"

"For what he's done to you?" Merrily scoffed. "*He* didn't push *you* down the stairs!"

"So? He's hurt me in other ways. Do you know how many doors closed to me when I ceased to be his wife? People who used to be my friends turned their backs on me—people who matter."

"People whose names get mentioned in the society pages, you mean," Merrily sneered, "people as vacuous and insincere as you and Kathryn."

"People with money!" Pamela exclaimed. "You wouldn't know what it's like to live as they do. You can't even imagine it because you're so far beneath them."

"And you're not?"

"I was meant for that world," Pamela declared, the fervency in her eyes bordering on the fanatical.

"And being a Lawler, Royce was your ticket in, wasn't

he? Well, you should've thought of that before you cheated on him.''

"It was just sex!" Pamela snapped.

"Oh, really? All those people who supposedly turned their backs on you don't seem to think so."

"It wasn't the affair!" Pamela contended hotly. "It was the divorce! People like that, people like us, aren't bound by the same silly conventions as the rest of you. We're beyond that."

"Guess not," Merrily rebutted succinctly.

"And whose fault is that?" Pamela hissed. "He cost me everything!"

"You did that to yourself!"

Pamela lifted her fists to her temples in frustration. "What I did shouldn't have mattered! Love is unconditional!"

"That works both ways," Merrily pointed out.

"I loved him!" Pamela exclaimed. "He's everything I ever wanted, wealthy, handsome and from one of the best families in Texas. He's invited to all the best parties, all the best homes. You should see the way they fawn over him. And he couldn't care less!"

"But you do," Merrily muttered, finally understanding the depth of Pamela's distorted reasoning. In truth, it bordered on insanity. "You can't understand that a man like Royce would never place value on something as shallow as that."

"Shallow?" Pamela sneered. "How would you know? I bet you were one of those girls around school that hardly anybody even noticed. *I* was the most popular girl in high school. *I* was the most popular girl in college! I should've been the most popular girl in San Antonio!"

"Don't you see that those people aren't worth agonizing over?'' Merrily asked. ''They only accepted you because you were married to a Lawler.''

''As I was meant to be!'' Pamela insisted. ''Don't you get it? He ruined it for me. Well, I warned him. He'll either fix it, or he'll pay.''

''He'll never take you back,'' Merrily said bluntly.

Pamela's face hardened. ''Then he'll pay,'' she gritted out.

Frustrated, Merrily threw up her arms. ''You'll only wind up hurting yourself. What are you going to do? Arrange another accident for him?''

Pamela reacted just as Merrily had always known she would, her eyes growing wide with alarm, perfect face paling. The next instant, however, a self-satisfied confidence replaced the flash of fear. ''You don't know what you're talking about.''

''Come off it,'' Merrily retorted. ''We both know you pushed Royce and that Tammy saw you do it.''

To Merrily's dismay, Pamela put her head back and laughed. ''My, my, you *are* as dumb as you look.''

Shaken, Merrily snapped, ''Even if Royce won't let her testify against you, one day it will come out!''

''My daughter,'' Pamela stated with chilling confidence, ''will never tell anyone what happened that night.''

It seemed incomprehensible to Merrily that Tammy would not eventually feel compelled to tell what she knew, but she sensed that Pamela believed wholeheartedly her daughter would never betray her. ''And why is that?'' she wondered aloud.

Pamela turned sly. ''Because she understands how dangerous her father is, of course.''

''Royce isn't dangerous.''

''You've no idea what he's capable of,'' Pamela insisted, eyes slitting. "If Tammy wasn't afraid, she could have him locked up for the rest of his life."

"That's a lie!"

"Is it?" Pamela asked coyly. "If a little girl said her daddy did something bad, wouldn't you believe her?"

Merrily felt physically ill. "Tammy would never say such a thing."

"She will if I tell her to."

Merrily shook her head, suddenly very afraid for Royce. "You're sick. You know that, don't you? You need help."

"No!" Pamela cried. "Don't say that!"

Merrily backed up a step, whispering, "You should be in a hospital."

"No-o-o!" Pamela suddenly flew at her. Nails raked Merrily's cheek and arm. "No! No!" She yanked at Merrily's hair, punched and kicked. Merrily threw up her arms, shielding herself as best she could, momentarily stunned. She remembered what Royce had said about Pamela attacking him and how he'd dared not fight back, but no such constraint applied to Merrily. Suddenly all her rage at the unfairness of what Royce and his children and now she herself suffered at the hands of this woman boiled over. She hadn't grown up the baby sister of three older brothers for nothing, by golly.

Hooking one foot behind Pamela's heel, Merrily shoved the flailing woman backward. Pamela went down like a sack a grain, but she flew up again, enraged, and ran smack into Merrily's fist. The blow merely glanced off Pam's shoulder, but it gave Merrily the chance to grab Pam's wrist, twist under her arm and flip the larger woman over her back just as she'd done her brothers countless times before they'd all grown too big to tussle. Pamela landed with a grunt and lay stunned. Merrily placed a foot square in the middle of her flat stomach and held her down. Bending over her, fists clenched, she laid down the law, just as she had once done to a teenage Jody when he'd smacked around Lane for no good reason she could see.

"Now you listen, and you listen good," she snarled, determined to penetrate Pamela's madness, "if anything, and I mean *anything,* the least harmful ever again happens to Royce or either of those kids, for that matter, I'll have you put away."

"Y-you can't do that!"

"Oh, yes, I can," Merrily bluffed. "You're not dealing with a man constrained by his own decency or a confused, frightened child now. I can give as good as I get, and I know people, doctors, who can put you away, have you committed. Do you understand me?" Pamela just glared at her, but the fear in her eyes was answer enough for Merrily. Stepping over the woman, Merrily moved a safe distance away.

Pamela scrambled up. "You don't know anything," she whispered, as if trying to convince herself of that.

Suddenly Dale called out from above. "Merrily? What's taking so long?"

Pamela ran, yelling over her shoulder, "You don't know anything!"

"Merrily!" Dale cried urgently, pounding down the stairs.

"I know enough," Merrily muttered at Pamela's retreating back. She lifted a hand to her burning cheek just as Dale skidded to a halt next to her. He took one look at her disheveled hair and yanked her protectively into his arms.

"I heard Pam. Where is she?"

"Gone."

The tires of a car screeched on pavement in the distance, punctuating Merrily's assertion. Dale turned her face up to the light. There at the foot of the hill, with the sun sinking behind the horizon, the shadows had deepened considerably over the past moments but not enough, apparently, to obscure her injury.

"You're hurt!"

Merrily glanced at her arm. Angry, red welts streaked down her skin. Blood flecked her sleeve. "It's looks worse than it is," she muttered, "but that's good enough." Looking up at him, she said firmly, "Pamela attacked me. I want to press charges. I've seen it done with less evidence than this."

Dale examined her arm, concern furrowing his brow. Finally he looked at her. "What happened?"

"She was waiting for me when I came down with the trash. We argued, and she attacked me. She's everything you said she was. You were both right, you and Royce. She's crazy, and she'll do anything to hurt him—unless we stop her."

Dale rubbed his chin. "It might work. It's certainly enough to get us a hearing, but, Merrily, you have to know she'll come after you for this."

"Not if we win," Merrily countered defiantly, lifting her chin.

"Especially if we win," Dale warned. "And Royce isn't going to like it."

As if summoned by the mere mention of his name, Royce chose that moment to call out, "Merrily? Dale? What's going on?" They heard him clumping across the deck on his crutches.

"Royce doesn't get to decide," Merrily said flatly, turning for the stairs.

"In that case," Dale said, coming up the stairs behind her. "I hope you'll let me recommend a good attorney."

"Oh, yes," Merrily answered, and steeled herself for the battle to come.

Chapter Fifteen

"You don't understand how dangerous she is!" Royce insisted again, looking up from the recliner.

"Oh, yes, I do," Merrily said. "The woman was lying in wait. She attacked me. I put her on the ground twice and practically stood on her to make her stop."

Dale hooted. "Wish I'd seen that! Bet she never expected little old Nurse Gage to knock her on her butt."

"She should have realized 'little old Nurse Gage' would be able to defend herself, given that she grew up with three older brothers," Merrily said.

"You may have bested her this time," Royce argued, "but Pamela won't make the same mistake twice."

"That's why I'm going to press charges," Merrily stated firmly.

"This is our chance, Royce," Dale added excitedly. "We finally have proof of Pamela's vicious temper and instability. With this ammunition we can fast-track the hearing and make a real fight of it. Dr. Denelo will back us up, I know it.''

''And what happens if it's not enough?'' Royce demanded.

''Then we keep fighting,'' Merrily answered.

''I'm going to level with you,'' Dale put in quickly. ''This is our first real chance. It's all been a desperate bluff until now. The nanny's deposition helps, but Merrily's testimony could put this thing away for us. We could actually win.''

For a moment naked hope lit those incredible blue eyes, but then Royce stubbornly shook his head. ''I can't let you do it, honey,'' he said to Merrily. ''Her hatred for me is too strong to be curtailed by something like an assault charge, and I couldn't bear it if anything worse happened to you because of me.''

Merrily went down on her knees beside him. Her heartbeat was pronounced but even. Oddly, now that the moment had come, all the petty fears fell away. Everything that mattered was sitting right here in front of her, frowning. She reached up and smoothed the crease between his eyebrows with her thumb, saying softly, ''Can't you see that my love for you is stronger than her hatred?''

For a moment Royce just stared as if he hadn't heard a word she'd said, but then his hand rose and his fingers traced a trembling path through the air over the livid marks on her cheek. ''I love you too much to take the risk,'' he whispered.

That was all she needed to know. She coiled her arms about his neck, and he hauled her up onto his lap. ''We have to find a way to stop her,'' she told him, ''because I can't live my life without you.''

''I can't live my life knowing I caused you hurt,'' he replied, lightly kissing her injured cheek.

"You haven't," she vowed. "Don't take credit for Pamela's sick viciousness. Don't let it rule you anymore. And don't make the mistake of thinking you can dictate to me, even for my own protection. I'm a grown woman."

"Oh, do I know that," he said, turning his head to place his mouth against the sensitive underside of her jaw.

Merrily's eyes fluttered shut, but she would not be deterred. "I'm going to do what I believe to be best," she went on breathlessly. "Now, you can help me, or you can fight me, but you can't stop me."

"Look," Dale said, "we'll drop the charges before they get to court. That way the case won't be pending when the custody hearing comes up so Merrily can testify on our behalf and we'll still have documentation."

Royce put his head back with a long-suffering sigh. After a moment he asked wryly, "Did you really put her down?"

"Twice," she confirmed with a grin, "and if she comes after me again, she'll be wearing the wounds to prove it."

"Just now, however," Dale interrupted, "we are fortunate that the wounds are on the other cheek, so to speak." He pulled his cell phone from his pocket, suggesting, "No one documents evidence better than our friends the police."

Merrily glanced at Royce, who frowned but finally nodded. She held out her hand. Grinning broadly, Dale punched in the numbers 911 and handed the phone to Merrily, who put it to her ear.

"Yes," she said in answer to the operator on the other end of the line, "I'd like to report an assault."

"What's this?" she asked, standing before the dancing flames on the dining room table. It was still early for the first fire of the season, but he had lit the dozen tapers in the magnificent wrought-iron candelabra.

"I thought we were due a celebration," Royce told her, balancing himself with one hand upon the cane for which he'd traded his crutches when the walking cast had taken the place of the stabilizer on his right leg. "It's been a long time since I got to cook."

For the occasion he had laid two places: copper charger plates awaiting his best china, ebony-handled flatware, crystal champagne flutes, crisp linen. He'd also carefully opened one seam of his best pair of jeans, in order to accommodate the cast on his leg, and donned them along with a lightweight, off-white cashmere sweater. If he wasn't looking his best, it was the best he could do at the moment.

"This doesn't have anything to do with tomorrow's hearing, does it?" she asked lightly, but he only smiled.

"Hope you like honey-glazed salmon."

"Where did you get salmon?" she asked suspiciously.

"I have my ways."

"And the champagne?"

"Now that I'm off all the meds, why not?" he asked nonchalantly.

"Why not?" she echoed, smiling.

He pulled out a chair for her and indicated with a sweep of his hand that she should be seated. Even while easing down into the chair, she said softly, "I feel under-dressed."

He glanced down at the simple T-shirt and brushed denim jeans she wore, laid his cheek alongside hers and whispered, "Overdressed is more like it."

She burbled with laughter, and he gave her a quick hug before straightening and hobbling toward the kitchen. "Can I help?" she called after him.

"Nope. You've waited on me all these weeks. Tonight it's my turn."

"Whatever you say."

The plates were already filled and waiting in a warm oven. One at a time, he carried them to the dining room, patiently limping first down and then up the sloping interior hallway. He had wrestled with this decision for days. Should he wait until after the hearing and the cast came off or take his chances now? One moment he was convinced that he should wait. If the hearing didn't go their way, Pamela would have a stronger hand and greater reason to torment him, which would likely make Merrily an even bigger target. In the end, however, he understood that waiting was pointless. He could not find the strength or means to convince Merrily that he didn't want her, so he might as well put away all pretense at chivalry and take a swipe at the brass ring.

That thought brought to mind the small blue velvet box now riding safely in the pocket of his pants. His heartbeat trebled, but he kept his smile in place as he laid her plate before her and took his own seat. Lifting the bottle from the ice bucket, he poured both of their glasses full of the sparkling, golden wine. Merrily lifted hers in a toast.

"Here's to tomorrow."

"All our tomorrows," he amended, and she smiled.

"All our tomorrows, then."

They clinked their glasses and sipped. Then Royce shook out his napkin, draped it over his lap and picked up his eating utensils. It was so good to have the use of both hands again. Despite the walking cast on his leg, he was beginning to feel whole again, alive again. If his hands shook slightly, well, he had ample reason for feeling nervous.

"Salmon's wonderful," Merrily told him, "so are these vegetables."

"It's a simple recipe," he said, and they talked casually of cooking techniques until their plates were clean and he refilled their glasses. They sat for a while, sipping champagne, then he asked casually, "Ready for dessert?"

"Gee, I don't know. I'm pretty full," she said, a hand going to her tummy.

"This ought to be just the thing, then," he said, slipping the tiny blue box from his pocket and placing it in front of her.

She stared at the box so long that he began to fear he'd rushed headlong into disaster. Then she reached out with trembling fingers to flip open the top half of the box, revealing the old-fashioned engagement ring inside. The center stone was a large, square-cut diamond of good quality, the four smaller stones flanking it were round stones in square settings. Without saying a word, she lifted a hand and covered her mouth. Suddenly he knew he'd blown it. Pamela had turned up her nose at this same ring years ago, declaring it hopelessly passé. He'd stashed it away in a bank vault, thinking that he might pass it down to his own son one day, and taken Pamela to pick out a ring more to her taste.

"It was my grandmother's," he said hastily. "You could wear it until you find something you like better."

Merrily looked at him as if he had a hole in his head, her eyes brimming with tears. "Your grandmother's! Oh, how wonderful."

He nearly fell into his plate. "It's okay, then? You like it?"

"It's beautiful! I love it!"

He wiped his brow with a shaky hand. "I think I could manage one knee if you like, but—"

"Don't you dare!" she interrupted, snatching up the box and plunking it down in front of him. Her hands twined tightly together, she waited expectantly.

He wanted to laugh, but he managed to swallow down the impulse and plucked the ring from the box. Licking his lips, he looked her in the eyes and asked, "Will you marry me?"

"Oh, yes! As if you didn't know." Then she laughed and held out her left hand. He'd had the ring sized for her tiny finger, but he and Dale had guessed at the fit. Hoping that he hadn't gotten it wrong, he plucked out the ring and, with shaking hands, slid it onto her finger. Close enough. They both laughed, and the tears began to fall. "What changed your mind?" she wanted to know.

"Well," he said softly, "I started thinking that maybe Pamela and I both had met our match."

"Do you think the kids will mind?" she asked, holding out her hand and admiring the ring.

He had to be honest with her. "I don't know. I hope not. Will your brothers?"

She smiled and blinked away her tears. "They wouldn't dare, not if they know what's good for them."

"I know what's good for me," he whispered, pulling her close for a kiss.

Now if only tomorrow would go so well.

Royce paced the antechamber, putting the cane and walking cast to good use. The pacing coupled with the habitual flexing of his still slightly stiff right elbow to render him a case of nervous motion. Dale contained his own anxiety by jangling the change in his pocket. Only Merrily sat calmly waiting, content to stare at the engagement ring Royce had put on her finger only the night before. She couldn't help smiling, and yet, oddly enough, having her own dream come true worried her. Was it too much to hope that today could go their way, as well?

Just then a tall, attractive woman with thick, black hair coiled atop her head strode through the double doors into the vestibule. Merrily came instantly to her feet. "Dr. Denelo."

"Merrily! I didn't expect to see you here."

Dale strode swiftly forward. "I'm quite sure I mentioned Nurse Gage by name when I first contacted you."

Pandora Denelo dismissed the attorney with a scant glance, concentrating on Merrily instead. "I never was certain of your connection to my patient."

Merrily held up her left hand. "I'm engaged to marry her father."

"Congratulations!" The doctor clasped her portfolio beneath one arm and hugged Merrily. "I guess I should say best wishes."

"Thank you, and please allow me to introduce you to my fiancé, Royce Lawler. Honey, this is Dr. Denelo."

Royce shook Dr. Denelo's hand. "Merrily speaks very highly of you."

"Coming from one of the most dedicated nurses I've seen, that's high praise, indeed. You're a lucky man, Mr. Lawler."

Royce smiled. "I think so. Oh, and, Doctor, I want to thank you for what you're doing for my daughter."

Dr. Denelo smiled with empathy. "I cannot, of course, discuss anything your daughter has said to me, but I assure you I understand your situation. Now, if you'll excuse me, I've been asked to report directly to the court clerk."

She started to turn away, but Dale adroitly stepped into her path. "I need to speak with you first, Dora."

The familiar use of her name had Merrily and Royce

trading surprised looks. Pandora Denelo, however, scowled. "I've already told you, Counselor, not so long as we have a professional connection."

Dale colored and said through his teeth, "It's about the case, Doctor."

Dora Denelo lifted her chin. "Oh." She smoothed a hand across the seat of her short skirt. "All right, then."

"Excuse us," Dale said with a nod in their direction, and, taking the attractive doctor quite firmly by the upper arm, he steered her to the far corner of the room.

"Well, well," Royce muttered, watching the intense conversation.

Merrily tilted her head. "Interesting."

"She is single, isn't she?"

"She was. I haven't heard that it's changed."

"Maybe it will," Royce murmured with a lift of a brow. "Maybe instead of a nurse of his own, Dale will get a doctor."

Merrily laughed. "Matchmaking, are we?"

Royce hooked his arm about her waist and pulled her close. "Maybe I'm just tired of him trying to steal my girl."

"Not a chance," she vowed as his head bent toward hers. She closed her eyes, enjoying the kiss. A cleared throat had them pulling apart only seconds later.

Dale grinned and said, "Just can't keep your hands off her, can you?"

"Look who's talking," Royce retorted, glancing around for the lovely doctor, who had disappeared. "Was that really about the case?"

Dale's expression sobered, and he cleared his throat. "Yes, as a matter of fact, it was. Listen, whatever happens, I want you to keep your cool in there."

Before he could reply, the antechamber doors burst

open and Pamela stormed into the room, exclaiming, "Don't tell me to keep my voice down, damn you! I've paid you a fortune to keep this out of court, but here we are!" She stopped abruptly, glaring at Merrily and Royce, who stood with arms linked. The harried attorney bumped into her from the back. "You!" Pamela sneered, focusing on Merrily. "You better be glad you wised up and dropped those charges."

Merrily regarded Pamela blankly, not giving away by so much as a twitch that dropping the charges had been the plan all along. Tammy and Cory, accompanied by their new nanny, entered the room then, obviously hanging back to avoid whatever scene Pamela was currently causing.

"Daddy!" Cory broke free of the nanny and ran to his father, but Tammy stepped closer to the plump, plain young woman. Visibly trembling, she seemed wary of everyone there. Merrily sent her an encouraging smile as Royce bent to hug his son. The attorney cleared his throat.

"Perhaps we should check in with the court clerk."

"Fine," Pamela snapped. "So check in."

He seemed to consider the merits of trying to bully her into good behavior, then simply gave up and pushed on into the hearing room. Pamela took a swaying step closer to Merrily and threw out one hip to park her hand on it. Royce tensed, but Merrily steadied him with a squeeze of her arm. Pamela raked her contemptuous gaze from the top of Merrily's head down to her feet and back up again, settling on the faint scratches still visible on her cheek. Instinctively Merrily lifted her hand to cover them. She had been assured that they would leave no scars, but they had stood out quite visibly in the photos the police had taken. Pamela's gaze, however, went to the ring on Merrily's finger, and she gasped. Snatching at Merrily's hand, she screeched, "That's my ring!"

Royce shoved her hand away. "Oh, no, it's not. You didn't want it. My grandmother's ring wasn't good enough for you."

"You're going to marry her?" Pamela bawled.

"I am," Royce confirmed, folding both hands on the gold head of his cane, Cory wrapped around his good leg.

"We'll see about that!" Pamela declared. Her hands curled into fists, and veins stood out on her neck. Then she whirled and stalked into the hearing room.

"Whew!" Dale said, adding in a murmur, "That's pretty over the top even for Pamela. She doesn't usually make public threats."

"Just goes to show how much we've rattled her," Merrily murmured.

Royce bowed his head, saying nothing. With her mother safely out of earshot, Tammy quickly moved closer, but to Merrily's side, not her father's. "Are you really getting married?" she asked in a small, urgent voice.

Merrily smiled. "Yes, honey, we are."

"You mean we get another mommy?" Cory asked, just a hint of hopefulness in his small voice.

"A stepmother," Dale clarified.

"I like the idea of another mommy best," Merrily said, smiling at the boy.

Tammy bit her lip, her expression worried. "Mother won't like it."

Royce said, "I can't help that, honey. I love Merrily, and I know you will, too, once you get to really know her."

"I already love you," Merrily assured them.

Tammy just chewed her lip, her face contorted with

thought. The door to the hearing room opened, and a small, wiry man addressed them. "The judge is ready for you now."

The nanny swept forward and ushered the children into the chamber. Dale followed, leaving Merrily and Royce with a moment to exchange looks before entering the larger room. Merrily's was one of encouragement, but Royce's was heavy with worry.

The hearing chamber was set up much like a courtroom but with some exceptions. Three tables had been arranged at the front of the room. The judge stood behind the long one in the center. An empty chair had been placed at one end of it. Facing the judge stood two smaller tables with three chairs each. Behind those, a single row of chairs had been provided for observers and other interested parties. Merrily moved to stand in front of one of these chairs, while Royce moved forward to take his place beside Dale at one of the small tables. Dr. Denelo had already claimed a chair a few seats down from Merrily, and the nanny herded the children into a spot at the far end of the row. No sooner had they had all filed in than a uniformed female bailiff intoned, "Judge Ann Sizer presiding. Be seated."

A thick-waisted, middle-aged woman with short, thick, salt-and-pepper hair and stout ankles, the judge wore her formal robes open over an austere business suit, a detail which did nothing to diminish her aura of authority. After taking her seat, she nodded, and the bailiff retreated to a chair in the corner. The judge performed the legal niceties herself, calling the court to order, reading the names of the plaintiff and defendant into the record and administering the oath for truthfulness to both. She then invited the attorneys to make their cases.

Dale was on his feet first, but the proceedings were

surprisingly informal from that point on, with one attorney often interrupting the other to make a point or refute an accusation and the judge asking questions as she saw fit of both Pamela and Royce. When Dale laid the former nanny's statement before her, she waved it away, saying that she had already read it. Then she looked sternly at Pamela and demanded, "What about that, Mrs. Lawler? Did you strike your daughter?"

Pamela bowed her head and gently admitted, "Yes, your honor. I had to. She was hysterical."

The judge lifted an eyebrow. "And what brought on this hysteria?"

"Well, from what I've gathered, Tammy really liked her friend's father, and I guess she was upset when she realized that her own would never measure up."

"I heard nothing to support that when I spoke with the parents of Tammy's friend, your honor," Dale interjected.

The judge looked at Tammy then and beckoned her forward. Reluctantly Tammy slid off her chair. But only after the nanny urged her forward with a whisper and a little push did she walk to the judge's table. The judge directed her to the chair at the end of the table and folded her arms on the tabletop.

"Now then, young lady, do you know what it means to tell the truth?"

"Yes," Tammy whispered. Then at the judge's behest, she repeated herself a little louder. "Yes."

The judge nodded and folded her hands together, asking sternly, "Do you promise to tell the truth here today?" Tammy bit her lip, then shrugged. The judge said impatiently, "If you won't tell the truth, we can't get to the bottom of this and make a good decision here today. I might have no other choice than to send you and your brother into foster care until I can question your friend and her parents myself. Now, do you swear to tell the truth?''

Tammy took a deep breath, her bottom lip quivering, and said in a tiny voice, ''I swear.''

Merrily glanced at Royce and found him gripping the edge of the table. Pamela simply folded her arms and crossed her legs, kicking one foot rhythmically.

''Do you remember the night your mother slapped you?''

''Yes.''

''Was that the first time she slapped you?''

Royce leaned over and whispered something to Dale, who clamped a hand down onto his shoulder. The judge repeated her question, to which Tammy mumbled, ''I don't know.''

''You don't know?''

''I can't remember.''

The judge grimaced and ordered impatiently, ''Tell the truth, young lady.''

Tammy began to cry silently. ''I don't know.''

Royce grabbed Dale's coat sleeve and whispered urgently into his ear. Frowning, Dale rose and said, ''We have another witness who can attest to Mrs. Lawler's vicious temper, your honor, and frankly my client would prefer that his daughter not be forced to testify against either parent.''

The judge sighed, but she waved Tammy back to her chair, saying, ''All right, Mr. Boyd, but this had better be to point.''

He beckoned to Merrily, who rose and smoothed the straight skirt that she wore with a pale-gold twin set. Pamela sat up straight and whispered angrily into her attorney's ear. He made a soothing motion and tried to calm her, until finally she fell back into her chair, pouting. Merrily, meanwhile, took the oath and sat down at the end of the judge's table. At Dale's urging, she described her encounter with Pamela, often over the objections of Pamela's attorney and Pamela's own rebuttal. Dale admitted bluntly that they had dropped the assault charges so Merrily could testify. The judge was scowling at everyone after that. It was impossible to tell what she might be thinking.

Dale then led Merrily on a careful recounting of the first visit the children had made to their father's home after his "unfortunate fall," and together they detailed Tammy's behavior that day. During this, Tammy bowed her head and hunched her shoulders, seeming to grow smaller the longer Merrily talked. The upshot of it all was that the judge once more called Tammy up to the table.

"When you tore up your room, Tammy, were you angry with your father?" the judge wanted to know.

Tammy shrugged and kept her head down. "No."

"Were you angry with your mother, then?"

"No."

"Then why did you do it?"

Another shrug, followed by, "I don't know."

"Miss Lawler, I'm losing patience with you," the judge scolded. It was then that Dr. Denelo rose to her feet.

"Your honor, if I may," she interjected. "Perhaps you'd allow me to question Tammy. As you know, I am her therapist, and I think together she and I might be able to arrive at some satisfactory answers for you."

Royce looked sharply at Dale, who leaned close and said something that clearly made Royce angry. "I object to this, your honor!" he stated firmly.

At the same moment Pamela came to her feet and laid her fist against the tabletop, exclaiming, "You can't do this!'' As the judge sat back with a wry smile, Pamela's attorney pulled her back down into her chair.

The judge parted a sly look between Pamela and Royce. "We seem to have agreement on one issue, at least, and this leaves me to believe Dr. Denelo is on to something. You may proceed, Doctor.''

Royce put his head in his hands, but Pamela simply glared at their daughter. Dr. Denelo pulled a chair close to Tammy's and sat down. In a low, gentle voice, she began to speak to the girl.

"Tammy, you remember what we talked about the other day, how sometimes when you love someone very much you'll do whatever they want, even if you don't really want to?'' Tammy nodded and wiped tears from her face. "Do you remember what I told you, honey, that the truth can make a bad thing better?''

Tammy sobbed, but she nodded again. Royce leaned his forearms on the table and looked at the judge. "Please don't do this. She's just a little girl.''

Her face stony, the judge instructed Dale to keep his client quiet and nodded at the doctor, who took Tammy's hand in hers. "Tammy,'' Dr. Denelo asked gently, "does your mother hit you? The truth now, honey.''

"S-sometimes,'' Tammy warbled.

"Every day?'' the doctor pressed.

Cory crawled up into the nanny's lap, and Pamela drilled a hole in Tammy's face with her glare. Tammy bowed her head and whispered, "Most days.''

"That's a lie!'' Pamela said loudly.

The judge pointed a finger at her. "Silence!'' She waved a hand at Dr. Denelo.

"Tammy, I'm going to ask you the most difficult question of all now, so the judge can understand. Don't be afraid.''

"Oh, God," Royce said, bowing his head and curling his hands into fists.

"Tammy," the doctor went on, "what happened the night your father fell down the stairs?"

"No!" Royce said, coming to his feet. "Leave her alone!"

"What are you trying to pull?" Pamela screamed.

For a moment all was pandemonium, with the judge shouting for order, both lawyers trying to talk their clients into behaving and Tammy sobbing loudly. Cory jumped down from the nanny's lap and ran to Merrily. She gathered him up, comforting him in a quiet voice while trying to keep an eye on everything else that was going on. Finally the judge rose and shouted everyone down, restoring order. Tugging on the bottom of her suit coat, she plopped down into her chair once more and glared at Tammy, instructing sternly, "Answer the question."

Tammy trembled from head to toe. Dr. Denelo took her by the shoulders and looked her in the eye, saying, "Tammy, why did you push your father down the stairs?"

Merrily gasped. Royce covered his head with both arms. At the same moment, Tammy wailed, "Mommy sa-a-id!"

Pamela lurched to the edge of her chair and began screaming, "You lying little bitch!"

Suddenly Royce jumped up and headed for Tammy, shaking off Dale, who tried to stop him. "It's okay, baby," he cried, falling to one knee and holding out his arms. "It's okay." Tammy slid off her chair and threw herself at his chest. "I know you didn't really want to hurt me," he said, gathering her close as she sobbed. "You saved me. You got help. You stayed with me, covered me up. You did everything just right.

"Oh, my God," Merrily whispered, covering Cory's

ears with her arms and rocking him. "Oh, my God." To think what lengths Royce had gone to in order to protect his daughter! Merrily's heart swelled with pride even as Pamela screamed.

"It was her idea! She wanted the money! She even said he deserved to die for everything he's done to us, to me!"

The judge was on her feet again and speaking to Pamela. "Sit down and shut up or I'll have the bailiff arrest you now!"

Dr. Denelo knelt on the floor beside Tammy and her father. Royce glared at her, but she wisely ignored him. "Tammy," she asked clearly, "how did your mother convince you to push your father down those stairs?"

Tammy turned her tear-streaked face up to the judge and said into dead silence, "She said if I loved her, if I wanted to make her happy, all I had to do was creep up behind him and give him a push." She swallowed down her tears and went on, her voice growing stronger. "She said it every time we went to spend the night. She'd make a noise, get him to come outside in the dark. All I had to do was wait until he got to the stairs and push him. She said he'd go to heaven, and we'd all be happy because she'd love me if I did it. Then she'd buy me something I liked, and she'd say it again and again and again. Just push him. Just push him."

Pamela sat down hard on the edge of her chair and began to cry noisily. Dr. Denelo looked at the judge, who was staring at Tammy with her mouth open. Royce gathered Tammy close and rocked her, whispering over and over, "It's okay, honey. I love you. It's okay."

"I'm sorry, Daddy." Tammy wept, her arms wrapped tight around his neck. "I'm so sorry."

"It's okay. It's okay." He turned to look over his shoulder at Merrily then, tears streaming down his face.

"It's okay," he repeated, his face full of pleading, apology and hope. "We're all going to be okay."

Merrily nodded, tears streaming down her face. "We're all going to be okay," she whispered, and then she gave him her most angelic smile, a smile made of pure love.

Epilogue

"Watch me! Watch me!" Cory called.

"We're watching," Merrily assured him as Royce carefully placed the ball on the tee wedged between the planks of the deck and stood back, crossing his arms over his chest in an effort to keep warm. Tammy huddled close to her side, wrapped in a bulky sweater that reached her knees and the tops of her retro-style leather boots.

"Don't choke up now," Royce coached as Cory took up his stance with the golf club. He looked so adorable standing there in heavy corduroy and a car coat, the ear flaps turned down on his matching hat against a brisk January breeze. Cory reared back, his tongue sticking out one corner of his mouth in concentration, and swung the club in a smooth, graceful arc. The golf ball flew over the railing and the back lane below landing yards away in the rough scrub at the foot of the hill.

"Yeah!" Merrily clapped her gloved hands as Tammy

jumped up and down beside her and Royce swung Cory up in his arms for a congratulatory hug.

"Good shot, son! Tammy want to try? You can use my club."

She shook her head. "Uh-uh. I'd rather watch golf than play it."

Royce waved his understanding and put Cory back on his feet before kneeling to right the tee and set another ball. This time he took aim, quietly instructing an eager Cory as he settled into his stance. Merrily leaned sideways and muttered out of one corner of her mouth, "You know we're going to have to watch these two play on a real course someday."

Tammy wrinkled her nose and rolled her eyes, but then she slipped her arm through the crook of Merrily's, giggling. "At least Daddy didn't buy us golf clubs for Christmas."

"He thought about it," Merrily whispered. "Luckily I convinced him that it was more of a father-son thing."

A sharp whack yanked their attention back to the guys. Royce dropped his club against his shoulder and shielded his eyes from the bright winter sunshine with one hand, watching the flight of the ball. Cory stood spellbound for a moment, then as the ball began to drop, started hopping up and down and hooting with delight.

"Wow!" Merrily called, impressed and sorry she'd missed the actual swing.

"Ohh, you're good, too, Daddy," Tammy said loudly, clapping her hands. "He is good, isn't he, Merrily?"

"Very good," Merrily replied, her voice rich with meaning.

Royce began lining up another shot for Cory, pointing out a target for him, coaching him on his stance and grip. To Merrily's surprise, Tammy's arms suddenly encircled her waist. Looking down, she saw tears glistening in Tammy's blue eyes.

"What is it, honey?"

"Happy," she said with a gulp. "It doesn't seem right."

"Oh, but it is, honey. You deserve to be happy. We all do. It's what your father's always wanted, especially for you and Cory."

"But it doesn't seem right when one person can't be happy and everyone else can."

"Tammy, remember what Dr. Denelo has told you. Happiness comes from inside, from doing the right things, valuing the right things. No one else can make you happy, Tammy. It's enough that they want you to be happy. But the happiness comes from inside you. It has to come from inside all of us."

Tammy nodded and whispered, "What's going to happen if Pamela gets to see us again? Will we still be happy then?"

Merrily smiled and smoothed a hand across her sleek, bright hair. "Tammy, your mother still has fifteen months to serve, and then she has to complete a long course of psychiatric counseling and evaluation before the doctors and the judge will decide whether or not she'll be allowed visitation."

"But I don't want to see her!" Tammy vowed, hugging Merrily tight. "I love you and Daddy!"

"Sweetie, that makes me very happy to hear. We love you, too, you know, but Pamela is your mother, and loving us doesn't mean that you have to stop loving her. She may never be quite well enough to love you back as she should, Tammy, but that doesn't mean you have to stop loving her."

"But I want you to be my mother," Tammy whispered.

Merrily hugged her close, her own eyes starting to tear up. "Honey, I am. Nothing can ever change that now, not in my heart, and when, *if,* you ever have to deal with Pamela again, your daddy and I will be here to help you."

"And Dr. Denelo, too," Tammy said, "and Uncle Dale."

"That's right, all the help you'll ever need."

"Woo-hoo!" Cory crowed, and they both turned to catch sight of the ball just as before it dropped out of view.

"Great shot!" Royce exclaimed, patting Cory on the back with pride.

"Do another, Daddy. I wanna do another," Cory pleaded excitedly.

"I'm afraid we're all out of balls, son. We'd better go down and hunt up a few." Taking Cory by the hand, he approached Merrily and Tammy. "Guess we'll go down and see if we can find some balls."

"I'll make some hot cocoa while you're gone," Merrily offered.

Royce slipped an arm around her neck and dropped an easy kiss on her mouth. "Thanks, hon. Sounds great."

Tammy, Merrily couldn't help noticing, watched them with glowing eyes. "That's okay, Daddy," she said, slipping away. "I'll go with Cory to look for the balls. Why don't you help Mom with the cocoa?"

Mom. Royce flipped a surprised look from Tammy to Merrily and back again. Merrily smiled, barely keeping the tears at bay. Cory had been calling her Merry Mom or Mommy Merrily almost from the day of their early November wedding, but this was the first time such a title had fallen from Tammy's mouth.

Royce wrapped his arm more tightly about Merrily's neck, bringing her close against his chest. "That'd be

great, Tammy. Thanks. Cory, do you remember where
you're supposed to look?"

"Yeah, yeah, just like last time, Dad," Cory assured
him, moving toward the steps. Tammy hurried after him,
a spring in her step, but Royce lifted a hand as if to hold
them back. "Kids!" They both paused, Cory almost at
the head of the stairs. Royce swallowed. "Be careful."

Tammy blinked, and for an instant the old shadows
flitted across her eyes, but then she smiled and reached
down for her brother's hand. "We will," she promised,
opening the gate.

They began sedately, taking the steps one at a time.
Royce turned slightly, wrapping his arms around Merrily,
holding her against him. With a sigh he propped his chin
on the crown of her head. For a long moment they simply
held each another. Then Royce murmured, "Ah, angel,
you know what you've done, don't you? You've put it all
back together, starting with my bones and then my heart
and now my family."

"Our family," Merrily corrected, turning her face up.

He grinned down at her. "How long do you think
they'll be, *Mom?* If we hurry we can get the cocoa on
and sneak in a little necking before they're back."

Merrily smiled. "Oh, I hope so. I think kisses are a
necessary for good cocoa, don't you?"

"I think kisses are the perfect sweetener," he said,
planting a quick one.

"Mmm, you are so right," she agreed, "but if kisses
are the sweetener, then love must be the binder, the es-
sential ingredient that holds it all together."

"Oh, yes," he said, "and with glue as strong as our
love, this marriage will hold forever."

"And the family will never come apart again," she
promised.

"I found one!" a triumphant little voice cried, and they both turned to see Cory at the edge of the trees, waving a golf ball over his head. They smiled and waved back in congratulations.

"I think we'd better hurry if we're going to get that cocoa properly sweetened," Royce murmured through his smile.

Merrily laughed, and arm in arm they went inside, a family, whole in body and spirit, bound in love and knowing that whatever came, the glue would hold.

* * * * * *

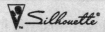

SPECIAL EDITION™

Coming in August 2002,
from Silhouette Special Edition and

CHRISTINE RIMMER,

the author who brought you the popular series

CONVENIENTLY YOURS,

brings her new series

THE SONS OF
CAITLIN
BRAVO

Starting with

HIS EXECUTIVE SWEETHEART
(SE #1485)...

One day she was the prim and proper executive assistant...
the next, Celia Tuttle fell hopelessly in love with her boss,
mogul Aaron Bravo, bachelor extraordinaire. It was clear he
was never going to return her feelings, so what was a girl to
do but get a makeover—and try to quit. Only suddenly,
was Aaron eyeing his assistant in a whole new light?

And coming in October 2002, MERCURY RISING,
also from Silhouette Special Edition.

**THE SONS OF CAITLIN BRAVO: Aaron, Cade and Will.
They thought no woman could tame them.
How wrong they were!**

Where love comes alive™

**Where royalty and romance
go hand in hand...**

The series continues in Silhouette Romance
with these unforgettable novels:

HER ROYAL HUSBAND
by Cara Colter
on sale July 2002 (SR #1600)

THE PRINCESS HAS AMNESIA!
by Patricia Thayer
on sale August 2002 (SR #1606)

SEARCHING FOR HER PRINCE
by Karen Rose Smith
on sale September 2002 (SR #1612)

And look for more Crown and Glory stories in
SILHOUETTE DESIRE starting in October 2002!

Available at your favorite retail outlet.

Where love comes alive™

Silhouette Books is proud to present:

Going to the Chapel

**Three brand-new stories
about getting that special man to the altar!**

featuring

USA Today bestselling author

SHARON SALA

*It Happened One Night...*that Georgia society belle
Harley June Beaumont went to Vegas—and woke up married!
How could she explain her hunk of a husband to
her family back home?

Award-winning author
DIXIE BROWNING

*Marrying a Millionaire...*was exactly what Grace McCall was
trying to keep her baby sister from doing. Not that Grace had
anything against the groom—it was the groom's arrogant
millionaire uncle who got Grace all hot and bothered!

National bestselling author
STELLA BAGWELL

*The Bride's Big Adventure...*was escaping her handpicked
fiancé in the arms of a hot-blooded cowboy! And from the
moment Gloria Rhodes said "I do" to her rugged groom, she
dreamed their wedded bliss would never end!

Available in July at your favorite retail outlets!

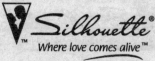

Where love comes alive™

Visit Silhouette at www.eHarlequin.com

PSGTCC

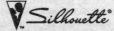

Silhouette®

COMING NEXT MONTH